Arx Epifcopi.

The Castilians

V.E.H. Masters

NYDIE
BOOKS

Books by VEH Masters

The Seton Chronicles:

The Castilians
The Conversos
The Apostates

First Published in Scotland in 2020 by Nydie Books

A CIP catalogue record for this book is available from the British Library

Paperback ISBN: 978-1-8382515-0-5

Also available as an ebook

Cover Design: Mike Masters

Map of St Andrews by John Geddy (1580) reproduced with the permission of the National Library of Scotland

www.vehmasters.com

For Mike, of course

And in memory of my parents

Morris and Elspeth Wilson, once of Newton of Nydie

StAndrews

collegium S. Saluatoris — Swallowgait

Northgait — ecclesia S. Saluatoris

franciscanorum
ædes — nemus
vrbis — Mercatgait

Ecclesia ferochia
ciuitatis

dominicanorum
ædes — Southgait

collegium D. Mariam

Castle

Epifcopi

Collegium
D. Leonardi

Cathedral

Part One

Bethia & Will

March to May 1546

Chapter One

The Burning

Bethia rests the book on her lap, its weight heavy across her knee. Head bent, she follows each line with her finger, lips moving, stumbling occasionally over a word as she translates. A thick lock of hair falls forward and she tucks it back into the ribbon, then tilts the book to catch the brief shaft of early spring sunshine seeping through the thick glass. A door slams, echoing through the house and her hand jerks, tearing the paper. She stares at the small rip, face flushing and then smooths it with shaking fingers. Perhaps Father won't notice.

Standing on the settle she opens the window and leans out in time to catch a glimpse of her brother disappearing around the corner. John's supposed to be studying his Latin, not allowing her the indulgence of reading alone, and Father ordered them to stay indoors. She's the eldest and he'll be angry with her – but it's John who'll get the thrashing.

She slips down the stairs, the smell of boiled cabbage stronger the lower she goes. The front door sticks, screeching over small stones and scraping white streaks across the flagstones.

'Bethia, come and give your obedience to Lady Merione,' Mother calls.

She flees instead, the freed door banging shut behind

3

her. Lifting her skirts she hurries along the street, ridges of mud hard beneath her soft slippers – foolish to forget to put on her pattens, but thanks be the ground is dry.

She doesn't look back in case Mother has come to the door, but turns down the pend towards the harbour. John is most likely headed there. He's forever clamouring to watch the ships come in, talk to the sailors and hear tales of mountainous seas and distant lands.

Mother doesn't like it when he goes there. 'An eight year old is the perfect age to be taken as a cabin boy.'

'They're welcome to him,' says Father, 'but any fool can see John is of good family.'

'That's all fine and well, as long as John's with you, but alone he can easily be spirited away and no one will know until the ship is long sailed.'

Bethia lifts her skirts higher, thankful Mother can't see her, and runs lightly down the hill. The wind blows chill off the grey sea, whipping across the water with a promise of snow. Shivering, she drops her skirts, tugging the shawl over her head. There's only one ship tied up harbourside amidst the cluster of small fishing boats.

'Where are ye going, my pretty blue-eyed lass?'

She jumps, turning around, skirts tangling, to find the source of the words. A sailor sitting astride the bow of the quayside ship, bare feet swinging, beckons. 'Come awa here and keep me warm.'

When he sees her startled face he grins, the few remaining teeth rotten stubs in his open mouth. She dips her head and hurries past, his laughter following her.

The harbour is deserted; no fishwives selling today's catch, nor any of their half-starved bairns either. There was plague recently in nearby Dundee when hundreds died; people didn't go about much then, but that has passed. Where is everyone, and where is John?

She looks over her shoulder; the sailor's still watching her. Reaching the end of the quayside, she clambers breathlessly up the steep steps to St Mary's on the Rock, the stones on the path sharp through her thin soled slippers. She touches the chapel wall with her fingertips and brings them to her lips; Mary, mother of Jesu protect and watch over John, indeed over both her brothers.

Her instinct is to hurry and find people, but she makes herself go slowly for she must tread the path with care as it narrows. The cliff edge is close; she can hear the low rumble of waves below. On her other side is the high wall which encircles the cathedral, built to venerate the bones it holds from the blessed body of Saint Andrew. She thinks of all the pilgrims who come to her city seeking comfort; and feels comfort herself to live in such a holy town as St Andrews.

There's a murmur of voices ahead as she passes through the postern and draws nearer to the castle. The sound grows harsher like the cawing of crows, and the smell assails her; a familiar stink of dirt and latrine that aye accompanies a crowd. They're in front of the castle; so many people, as if on a fair day or a street performance of the mystery plays, but this is no joyous gathering. People are muttering to one another as they stare at something. She stands on tiptoe, shifting from one foot to the other, but she cannot see.

They fall silent and she clutches her shawl with clammy fingers. There's a flare of light and the soft whuff of explosive. The crowd shifts with a collective sigh and a gap opens. She glimpses a pyre of wood with a man upon it, a rope around his neck and a chain wrapped tight around his chest, binding him to the stake at its centre. She touches hand to mouth, eyes wide as the flames flicker, unhurriedly creeping towards him. He stands tall, yet cannot help but flinch – and the fire so paltry that it will take many hours for him to die.

Bethia's seen hangings before at the Mercat Cross, the bodies swinging in the wind for days, and the occasional ear or tip of the nose sliced off. Although they are quick, a just punishment for thieves and vagabonds, she always looks away, sickened by the blood and fear – and the watching crowd's excitement. She stares at this man, gripping and loosening her fingers, a rushing noise in her ears and her bones gone soft as calf-foot jelly.

She's about to creep away when she glimpses John's yellow-red hair and small freckled face beyond the fire. His eyes are wide as he peeps out from between two of the town burghers; a couple of fat sentinels, arms folded, observing the scene with expressions of satisfaction.

Making her way through the crowd towards him, she's jostled as people push and shove to see, and finds herself funnelled towards the fire. The heat is puny as it smoulders and smokes, but a sudden gust of wind fans the flames setting them leaping. She's uncomfortably close now and afraid of being burned herself.

The man at the stake looks down upon her; there's an innocence about him, despite his black beard. This must be George Wishart; her brother Will has heard him preach. Father was very angry, but Will said Wishart spoke the true word and is a man full of God's grace. That made Father even angrier. She wonders why Wishart returned to Scotland instead of staying safely abroad like a sensible man – perhaps he's chosen a martyr's death. He may regret it now: the rope binding his neck to the pole is twisted tight so that he strains against it, a slow throttling – and the skin on his legs is sizzling, like roasting pig.

Pushing blindly she stumbles to the edge of the crowd and leans over, hands resting on her knees as the bile rises. She swallows it, bitter and stinging down her throat, only standing up when she can breathe again. There are soldiers in front of her, faces grim and weapons at the ready. They guard the gateway to the castle, but are also pinioning the townsfolk around the fire, no doubt to make sure everyone stays to watch the burning – and takes heed. It will be difficult for her to escape home, even if she can get hold of John. Standing, uncertain, she's biting down on her lip when someone grabs her shoulder. She flinches, heart thumping, and twists to get free, but the hand grips all the tighter.

Chapter Two

Escape

'Heavens Will, let go! Why so rough?'

Will releases her and glares. 'What are you doing here, Bethia? This is no place for you; what'll Father say?'

'I doubt he'll be any happier to know you're here.'

Her brother draws himself up to his full height. Although he's a year younger, he's grown recently: long legs and long arms, but scraggy with it.

'I'm a man. 'Tis fitting I am here, but you must go home.'

She snorts. 'I'm fetching John, he's somewhere over there.' She waves her hand vaguely.

'Come!' He gets hold of her, by the arm this time, gripping it tightly as though expecting resistance. But before she can shake him off, the preacher speaks and Will lets go.

'This flame is troubling to my body but hath in nowise broke my spirit,' he shouts hoarsely, eyes staring up at the castle.

All heads swivel to look. Silk banners hang from its windows as though it is a holy day; she tips her head back to stare up, and sees the tips of cannons poking out from the battlements. The helmets of the soldiers standing by them are visible too, no doubt ready to fire into the crowd should there be any attempt at rescue.

'Aye, there he is, and wearing the crimson robes.' Will points.

Standing at the tall window above is Cardinal Beaton, in his full regalia, stroking the pointed beard on his long chin as he watches the scene below. The crowd mutters angrily, for it is the Cardinal who leads the Council that condemned the preacher.

''Tis a fine thing to wear those clothes; easy to show he will defend the faith unto death, when it is someone else's death,' Will shouts. 'He maun take care for it may be his own next. That would be a true display of his faith.'

People turn to stare, some nodding in agreement but most looking fearful that he should speak so openly. Bethia tugs on his sleeve.

'Hush Will, stop this heretical talk, or they'll take you too.'

He knocks her hand away, still staring at the Cardinal. She sees he has all but forgot her. Whatever is going through his head she doesn't care. She must find young John and leave.

She turns around, seeking the landmark of the two fat burgesses and stumbles into a soldier, jumping in fear as he catches her. He lets go as soon as she steadies and, by his manner of dress and air of authority, she sees he is an officer.

He nods his head towards the close behind. 'Get thee away home, lass.'

'I must find my young brother first.'

'He's here?' the soldier asks, eyebrows raised.

'Aye, I saw him.'

'Show me.'

She studies him. He has a long scar running down one side of his face, the skin red and puckered; it's lucky the sword missed his eye. Yet, he has a stocky solidity that is reassuring.

He follows her as she ducks behind the two portly men, but John has disappeared. She turns, catching sight of his back as he slips away, and points. The officer leaps forward grabs John, who tries to wriggle out of his jerkin, while the burghers complain loudly about being knocked aside. They fall silent when they see the officer.

He snatches John up and John kicks wildly, opening his mouth to howl, but she rushes forward and clamps her hand over it.

'Wheesht, or the soldiers will take you.'

He glowers at her, but stops kicking.

'Will ye be still?' the officer asks.

He nods his head; after a moment he is carefully lowered to the ground, and Bethia grabs his hand.

'I'll divert my men,' the officer whispers, leaning so close she can count the individual hairs of the red beard springing from his chin. 'Once I do, you maun take this errant knave…,' he grins down at John who stares back, sticking his lower lip out, '…and run fast as you can down the close between the houses. I take it that a lady such as yourself can run?'

She sniffs, then realising he's making fun of her, nods, gripping John's hand tightly. But there's no need for a diversion.

The preacher is gasping in pain. He shouts a hoarse warning at the Cardinal. 'He who proudly looks down upon me shall soon be thrown down himself.'

The Cardinal raises his hand as though to signal, but, before he can drop it, there's an explosion. The flames dance high lighting up the grey day, while those closest to the fire shriek and push to escape.

Bethia draws John to her and huddles beside the officer.

He pats her shoulder. 'It was the gunpowder hung around the preacher's neck exploding. Cardinal Beaton does have compassion, whatever people may say. It was he who made sure plenty was used, so the burning would be over quick.'

The smell of cooked flesh has her swallowing hard.

'Go now,' he says, waving his hand in the direction of the close as he watches the pyre.

Dragging a reluctant John, she flees past the gawking soldiers, down the vennel, across Northgait and into the deserted Mercatgait. There she pauses taking in deep breaths of smoke-free air. A smirr touches her face and she looks up to the sky gratefully, although the Lord has sent too little rain too late to save his faithful servant George Wishart.

John tugs his hand out from hers. 'Let me go. I wanted to see. I'm going back, you can't stop me.'

'Don't be foolish. Do you want Father to find out and whip you?'

John considers, head bent and kicking at the cobblestones. 'Anyways you'll get a skelping from Mother if she sees you've been out in the streets wearing only slippers.'

She smirks, he knows she's too old for whippings, then her smile fades.

'We will both be in much trouble if Father finds out we disobeyed him and left the house.'

They cross the street and John reaches out to take her hand again.

'The man, he took it bravely. Why do they do such a wicked thing to him?'

She sighs. 'He translated the Helvetic Confession of Faith into English, among other things.'

'A book is a reason to burn someone?'

She squeezes his hand. 'You think it torture enough to be made to read, don't you?'

John nods, his head bobbing like a duck on the sea. Then his lower lip wobbles.

'He had a kind face. When his executioner kneeled before him to beg forgiveness, the preacher told him to stand; he kissed the executioner upon the cheek and said he forgave him. But the executioner still tied the noose tight around his neck and chained him to the stake.' John rubs his eyes hard. Then he brightens. 'It was a grand explosion. Did you see the flames, and how people

11

jumped for the fire was singeing them? All of his body bursted apart – I saw a bloody arm fly through the air!'

She swallows again. 'Enough, John. Let's leave the poor man, knowing his torment is over and pray he is at peace. Come, we'll go around the back and in by the byre.'

'Can I stop and speak to the cows?'

She shakes his arm. 'No, you cannot, we must hurry.'

They rush in through the kitchen door startling a flushed Agnes as she bends over her cooking pots; the heat of this fire is welcome after the chill outside. Bethia brushes down her skirts, smooths her hair and takes off her slippers. She dampens a cloth, rubbing hard to remove a boot print from the pink silk.

Agnes shakes her head. 'Ye canna save they now, lassie.'

'I fear you're right.'

She gives up and slips them back on, tucking her feet under her skirts. She'll have to take small steps to hide the toes.

She comes slowly into the hall, John following so closely he's treading on her skirt. The door closes behind them and they stand listening in the dim passageway. All is quiet – maybe Father isn't home yet. She takes a step forward, poised to run upstairs.

'And where have you been?' Father's voice growls from the darkness.

She jumps, heart thumping.

'Come here and tell me all. The baith o' you,' he barks as John turns to creep back to the safety of Agnes and the kitchen.

Dragging their feet, they come to stand before him.

'And while you're explaining your whereabouts, you may also give an explanation as to why I find my book in such a state.'

He holds the open book out, his finger resting on the torn page.

Chapter Three

Evil Deeds

Will cannot believe the hard heart of his mother. She visited the great tower of the Ruthvens by Perth when she was a child, and has desired a painted ceiling ever since. Finally she's worn Father down and now her ceiling is all she can talk about. The wickedness of Cardinal Beaton, the evil done to George Wishart, even his sister huddled in her corner – all are as nothing to her ceiling.

He stares at Bethia; her blue eyes look huge. Normally so calm and controlled, she's shivering; hunched over, arms wrapped around herself. He should've got her away to safety, and ignorance, but then she shouldn't have been there – she can be too interfering, and John can look out for himself.

'The Place of the Ruthvens has patterns in a Celtic knot style, but patterns are commonplace,' chatters Mother, disregarding the daughter shaking on the settle, the husband glowering at the board and John squirming in pain on his cushion. 'Lady Merione says the coming thing is cherubs, angels and much scenery – mountains and rivers and the like. And we need strong colours. I favour the yellow-red of orpiment.'

Father tugs on his beard and Will thinks it's not so far off the colour Mother is seeking for her ceiling.

'What's wrong with cow's blood mixed with a bucket

of lime? It makes a bonny pink when painted on a plastered wall,' he grumbles.

Mother sniffs.

'Where do you expect to find orpiment anyway? There's no exactly a volcano nearby.'

'You're a merchant and can get anything you want.'

'God's death woman, give it a rest.' He strides from the room, slamming the door behind him. His children look to one another and suddenly Will can bear it no longer. He leaps to his feet and paces up and down, fists clenched tightly, wishing there was something, or someone, to swing them at.

He can hear himself talking, talking about the burning, the cruelty of the Cardinal, the corruption amongst the clergy, and, most of all, about George Wishart.

'He was such a good man, such a good man,' he repeats over and over. 'Did you know he returned to Dundee after the plague broke out? He was already safe away and he went back to help the sick. He was kind and courteous, and he kissed his executioner and forgave him.'

He sees Bethia open her mouth and talks louder to forestall her.

'And abstemious, he ate only one meal a day and shared it with the poor. Not like the Cardinal, fathering all they children with the whore Marion Ogilvy, and as many more with other strumpets. Some say he has as many as twenty bastards!'

Mother picks up her needlework and sits up, back straight. 'William, I will not have such talk in my house.' She leans close to the candle-light screwing up her eyes to thread the needle.

Will throws himself down upon the settle making it rock, not caring that his sister, perching on the other end, is nearly catapulted off. The candle is smoking, the smell of animal fat reeks, and mother wipes her watering eyes. Will tugs his jerkin off, flings it upon the bench, and is off again, pacing and talking.

'And the Cardinal, you know what evil he did in Perth these three years past. I was but a lad and didn't know of it, till Norman Leslie told all yesterday.'

'You're but a lad still,' mutters Bethia, gazing at the floor.

Will frowns, and stretches. 'I may only be fifteen years of age, but I'm taller than most full-grown men and I bid you listen, for these are evil times we live in. Beaton had four people accused of heresy in Perth, and one of them a woman with a newborn bairn at her breast.'

'Stop this at once, or we'll all be accused of heresy if it comes to Cardinal Beaton's ears,' orders Mother.

Will ignores her. 'Do you know what the woman was accused of? Not praying to the Virgin more, and especially during the time she was brought to childbed.'

Bethia presses her hands into her stomach and rocks, but Mother says, 'we should always remember Our Lady, and she is aye there for us in times of great need.'

'Why, and is not to call on her worthy of drowning? This worshipping of Mary is all a trumpery anyway.'

'The woman was very wrong not to pray to our Holy Mother. And I'll have no more of this talk.'

Before he can continue Father returns, carrying his daybook. Will thuds down onto the settle. Out of the corner of his eye he can see Father opening the book and glancing at him. He stares at the floor. This isn't the time for studying petty transactions; indeed, as far as he's concerned, it's never the time.

'Bethia, lass, fetch me a cup of ale.'

Will hears the weariness in Father's voice.

Mother looks up and waves Bethia back to her seat. 'Agnes will bring your ale.' She rings the little bell on her sewing table. The bell is rung several times with increasing vigour before Agnes's daughter appears in the doorway, water dripping from her hands.

'What are ye wanting?'

15

'A curtsy first Grissel, to your master and mistress.'

'You called me from the cleaning o' the plates to make a curtsy?'

Mother's lips tighten and Father winks at Will, but he pretends not to see.

'Fetch the master a cup of ale, girl, and be quick about it.'

Grissel clatters out of the room, leaving the door wide so the cold air from the passageway flows in. Will reaches out a long leg and kicks it shut.

'It's time we had new servants, Thomas, some who know what it is to serve,' says Mother.

'I won't turn Grissel or her mother away. Agnes has been with my family since she was naught but a bairn. She has served us well, in her own way.'

'At least let us have one decent servant to wait upon us. I was mortified today when Lady Merione came to call and Agnes sent that child in her dirty apron and great red hands.'

'The child's hands are red raw from all the work she does to care for us. It's not the time to hire more servants anywise. Ye ken we're still recovering from the impounding of the Isle of May and its goods confiscated at Veere, although if I had my son as a helpmeet rather than gadding about the county on his seditious pursuits, our fortunes would revive faster.'

Mother puckers her mouth and stabs the needle into the cloth.

Will rises, trips over mother's footstool and staggers to right himself. He flings the door wide and it bangs off the wall with a satisfying crash. Running down the stairs he grabs his cloak and escapes the house, and his family, in search of some serious, God-fearing discourse.

Chapter Four

The Family

It's washing day. Agnes and Grissel are up before dawn on this mild April morning, drawing bucket after bucket of water from the well and stoking the fires to heat it. When Bethia comes down, the washhouse is full of steam and Grissel is in disgrace. She's tripped over a tub of linens soaking in urine to bleach them, creating a flood across the rough stone floor, and drenching Agnes's feet and the bottom of her dress.

Agnes, up to her elbows in hot water, scrubs furiously at stains on John's breeches. Bethia can see by the frown on her wrinkled face it is not the time to point out that the oatmeal is not boiled, a rat has been at the pigeon pie and someone, Grissel she suspects, has broken the butter crock. She slides away, but Agnes calls her back to fetch lavender for rinsing the linens.

'And I'll have to soak myself in herbs as well or else carry the stench of privy with me, till I get the time to wash my only skirt,' Agnes says, glowering at Grissel.

Grissel, face red from the heat and effort of wringing out clothes, grins at Bethia, behind Agnes's back.

Bethia returns to the kitchen. The fire here has been neglected in the washing frenzy and she crouches in front of it, blowing on the embers to encourage the firewood to catch. She can see now why Agnes complained about the woodman's recent delivery; these logs are too fresh cut to burn well. She digs around in the woodshed and finds a tumble of gorse in the corner. Wrapping her hands in her shawl she carries the prickly bundle inside and, holding it wide from her body, feeds the fire. The gorse is well-seasoned and the fire takes. Before she knows it the pot of oatmeal is engulfed in leaping flames. There's a shriek from behind and Agnes rushes in.

'By God's bones, lassie, what are ye doing?' Agnes picks up the poker and knocks the fiery bush to the side of the hearth. 'All my good whin that I was saving to get the fires going.'

Bethia stands up and backs away, arms behind her and head down. 'I was only trying to help.'

'You've got a curious way of helping.'

'Agnes,' says Mother as she glides into the room, 'what is all the fuffle about?'

There is a pause. 'Sorry, mistress,' says Agnes and bobs a small curtsy.

Mother stares at Agnes and goes to speak, but as she opens her mouth Father strides in.

'What is yon smell?'

Agnes rushes to stir the porridge, burnt and sticking to the bottom of the pot.

John and Will clatter in and slide onto the settle to eat. They both gaze at the meagre board. John opens his mouth to complain but Bethia, next to him, gives a sharp pinch.

'Ow,' says John, jumping. 'Why did you do that?'

She stares at him, opens her eyes wide and shakes her head fractionally so Mother won't notice.

Will gazes into his bowl of charred porridge. Mother studies her own plate of food and bemoans, yet again, what poor servants are to be had in their town, not what she's been brought up to expect. Bethia blushes, knowing Agnes can hear, indeed is meant to hear, every word.

'What's eating you, son?' asks Father.

Bethia looks at Will's sullen face.

'As if you dinna ken,' says Will and the arguments begin again. Father doesn't want to hear what he has to say and she can see Will understands this, but he cannot stop himself. John twitches on his stool, keen to be excused, but she grows more curious about Will's ideas the more he talks.

Father however is not to be swayed by Will's opinions. 'I hear all that protesting nonsense when I'm trading in the Low Countries, making money so you may have the leisure to indulge your ideas rather than putting in a hard day's work. 'Tis a great pity Martin Luther wasn't drowned at birth, Scotland is like to become infested with his pestilential heresies.' He wags his finger at Will. 'There's nae place for monks and preachers in our family. You are for business, my lad, and dinna forget it.'

'You're not listening Father. I don't want to be a priest. They're an unnecessary block between Our Lord and his flock; the supreme authority is Scripture, and not some man in faraway Rome. If the Bible was translated into our own Scots tongue so all could read it, we wouldn't need priests at all.'

'And what of they who canna read?'

She sees Will hasn't considered this, but he soon recovers.

'We can teach people to read and, in the meantime, they'll hear the word in the kirk so they can still answer to God themselves and not have a priest speaking for them.'

'And where are all these bibles to come from – we're no exactly flooded with printing presses in Scotland – and, more to the point, who is to pay for them?'

'We will find a way.' Will's voice tails off into a squeak.

She watches as they go back and forth. John's eyes too shift from Father to brother and brother to Father. It is like the game of caitch Father told of, that they play on the caitchpule at Falkland. King James himself, who died not three years since in that very palace, was fond of the game. Only, instead of a ball, it is ideas being hit between them.

'Enough of your blasphemous talk, enough, enough!' roars Father

The veins stand out on his face like to burst, and she fears for him.

'In my ane house I will have no more.'

'Then I'll leave.' Will slams out of the room and John seizes the opportunity to follow.

'I sent him to the university to learn Latin and Greek, not to debate religious tracts. He wants to be his own man, but riding the horse and wearing the clothes paid for by the trade which he's too grand to engage in. It's all your doing,' he says to Mother.

Mother glares back, but Father isn't finished.

'If you didn't encourage him to think he's better than a merchant's son, he'd be far ower busy to have time to play the lord of leisure and mix with the lairds and their sons talking sedition.' Father pauses. 'But it was a terrible thing done to George Wishart, I hear he was more roasted than burned.'

A shudder runs through Bethia. The smell of burning flesh is still acrid in her nose and she cannot seem to rid herself of it, even when she buries her face in dried rose petals. By night she manages barely any sleep: dancing flames; the innocent face of the preacher; and the story of the poor drowned woman of Perth haunt her dreams. She does not want to hear of it by day.

Father tugs on his beard. She goes to him, laying her hand upon his shoulder and wondering if he knows he has a bald spot at his crown.

'Father, can I do aught to help?'

He reaches up and pats her hand. 'It's a great pity you're but a lass. You've the mind and spirit of a son to make any father proud, all wasted in a woman's body.'

She's glad Will is gone out. It's not the first time Father has told her she's as quick-thinking as a man, but she doubts Will would've winked about it today.

'You cannot go about the stores or the ships; it's neither safe nor fitting. But...,' he inclines his head, '...the ledgers, now that would be a fine thing. I aye hoped your mother would be my helpmeet but she has nae interest, and as for Will... anywise there is no harm in teaching you as well as him.'

Mother sniffs. 'Never mind your accounts, it's time we find her a husband.'

Bethia goes rigid by father's side.

'You want her wed? She's naught but a bairn.'

She relaxes her shoulders, but Mother's next words set her heart to thumping.

'I was married at sixteen and had a child soon after, and I didn't notice you being overly concerned about my youth.'

'Aye, you were a bonny lass.' Father smiles at Mother and, after a moment, she smiles back.

Bethia remembers how beautiful Mother once was, before the pox left the skin of her face as pitted as pick-hacked stone.

'We'll wait a wee whilie yet, Mary. There's nae rush.' His face brightens. 'And if she learns book keeping, it'll make of her a useful wife.'

Mother shakes her head. 'Bethia is *not* marrying one of your fellow merchants. She can do better.'

'Aye and that's no what you thought when you married me, and glad enough your father was too, with no dowry to give.'

'And glad enough you were to get the daughter of an earl.'

Bethia slides out of the room. It might not be so bad to be married and have her own home, rather than listening to an endless repetition of the same arguments. But if Father is thinking of marrying her off to a local merchant, she's not so willing, for there are none under forty years of age. No, better to stay where she is; he'll not send her away if she doesn't want it.

She stands by the casement in her chamber gazing out, and spies the top of Will's head below. There's dust on his cap; she'll make sure and brush it for him when he returns. He strolls away, tossing a ball in one hand and his club over his shoulder. He's off to play at the golf, no doubt in the streets, even though it's been banned. She feels oddly disappointed in him. After all his shouting he should be thinking higher thoughts – not indulging in a boy's game.

Chapter Five

The Great Michael

Will, leaning against the workroom wall awaiting Father's pleasure, can hear him grinding his teeth. The noise makes him grit his own. He tries to shut his ears to it, but Father, bent over his books, keeps on.

'What's got you all perturbed, Father?' he asks, hunching his shoulders up to his ears and awaiting a bellow of "mind yer cheek". Unusually, he's given a full answer.

'Those blethering fools on the town council have decided all merchants must plant trees. What are trees to me? I cannot make any profit from planting something that'll be full grown long after I'm dead.'

'I can see that is a difficulty.'

Father glares at him from under bushy eyebrows. 'I can do without the sarcasm, laddie.'

'When I was a girl and first came to Fife, it had so many beautiful oak trees,' says Mother, appearing in the open doorway.

'Aye and they were all taken for King James IV's grand folly, to make his big ship.' Father pauses and a faraway look comes into his eyes. 'Ye've never seen such a sight as yon ship. The Great Michael they called it, and my it was big, like a fort at sea. Bigger than yon wee carrack Mary Rose which Henry of England built.'

23

Will blinks.

'You ken, King Henry's ship that was sunk last year by the French.'

He shrugs.

But Father's in full flow. 'All the ships that Columbus went to the Americas in coulda fitted inside the Great Michael, and room to spare. I saw it myself; your grandfather took me to Newhaven for the launching. There was a grand fanfare with music and trumpets blaring and all the people cheering and the king smiling all over his face.'

Will glances at Mother, who's leaning forward no doubt waiting to interrupt. It's a relief to see Father in a good humour, and he hopes she's not about to spoil it.

Father's done anyway; the absent look leaves his face to be replaced by one of more customary annoyance. 'Aye, the king's smile didn't last long. He chopped down all the woods in Fife to build it, excepting he didn't cut down any trees around his palace at Falkland mind; oh no, wasn't going to spoil his hunting. Left the rest of the countryside raped bare, spent 30,000 merks in a time when people were starving from war and poor harvests, and then he went off and got hisself killed at Flodden.'

'What happened to the ship?' He's not much interested, but it's better to keep Father talking about ships and trees than be instructed on trading and ledgers.

'It was sold to Louis of France and I heard tell lays mouldering on some French beach. So rests Scotland's folly in wanting to be a grand power and not enough food for its people, and the upshot is now I have to waste my hard-earned money on planting trees.'

Will rolls his eyes. 'I heard tell that the reason we've still one of the largest navies in all of Europe is to stop King Henry blockading our ports.'

Father leans forward, twisting a long eyebrow hair between his fingers. 'Aye, and you would do well to remember it. Henry Tudor is no friend to Scotland. Your

24

ane mother, as you well know, has suffered at the hands of England. Her family was expelled from there for no other reason than being Scottish, and all their property confiscated – so tread carefully, for the Tudor king can never be trusted.'

'That is very true,' says Mother. 'We were a wealthy family of high repute, and were left with nothing.'

Will humphs. He's heard this story many times.

'But Thomas,' says Mother. 'I wish to speak to you of which maxim can be writ large upon the ceiling, for I think it would look very fine to have one.'

Will stifles a laugh at the expression on Father's face.

Mother continues regardless. *'Verbum emissum non est revocabil,* is most suitable,' she says, stumbling over the pronunciation. 'It means, "a word once uttered cannot be recalled".'

'I know what it means,' growls Father.

Mother can barely read and certainly doesn't know Latin. It's most likely Bethia who's feeding her this, although Mother does not encourage his sister's learning. He's heard her tell Bethia many times that she need know only how to figure out simple transactions, enough to run a household, and write her name, and it does not make a woman desirable to be overfull of learning – but no one can keep his sister away from books.

'Can it no wait, I'm ower busy to talk about this just now.'

Mother continues as though Father hasn't spoken, 'Or is this better, *pietas filorum in parente;* "duty and respect to parents"? Shorter too. Yes, I prefer it, it will look very fine.'

'The maxim to go upon my ceiling will cover a wife's duty to her husband, and especially to hold her tongue,' Father roars. 'Christ's death woman, give us some peace.'

Mother turns on her heel, slamming the door behind her and Will sighs; the work is tedious enough without having Father in an ill humour.

'Stop your indolence and get over here.' Father bends over his ledger and Will glowers at his bent head, but comes to stand next to him. Father looks up. 'I am going to say one more thing and then we will get on with the work. I don't know what those protesting friends are telling you but they're all being played by Henry Tudor. A trickster he is, a trickster with a long life. He's outlived two of our kings and will no give up till Scotland is fully in his power.'

Will shakes his head and goes to speak, but Father is off again, pointing his finger at Will. 'You maun take care son; here's a man burnt at the stake because of his heretical words. This is no some laddies' game.' He sighs and slumps onto his seat.

Will feels a rush of rage. 'How can it ever be a laddies' game to have a man die in agony for wanting reform?'

Father sits up again. 'You think this is about reform, well you're wrong. It's got nothing to do with reform.' He stands up and pokes his finger in Will's chest. 'Most of those great friends of yours, the lairds, are in Henry's pay. After we lost the battle of Solway Moss, and Flodden too, half the gentry of Scotland swore fealty to him in exchange for their freedom – his *assured Scots* he calls them.'

The finger pokes once more and he steps back; if Father touches him again, he swears he'll swing for him. He glares down, thrusting his face close to Father's. 'If Henry wants Scotland so much he'd have taken us by now, after all they defeats. The lairds are for reform of the kirk, not for Henry.'

'It's France Henry wants,' Father bellows, spittle flying. 'He's just getting us out of his way, like an annoying wee dog.'

'And what of France, who aye wants Scotland to do her bidding?' Will shouts back, wiping his face with his sleeve. 'There's the Queen Mother sitting like a spider in the centre of her web, pretending all is for her daughter when she is *only* about promoting the interests of her French relations.' Will takes a deep breath to calm himself. 'But what has this got to do with George Wishart and the true words he spoke on the need for change?' His voice trails away. 'It should have nothing to do with it… nothing.'

Father drops into his chair. 'Aye, you would think that, but I do not trust the lairds or their motives.' He looks up at Will. 'All I ask, son, is that you heed my warning and take care. Cardinal Beaton is in their way, and it has little to do with the martyrdom of the preacher, and everything to do with what King Henry of England wants – our wee Queen Mary married to his son, and Scotland finally under his control.'

Chapter Six

Mayday

Beltane comes and Bethia rises with the sun. She joins her friend Elspeth and the flow of girls heading for the Braes to wash their faces in the Mayday morning dew, which will bring good fortune for the coming year. It should be a joyous renewal but the town feels heavy, as though someone is pressing a lid down on a boiling pot that may blow off at any moment. Bethia thinks that even if she and all the lassies of St Andrews immersed their whole bodies in dew, it wouldn't create enough good fortune to prevent the explosion that's building. After the subdued festivities, she drags her feet homeward, already weary of the day.

When she emerges from Louden Close into Southgait, she sees Will hurrying past Holy Trinity, head down. It's a relief he won't be at home and she can have Father's undivided attention – and a break from arguments. But where is he going in such haste? She hesitates, then follows at a distance. He crosses Mercatgait, weaving his way through the busy market stalls.

'That brother of yours aye looks to be on some furtive business,' says a neighbour, grabbing Bethia's arm as she goes to pass. 'And he's got some fancy friends these days, he'll be getting ower grand to speak to us soon.'

Fortunately the neighbour is distracted by the stall

holder arguing the price of a bundle of kale. Bethia squeezes through the crowd and runs down Rotten Row. She sees Will ahead, striding past Fishers Cross watched by the fisher wives redding and baiting lines as they sit chatting on their doorsteps. He turns into Swallowgait and she peers around the corner. Will's stopped in front of a house and is looking back up the street. She ducks her head in, then peeps out again in time to see him disappearing through the opened door.

She walks up the street and stands in front of the house frowning. Who lives here, boarders from the new St Leonards College perhaps, but she can't think what Will could have to do with them. She stands on tiptoe but the lower shutters are closed and she cannot see through the upper mottled glass.

Conscious a pedlar leaning against a nearby wall is watching her, she walks away. Two men brush past her; she recognises them and shivers. The Leslies are powerful and dangerous men. It is said the nephew, Norman Leslie, has quarrelled with Cardinal Beaton and John, the uncle, has spoken openly of vengeance. She turns back to watch them. They too stop at the door and are admitted.

She bites at the skin around her thumbnail, wondering if she should tell Father where Will is, and sighs at the prospect of the shouting match which will inevitably follow. Anyway, Father seems unable to stop Will in anything he's put his mind to. No, better to say nothing, there's no point in causing more arguments.

When she reaches home, she finds the painter has come and gladly forgets about the Leslies.

Mother has cornered Father again. 'We must have vermilion, made of crushed snail shells from the Orient.'

'I know what vermilion is made from – and more importantly how costly it is. What I don't know is why we must have it.'

'There's to be an indigo for blue skies and the angels'

gowns, and a tracery of stars and moons along the beams. It will be exquisite. There won't be another ceiling like it anywhere.'

Father rubs his head, then touches it again, forehead wrinkling. He runs his fingers around the bald patch, stroking and touching. 'Fine, I will speak with the fellow.'

'But I will have my vermilion.' Mother raises her eyebrows and gives a slight nod.

A smile creeps over Father's face. Bethia knows Mother will indeed get her vermilion, and Father his rare reward.

Bethia leaves them and goes to have a look at the painter. She finds him perching on a ladder; he glances down, sees her and winks. Blushing, she hurries from the room, returning later with her friend Elspeth.

The painter has built a scaffolding of planks and ladders, and is laid on his back when Elspeth calls up to him. His hand jerks and the line of the pyramid he's painting smears into its neighbour. He tuts, cleans it off, then leaps down from his eyrie to stand in front of the girls. He has the deepest brown eyes, thick brown curls and a broken nose – which somehow makes him more, not less, attractive. Her tongue cleaves to the roof of her mouth; she could not speak even if she could think of anything to say. Elspeth has no such issue.

'Where are you from?' she asks, and Bethia flinches at her bluntness. A "good day to you", first would be more courteous.

'I from Firenze.' His eyes slide from Elspeth to Bethia as he speaks. Elspeth nudges her.

'Che bellissima,' he mutters to himself.

The heat starts at her neck and crawls up her face.

The door opens and Mother drifts in. 'Antonio, how does the work progress?' She looks up at the ceiling. 'I do hope you're not being interrupted.'

'Ah, signora, the daughter?' He waves his hand towards Bethia.

'Yes, this is my daughter, Bethia.' Mother pauses, not looking at Elspeth, 'and her friend.'

He catches Mother by the elbow. 'The daughter, I must paint.'

Mother looks down at her arm and detaches it from his grip. She opens her mouth to speak, but he forestalls her.

'Mamma e figlia,' he says, 'both the beautifuls. We will have the portrait together, the mother and the daughter, and no one he will know who she is the mother and who the daughter.'

Mother frowns.

'Only one figlia, one she child?'

'Only one living,' says Mother, and looks more kindly upon Bethia than she can remember in a long time.

'Then the portrait we must paint,' says Antonio, sweeping his arm out to take Mother's hand in his, and bowing low.

Mother hesitates, but he kisses her hand and releases it.

'I will speak with my husband.'

Bethia sighs as she thinks on Father's reaction.

Mother opens the door. 'Come girls, we must let Antonio work.'

As Bethia goes to leave, she glances at Antonio and he raises his eyebrows. A giggle escapes from the watchful Elspeth. Dipping her head to hide a smile, Bethia closes the door carefully behind them.

But soon it is Elspeth who's constantly with the painter. At first, Bethia feels she must stay too, she should not leave Elspeth alone with the vibrant Florentine; anyway, it's her hand he bows over and her he calls bellisima, not Elspeth. Yet the more often he takes her hand, the less she likes it, thinking he relies too much on his pretty face to get what he wants.

She's annoyed with Elspeth too. She's seen how, recently, Will grows silent and red-faced when Elspeth is near. She knows, next to the Italian, he's only a boy, but he is her brother. Yet, as the work progresses she realises that Elspeth is more interested in the painting than the painter – asking about the making and mixing of colours, the angle and sweep of the brush and how he creates the cherubs, crosses and fleurs de lys. She's even broached with her parents that they could have a painted ceiling with herself as the artist. Her mother will let Elspeth do as she wills, as long as it is safe, but her father says that no daughter of his is to be an artisan, and laughs at her ambitions. So, under the pretence she's visiting Bethia, she spends as much of her days as she can in the room with the painter, and soon Bethia is unaware Elspeth's even in the house. Anyway, she's preoccupied, the skin around her thumb nail bitten raw – Will is in a strange mood, and she doesn't think it's got anything to do with Elspeth.

Chapter Seven

The Cardinal's Entourage

As the sun finally drops low in the sky, Bethia finds Will reading. He's crouched in the window seat with the lower unglazed shutters open to catch the light, shoulders hunched against the chill breeze. She watches unobserved and then looks out past his bent head to where the golden light brushes the top of the New Inn, the house given to Mary of Guise on her triumphal entry to St Andrews.

She remembers the beauty and foreignness of the new Queen when she arrived from France: the richness of her clothes; her vast retinue including her own father come to check his daughter would be treated with care and full honours; the angel that handed her the keys to Scotland; and the forty days of jousting, archery, hunting, dancing and masquerades which followed. It was the most exciting event of Bethia's life. But now, only six years later, both sons Marie birthed for James are dead, along with King James himself, leaving only the unwelcome baby daughter as queen, and a group of nobles power-broking to control the regency.

But what is Will, who rarely reads, studying so intently he's unaware of her presence? She draws closer and he jumps, closing the tome with a thump and fastening its clasp.

'Come Will, you need never hide a book from me, who loves them above all else.'

Will laughs. 'And that's the truth, my bookish sister. Take care for men do not like a wife who has more knowledge than them.'

She tosses her head. 'Then I will find one who will take pride in a clever wife.'

'Good luck in this town.'

'But what are you reading?' She nudges him so she can squeeze into the narrow seat too.

''Tis better you do not see,' he says, covering the title with his hand.

'Oh Will, it's some heresy. I know it.'

'Well, since you know I need tell you no more.'

She elbows him. 'Come on, where did you get the book?'

Will grins. 'Father's ship brought it.'

'But how?'

'How do you think? The sailors bring them to sell, for there's a ready market in holy St Andrews. Even the priests want to read what Calvin, Erasmus and Martin Luther have to say.'

'Please let me see.' She presses her hands together in mock prayer.

Will bows back and passes her the book. She unclasps it, spreading its weight across her lap.

'It's in Greek!' She's surprised, Will is choosing to read anything in Greek when he complained so often about having to learn it. 'By God's good heart, it's the New Testament translated into Greek.' She looks at him. 'Oh Will, when it's one of the reasons they burned poor Wishart. This is perilous, not only to your life but to your eternal soul. You're questioning our Holy Father in Rome.'

'Stop going on. I don't need you to play the big sister *all* the time. And what is the harm anyway – to read it in Greek, or to read it in Latin?'

She throws the book at him as though it is poison, which in a way it is; poison to question the true faith. She does not understand why Will is getting drawn into this new doctrine, he was never a scholar. She cannot stay in the room, she needs to breathe.

Out she goes into the twilight in time to see Cardinal Beaton's entourage returning to the city. He's not there, no doubt ridden ahead with his guard of soldiers tight about him, the townsfolk made to line the streets and bow as he passes. The baggage train, although well guarded, will travel too slow for his safety. She'd heard it was recently attacked but, not finding the Cardinal, the ruffians indulged in a spot of thievery, stealing a chest full of gold coin.

A small crowd is still there. They've seen it many times, for the Cardinal never travels lightly, but the wonder of all the carts carrying food, fine wine, bedding, clothing, silver plates, fuel, a hundred servants both French and Scots, and the final crowning glory, his four-poster bed perched upon a broad cart, never fails to entertain – although she can hear angry muttering too. She turns to leave after the passing of the bed, and finds the lanky figure of her brother behind her, his face dark with anger.

'You know it is his fault.'

'What is?' she says, wearily. She's cold, and in no mood to stand listening to another of Will's rants, as well as fearful someone might overhear him.

'Come, let me show you.'

He turns and marches for home and she trails behind. Waving her to wait, he disappears up the spiral to the attics. She stands warming herself, her back to the fire, longing for the unseasonably wintry May to pass. She can hear Will rummaging in the room above, boards creaking, and then he's thundering back down the stairs, bursting into the room waving a paper.

'Shut that door.'

He kicks it shut, flapping the paper in front of her face. She snatches it and he hauls her away from the fire. There's an eye-watering smell of scorched wool and he beats at the back of her dress with his hands.

'It's as well Mother isn't here to see you do this, yet again.' He grins at her.

She smiles back ruefully, then smooths the paper crumpled in her fist.

It's a notice. She can see the hole where it was once pinned to a church door or a tree, or, most likely, a Mercat cross. She tilts it, trying to read in the firelight.

'You may thank your Cardinal for this…' it begins.

She looks at Will questioningly.

'When Henry Tudor's troops sacked Haddington and all the other towns, and even burnt the kirk at St Monans, over the past two years, they left a notice each time with these words,' he explains.

She feels the fear, like a punch to her belly. 'And how is it that the King of England invades our country and it becomes the fault of our Cardinal, who has been the great defender of Scotland? Take care, Will, this is anglophile talk, and treason forby.'

'It was us who broke the treaty promising our infant queen in matrimony to King Henry's son,' he mumbles, looking down at his feet.

'It is a too rough wooing of our wee Queen Mary,' she says angrily.

'Why can't you understand Bethia – we must have reform of the church, and Cardinal Beaton is blocking it. And, as the Bishop of Mirepoix, he's all about supporting French interests, for they align with his own.'

She reaches up and touches his face. 'Will, please don't listen to those lairds. Father says they are not good men.'

He knocks her hand away and leaves the room, slamming the heavy door behind him.

Chapter Eight

Conspirators

Will is still so angry he might burst. He can picture it, his guts spilling across the floor and a great steam-cloud of fury rising from them. The wickedness of Cardinal Beaton to do what he did to that gentle soul, George Wishart, makes him question God. For surely a just God would strike the Cardinal down; smite and smite and smite him. But the Lord God Almighty has withheld his gracious hand, and the Cardinal still rides out freely, living a life of greedy self-interest, swelling his own coffers by the wicked selling of indulgences and at the expense of the people of his vast diocese, especially the poor.

He sits in the family pew in Holy Trinity, his back resting where the family's name has been carved into the wood. He's hoping to find some calm in this church of guilds, merchants and craftsmen; the church of the people of St Andrews. The sun glints through the coloured glass, staining the Hammersmith's altar pink and green. Next to it, through the lattice of the screen, the priest sways as he chants the words of the mass; the standing congregation sway with him. The familiar words of the liturgy wash over him, and peace does enter his soul.

It doesn't last long. Again angry thoughts race

through his head until he's ready to bang it off the polished knob which decorates the end of the pew. He knows God can only act through his true servants, which he and his fellows are. He has no choice, he must work with them to bring down the Cardinal.

Nearby, John is swinging the thurible with enthusiasm, the smoke from the incense enveloping him. If he swings it another hands-width wider, he'll give the priest a good whack across the back of the legs with the burner. Will thinks how much he would enjoy that. The priest ends his Latin babble and the boys of the Song School line up, John included, to deliver their pricked song and descant. The purity of their voices soars into the vaulted nave, and brings a tear to Will's eye.

He bends forward to rest his elbows on his knees, face in his hands. He knows that he must be bold but he feels shaky inside. It's his, and his fellows', task to deal with the Cardinal, in the name of the Lord God Almighty. He kens how to shoot an arrow for he's spent enough time at the Bow Butts, as all boys are required to, but he's never attacked anyone. The most he's ever done was to wrestle and swing a few punches, when he was no older than John. When Bethia, squashed in next to him, touches his arm to inquire if he's ill, he glares and knocks her hand away. He's not ill, he's scared.

After dinner he goes to meet with his fellow conspirators in the house by the Swallowgait. He's a minor player in a great game, being only the son of a merchant. It is the lairds, the grandees of Fife, and their sons, who are taking the lead in making plans. Will's included because his friend James of Nydie, is here. And he does most fervently believe in the need for reform, and the doctrine that salvation comes through individual faith and constant reading of the scripture in the vernacular, none of which is sanctioned by the Pope's church.

When he joined the group, he expected much

discourse on such topics but it hasn't happened. He thinks his fellows have forgot why they're here, overtaken by their hatred of Cardinal Beaton and their determination to bring him down. True, Beaton is a wicked and corrupt man, who must be held to account for what he's done to Wishart, and others, but surely there should be some talk of the spiritual amongst the political?

The key conspirators sit along the long board, while the lesser players, who include Will and James, are standing. Will is hard against the wooden panelling that lines the walls in this comfortable home, ridges pressing into his back, with Nydie tucked in next to him. He wonders if it's necessary for James to be quite so close. James is forever touching; a nudge here, a wee pat on the arm there. Actually, today, he finds the prospect of a wee pat on the arm comforting – in view of the plans that are being made.

He studies the conspirators as they talk. Most notable are the Leslies, the uncle John and his nephew Norman, but really it should be said in reverse – for Norman Leslie, Master of Rothes, is a leader of men. He fought at Ancrum Moor last year, leading three hundred bowmen from Fife; a battle against the English where, for once, Scotland was victorious. Norman's certainly taking the lead here, insisting that they must act against the Cardinal, now.

'We will take him where he feels most safe… in his castle,' he says banging his fist upon the board.

'And he *is* most safe in his own castle. I do not think it a wise course of action,' says Henry Balnaves. 'We're not an army, not yet. And although, with wider family members and our servants, we may number over one hundred, most of our followers could not successfully be pitted against Beaton's trained soldiery. We need to take him when he's out from his stronghold, on one of his many processions across the countryside.'

'We've tried, as you well know, and failed. He rides out with too strong a guard. Gaining entry to the bishop's palace is the way to go. I know my way around, am well kent by the servants, and we can enter quietly as a small group claiming to have a meeting arranged.'

'Aye, you are a great friend to the Cardinal,' says Peter Carmichael.

Will doesn't like the man, nor his habit of sneering at others.

'Many of us have been a great friend to Cardinal Beaton – in the past,' says William Kirkcaldy of Grange.

'But not sworn an oath of loyalty to him,' says Carmichael.

John Leslie leaps to his feet, sword in hand. 'Take that back!'

'Sit down John,' says Norman. 'It's true, as we all know. But as we also know Beaton has been ower greedy. When he reneges on a bond he has made to us and takes land that's rightfully Rothes land, then he is no longer deserving of our loyalty.'

'God's death, we've all suffered at the altar of Beaton's ruthless ambition,' says Kirkcaldy. 'My father,' he waves to the man sitting opposite, 'removed from his position as Treasurer of the Realm, Balnaves taken down as Secretary of State, and both imprisoned, as well as your land unlawfully seized. Where we once all worked alongside the Cardinal for the good of our country, he is now too self-interested to ever place its higher good before his own.'

There's much nodding around the board.

'Beaton was himself held prisoner in Blackness Castle for a time,' mutters Peter Carmichael, but he is ignored.

Will tries unsuccessfully to block the memory of arguing with Father about the lairds' motives. Their group is all about curbing Beaton and instigating reform and is not, as Father claims, driven mainly by the advantages the lairds receive from supporting King

40

Henry in his ambition to control Scotland. He does not believe that Balnaves, the Kirkcaldys and the Leslies all receive a regular pension from England to further Henry's cause. Father even says it is only thanks to Cardinal Beaton's valiant efforts to exclude them from power, and to maintain the French alliance, that King Henry's ambitions have not yet been achieved. France is Scotland's puppet master, but Father aye ignores that.

The room is stultifying; Will wipes the sweat from his face and shakes his head to clear it of Father's words. Father has misunderstood the main point, which is surely the desperate need for church reform, and to hold the Cardinal to account for instigating the burning of George Wishart.

It seems James Melville of Carnbee, a close friend of the dead Wishart agrees, for he leaps up making the shared settle rock violently, his companions either side grabbing at the board to prevent being overturned. 'We are not here in service of personal vengeance.' He glares at the Leslies. 'And we are not here in service of King Henry of England.' This time it is Balnaves who receives the venomous look. 'We are here to avenge the death of a good man, whose only crime was to challenge corruption within the clergy, and whose only desire was to bring people to a right and true faith. He chose a martyr's death, as the good Lord wished, and now it is our turn to show ourselves loyal servants of the Lord.' Melville sits down and folds his arms, chin pushed out, daring anyone to challenge him.

There's some shuffling and looking at the floor until Norman Leslie once more takes over, and dour Melville is sidelined. 'We are agreed to take action then,' he says firmly. 'Let me lay the fruits of our discussion before you so we may all be clear.' He rubs his face and takes a deep breath. ''Tis true we never thought to take the Cardinal in his own palace, but it seems our best chance is in the place where he feels most safe. You are in agreement so far?'

There are nods from the group, although Balnaves stares at the board.

'The building work the Cardinal is undertaking to strengthen his castle against attack from England has left him vulnerable, and he seems unaware of this weakness in his defences.' Leslie looks to Balnaves, who nods slowly. 'Indeed, so great is Beaton's confidence in his own power and infallibility, that he's allowed much of his garrison leave to be away, including the Captain of his Guard. At present, he is less well protected than we are ever likely to find him again. Although it was never our intention to take this bishop's palace, it is too good an opportunity to lose. What say you? Shall we seize our moment, take the castle and its Cardinal?'

There's a great cheer, and the men turn to slapping one another's backs as though they've already won a victory. Will watches Leslie look around the group for any sign of dissent, but no one gainsays him.

'Good. And there is an added benefit. In his fear that the castle will be attacked by England, the Cardinal has built up a large stock of powder and lead, as well as purchasing more cannon. Once we're safe inside they will find it almost impossible to dislodge us, giving Henry Tudor ample time to come to our aid.' He pauses and Will sees him take a deep breath. 'We will act, early tomorrow.'

There's another cheer, which Kirkcaldy of Grange hushes in his deep voice. 'We must be discreet. There's many a good plan destroyed by a loose tongue. No word, I mean NO word must leak out, or we'll be undone before we've even begun.'

The jubilation dies quickly and they fall silent in front of this man who exudes great authority.

Kirkcaldy stares at Norman Leslie. 'And to be clear, Cardinal Beaton is to be imprisoned and tried before us all.'

Leslie nods curtly and takes up the reins again,

allocating tasks to those who will enter the castle first. Balnaves is to return to Stirling and will be their eyes and ears outside. William Kirkcaldy will represent his large clan and Norman and John Leslie theirs. James Melville is included in the first wave too, although Will thinks he's unlikely to be handy with a sword. He's surprised to be among the group. He supposes he must have a more warlike appearance than he realises, to be so included. He's less pleased when it transpires he's to gain entry by posing as a workman, because his looks and age fit the part of an apprentice, and even less satisfied when he discovers he must dress in rough clothing and cannot carry any weapon beyond a stonemason's hammer.

When some complain about being left out Leslie says, 'remember, we're doing this by stealth. The rest of you will join us as soon as the castle is safely in our control. It may be the vanguard who take the lead, but your turn for bravery will come later.'

James grins at Will. 'We are the brave vanguard.'

He tries to smile back but he has to grit his teeth to stop them chattering. Once he's out on the street, his courage recovers when Nydie reminds him how easy it will be. He swaggers home, doesn't sleep all night and hours before dawn is up. He dresses in the workman's clothes Melville gave him, which smell of dirt and sweat. Tucking his own clothes into a small sack which he ties around his waist, under the shift, he is ready for action – if he could only control the shaking.

Chapter Nine

The Storming

It is early on the morning of the 29th May in the year of our Lord 1546. Bethia hears the bells for the first mass at the cathedral, then Blackfriars, soon overlapping with a more distant Greyfriars. The noise wouldn't usually call her to wakefulness, there's forever a bell ringing somewhere in St Andrews. It is the squeal of the heavy front door being edged open, but not carefully enough as it grates over the stone floor, which has startled her awake. Thoughts buzz around her head, like bluebottles around a carcass, and she knows she won't get back to sleep.

She slides out of bed, then goes still as Mother turns her head restlessly against the bolster. Mother's slipped down in the night and it's dangerous to lie flat when you sleep – otherwise the Devil may tempt you with his sweet songs; lying flat is only for your coffin. It's not so dark now, no corners for him to hide in; Mother will be safe enough.

Pulling on her skirt she ties the strings tight around the waist then laces her bodice, still surprised by how large her bosom is become, and draws her shawl over it. She creeps down the stairs and leaves the house without any of the racket Will made, for she's trained herself now to check for pebbles on the floor, so the door won't stick.

She assumes it must be him: Father wouldn't bother to sneak; John was asleep in his truckle bed as she arose; and Agnes and Grissel, sleeping in the kitchen, leave by the back door. Maybe today she'll uncover what Will is doing that requires such stealth, and so early.

The air is fresh, a sky of purest cobalt. She thinks how much she'd like to have a dress this colour, but it's difficult to get the dye right for such a pure shade. Mother says she'll get one as a bridal gift, but she's not ready to claim her tocher. She crosses her arms over her breast and hurries down the street.

There's few people abroad so early and they mostly workmen, yet the sun is already climbing. She loves the clean newness of late spring: the green buds on the trees unfurled and reaching for the light and hope of heat; the loud song of birds busy about their nests; the recently sown crops in the riggs behind the houses thrusting through the soil.

Instinctively she heads for the house by the Swallowgait and waits in a nearby doorway. The sea is as blue and still as the sky; it's hard to see where one begins and the other ends. There's barely a ripple as the waves touch the shore at the dunes over by the West Sands. All would be peaceful, were it not for the dark mass of the castle to her right.

A woman passes, trailed by her servant, head bent and muffled in her cloak as she hurries up Fishergait. It is Marion Ogilvy, the Cardinal's mistress and mother of nine of his children, leaving the castle and heading for the house he keeps for her in Southgait. She thinks of Will's indignation that Cardinal Beaton has a mistress.

'What does it matter when George Wishart himself said a priest should marry?' she'd said.

'Because it's honest and above board to marry,' Will roared. 'And dishonest to keep a whore and a pack of bastards that you're busy finding livings for, good livings which belong to the church and are not the benefice of

Beaton's to give away at will.'

She gave up the argument then, for Will always has an answer, and even when he doesn't, he shouts her down. Privately she considers that it's right the Cardinal looks to care for his own, and she does not think any less of him for it.

Suddenly there's movement, and she forgets about Marion Ogilvy and her children. Pulling the shawl over her head, she slips into the close, the smell of the byre strong. Will and three others, all dressed as workmen, stride past the end of the close; heart thumping, she follows.

He's dressed in dirty hessian and all four carry tools. A group of workmen amble ahead, and the four move faster to tuck in behind them. One workman turns to look at the newcomers and, as quickly, turns back. Bethia, now, only a short distance behind, sees fear on his face – and feels it gripping her own belly too.

They're in the shadow of the castle now, early sun glinting off the windows high above. She speeds up, determined to stop Will, to save him from whatever he's got himself drawn into – doesn't care if she embarrasses him in front of his fellows – but she's too late. The whole group are crossing the bridge over the dry moat, while the porter holds wide the gate and bids them enter. She stands uncertain, but the bishop's palace is closed to her. She's never been inside and can think of no reason whereby she could convincingly request entry now, for she's neither a servant nor a whore.

The rhythmic thump of hammer hitting stone begins and, hanging in the still blue sky, a seagull calls. There's the ghosting of last night's moon above and the whisper of water touching the rocks below: a perfect day – yet she's standing close to the spot where George Wishart died in agony, and she shivers; his ghost has touched her.

She hears voices coming from behind and shrinks against the castle wall. A party of men are striding down

Rottenrow, talking loudly. Unlike Will and his co-conspirators, these men are bright in cloaks, feathered caps and pantaloons. They too cross the moat. Bethia gasps, she knows at least two of their number: Norman Leslie and the young laird of Nydie, Lady Merione's son. James turns his head, and gestures urgently for her to leave, but he doesn't stop. She can hear Leslie demanding loudly that they're here to speak with the Cardinal, that he's expecting them. The porter again opens the gate and they too disappear through the gateway.

All is still once more. The servant from the house behind is in the byre, talking to the cows. The gate opens wide and out she comes, leading the beasts to pasture. Bethia rocks from one foot to the other; should she go home and fetch Father? A group of men, including John Leslie, come charging down the street, alarming the cows who grow skittish and scatter before them, knocking her out of the way.

The men are armed and their blood is up, ready for a fight. The porter, alarmed, tries to close the gate – but they're too quick. They leap onto the bridge and she can see the raised arm of the foremost, dirk glinting in his hand and then the quick slash as he stabs the porter once, then twice, in the chest. Then he's tossed into the dry moat, like a slaughtered beast.

There's a wail from behind. The servant too has seen the porter stabbed, and sinks to her knees. She screams, long and loud, until Bethia kneels to hush her, when she settles to whimpering. High above a figure appears at a window, gazing down upon them, and then vanishes.

The men have disappeared inside and the gate is unguarded. She crosses quickly but there's a great shouting from within and she hesitates, then retreats to the shelter of the house. The servant girl has run away and left her cows milling in the street, while people spill from their homes, looking to one another for an explanation.

She must get Will out, otherwise he'll go the way of

47

George Wishart. She knows he believes in the preachings of Martin Luther, but surely that does not condone the brutal killing of an innocent porter. But no one has looked; perhaps the porter is still alive. The idea of clambering into the stinking fosse has her skin crawling, but the thought of how long she'll be condemned to purgatory if she leaves him lying injured drives her forward. The shouting from inside the castle grows louder as she again crosses the unsafe space between it and the houses. Teetering on the edge of the deep ditch, she slides down on her buttocks. By God's bones, it smells bad. The porter is lying, arms outstretched, atop the rubbish. Drawing closer she sees his eyes are wide open, no doubt surprised to be catapulted into purgatory so abruptly. She'll pay for masses to be said for his soul; then his time there should be as swift as his dying, she hopes.

She clambers back up, resolved to race up the ramp into the castle. Then she will find Will and drag him home before he destroys his own, and his family's, future. She's nearly at the top of the fosse when suddenly men are running out through the gate. She can see their bare feet level with her eyes. Where are their boots? Her eyes travel upwards; driven from behind like cattle, they're naked as newborn babes, their pizzles slapping against their legs as they escape down the drawbridge and across the castle forecourt.

The townsfolk crowding in front of the castle, watch open mouthed, while Bethia peeps through her fingers. The last naked man is chased out, followed by a great herd of workmen. At least they have been allowed to keep their clothes. Then the gate is shut. She hesitated too long and won't easily gain entry to the castle now. She runs back to join the watchers. Someone grips her arm. It is Father, but she's too stunned by what has happened to be afraid of his anger.

'What are ye doing here? This is no place for a lass,

and with all they naked soldiers running about.'

Soldiers? By the blood of Christ, Will and his co-conspirators have made the soldiers strip and chased them out. She leans in to whisper to Father that Will is inside, that they must get him out, but the Provost, Sir James Learmonth, is shoving his way in on Father's other side.

Learmonth's face is puffed up with anger. 'What *is* this disturbance, and so early on a May morn?' he demands.

Before Father can reply, there's a cry from high above, a cry as if a boar was shafted. The Provost staggers and Father lets go of Bethia's arm to steady him, while the crowd falls silent.

Chapter Ten

Inside the Castle

Will feels powerful as they chase the soldiers, as if he truly can be a warrior – except his fellows have swords and daggers, while he only has a mason's hammer. Nevertheless it's exciting. Shouting and waving the hammer, he's one of the ring around the soldiers making them strip, although many are only half dressed anyway, having been rudely awoken from their slumbers. When his heart stops thumping and his brain is clear again and he looks at the few naked scrawny soldiers as they drive them out through the gate, it's not such a triumph after all. He knows they wouldn't have succeeded, or at least not so easily, if most of the officers hadn't been from the castle. They round up the servants and workmen next to push them out, although some choose to stay and join their garrison. That feels good; makes what they're doing seem right.

He's getting his breath back when young Nydie beckons. He runs over, slowing when he sees James smiling at his eagerness, and adopts a swagger for the last few steps.

'That wasn't too difficult, Nydie.'

'Aye well, now you can come help with something more challenging,' says James.

He feels a prickle of irritation; Nydie's only a few

years older than him, and considerably smaller. He has no right to patronise. Then he notices the sword twitching in James's hand and realises James is as scared as he.

James tells how they've found the Cardinal, barred in his room. Will strips off the hessian and quickly changes into his clothes, then runs to catch up. He mounts the stairs at the back of the group, behind Nydie's vivid green jerkin with its gold braiding. In different circumstances he'd be pushing to the front, but he's more than happy to bring up the coo's tail today. Ahead John Leslie is hammering on a studded door with ornate iron hinges.

A voice calls from within. 'Who dares disturb my peace? Begone, before I set the guard upon you.'

Will can hear how shaky the voice is.

Leslie laughs cynically. 'Go ahead, call the guard. We will await your pleasure.'

He nods to the man behind him and steps to one side. The man has a long heavy mallet and he swings it, hitting the door with an almighty thwack that reverberates down the passageway. There's a shriek from inside, then the scrape of something heavy being moved; the door shudders. The hammerman swings his mallet once more but without much enthusiasm. It's obvious to all that he doesn't have space to wield it to good effect, especially against such a sturdy door.

John Leslie, Peter Carmichael and James Melville draw back. There's much whispering, then the hammerman and Carmichael leave, pushing past Will as they hurry down the turnpike of steps. They soon return carrying armfuls of straw and wood. It seems the Cardinal is to be imprisoned within a smokehouse, much like the haddock landed from the fishing boats. Will shudders. Nydie hisses that it's justice for the Cardinal to burn, or it would be if only someone had remembered a means of lighting the fire.

51

'You at the back,' shouts John Leslie.

Everyone turns, including Will, but there's no one behind him.

'Yes, you, you glaikit lump,' Carmichael roars.

He can feel his face flushing.

'Get to the kitchens and fetch some embers.'

He opens his mouth to complain that he doesn't know the location of the kitchens, or indeed any room in this great bishop's palace, but thinks better of it. He runs down the winding stairs so fast he's dizzy. He can't think why Peter Carmichael has taken so agin him, roaring at him in front of his fellows? He's done his part in the taking of the castle. He would have shed blood if it'd been necessary, although he is not entirely confident he could deliberately stab another of God's creatures.

He steps out into the portico, hoping to quickly find the kitchens or indeed any room which might have a fire burning. The Cardinal will probably have one in his chamber, but he's hardly likely to respond to a request for hot coals. He can see some of his fellows standing guard near the main gate, but otherwise the bailey is empty.

The courtyard is cobbled with a large well in the centre and is clearly regularly swept, since Will sees a broom lying, where the servant must have dropped it when he fled. To his right is the great hall, obvious by its long windows, to his left more high walls with stabling below them for horses, and a few hens perched upon its roof. The kitchens will be on the far side, away from any living quarters and the danger of setting them alight. He heads towards them.

He can hear shouting coming from the great hall, Norman Leslie and Kirkcaldy of Grange must be inside taking control. He slides through a narrow doorway, below an outer flight of wooden stairs, and twists down two or three stone steps. He can dimly see a hole in the floor with the trap door raised behind it, and peers over the edge. It's a dark space, deep and dank smelling. He shivers and retreats. It's most probably the infamous dungeon dug out of the rock and shaped like a bottle, where they'll likely imprison Cardinal Beaton – once they've captured him.

In the corner tower, beneath the flight of wooden outer stairs, a door stands wide, and Will steps down onto the rough floor; no smooth flagstones here. It's also dark, lit only by the small unglazed embrasures along the sea wall. A broad trestle runs the length of the arched cellar and Will can see signs of hasty departure – oatmeal spilt, a broken egg upon the table and a pot hung in the huge fire pit. He pokes at the heap of ashes uncovering a soft orange glow. Snatching up the scuttle, he shovels hot coals onto it. He moves quick as he can to return to his waiting fellows, arm outstretched to keep the burning heat away from his face.

John Leslie's grim faces lightens when Will's head appears.

'At last, did you go to Hades itself?' Carmichael calls.

But Will is too intent on blowing the coals to keep them alight to pay heed.

The straw takes quickly, the fire leaping high, and soon the wood they brought is burning merrily too. It's a well-made door of good Scottish oak but the flames are licking it, creating long black scorch marks which rise higher and higher. Nydie, this time, is sent to fetch more wood to get the fire even hotter. Smoke is rising from the door, creeping up the turnpike and along the wooden roof timbers. If they feed the fire enough, not only will it burn through the door, but set the roof alight.

There's a scraping noise from behind the door, then cries from within. A voice shouts, 'leave the armoire in place, that is an order.'

The noise of someone pushing something heavy continues. They hear a ringing slap, even above the crackle of the fire.

John Leslie leans as close to the door as he safely can.

'Give yourself up man, or it'll go ill for you.'

'Is that Norman?' calls the Cardinal.

'No, it is John, John Leslie.'

'I will have Norman, for he is my friend.'

Leaning in to listen, Will thinks, Norman is not your friend, not anymore.

'Content yourself with such as are here, there are no others.'

Will shivers, for Leslie's voice is cold as a bucket of icy water tipped ower him.

'I will open the door if you promise me safe passage,' the Cardinal pleads.

There's a snort of laughter from Carmichael, and Leslie raises his eyebrows, finger over his lips.

'We promise you safe passage,' says Leslie leaning into the door. 'Safe passage to hell,' he mutters to Carmichael, who smirks.

James Melville steps away from them. Will can see he disapproves of Leslie and Carmichael's levity.

'You will not kill me?' Beaton asks, so softly Will strains to hear the words.

'We will not kill you,' Leslie says loudly.

They wait.

There's a shuffling as the servant is presumably permitted to push the armoire aside and then the door is slowly unlocked. Leslie, Carmichael and Melville leap over the fire and rush into the room. Nydie follows, while Will and the hammerman kick the fire and stamp on the scattered embers. Will coughs and coughs on the smoke.

Chapter Eleven

Cardinal Beaton

Cardinal Beaton sits upright in his chair, hands holding his belly. He's dressed in his red robes and even his cardinal's hat, just as when he watched poor Wishart die from on high. Will rubs his watering eyes, thinking things might go better for Beaton if he wasn't wearing these robes. The servant edges towards the door and Will blocks his exit.

Leslie and Carmichael stand before the Cardinal, who gazes at them. There's a glint of steel and suddenly Leslie has a jagged edged whinger in his hand, and Carmichael is fumbling at his breeches to release his dirk. Will snorts as Carmichael struggles with his clothing. He covers his mouth with his hand, can't believe that such a sound escaped him. Carmichael glances over his shoulder, glaring at Will.

Beaton's expression changes from one of outraged hauteur to terror when Leslie points the whinger at his face. He flinches. 'You promised!'

'We make no promises to a viper,' hisses Leslie and stabs at the Cardinal's chest. Beaton raises his arm to protect himself and the point slices deep into his flesh. He screams, and Leslie tugs on the knife to release it.

'I am a priest,' shrieks Beaton, face twisted in pain, clutching the arm as the blood runs from under his sleeve to drip on the floor.

Leslie's only response is to lunge again, and this time he hits the collar bone.

Will winces, puzzled; they'd agreed to take the Cardinal hostage, not kill him. Perhaps they intend only to maim, for surely he's more use to their cause alive than dead? He does not want to watch an attack on Beaton, any more than he wanted to watch the slow burning of Wishart, but, yet again, he cannot draw his eyes away.

Carmichael's finally freed his dirk and raises it high, stabbing down. Beaton tries to block the knife point with his uninjured arm. Leslie takes the opportunity to thrust his knife below the raised arm but the Cardinal hunches, protecting his heart. This time Leslie's dagger bounces off Beaton's ribs.

'I am a priest, I am a priest! You cannot slay me.'

It seems to Will that the Cardinal is taunting them with his invincibility. Faces flushing in the fury of the kill, Leslie and Carmichael raise their daggers to stab again and again, for Beaton may be a cardinal but he cannot be allowed to believe he's under God's protection, not after the burning of Wishart and others too; that was the Devil's work.

But before they can hack him to pieces James Melville awakes from his torpor and shouts. 'Stop!'

Leslie and Carmichael both stop, Carmichael with his arm raised high, and stare at Melville. Beaton, hunched over, blood soaking his clothes, looks to his rescuer. Will looks to Nydie and his eye catches Beaton's forgotten servant. He knows all three of them are waiting for an excuse to leave the slaughter.

'This is not the way,' Melville says. 'The judgement of the Lord will be dealt out wisely, soberly and justly, not in an ill-managed frenzy.'

Carmichael lowers his dirk and yields to Melville. After a moment Leslie steps back too.

Beaton twists in his seat, holding his arm and pressing

his elbow into his ribs to stem the bleeding. 'You must protect me,' he appeals to Melville. 'I am a servant of God and he will reward you for saving his own.'

'Don't listen to him.'

Will looks around and is astounded to see it's the Cardinal's servant speaking.

'You deserve to die,' the servant hisses at Beaton.

The Cardinal glares back, clearly incensed that his servant should speak to him thus. 'Get thee awa, Guthrie. You have failed to protect me and have no place here, nor ever will again.'

Guthrie stares at him, then hawks and spits. He pushes past the men and goes to leave the room. This time Will doesn't stop him.

Beaton stares at the lump of yellow mucus defiling his red robes.

Carmichael raises his dagger once more, but Melville raises his hand. 'Let all things be seemly in the sight of our Maker.'

Beaton looks up hopefully, but Melville shakes his head.

'Careful, Cardinal, Prince of Darkness, you are on your way to the eternal fires of judgement. Do you repent of your wicked life, and especially of the shedding of the blood of that notable instrument of God, Master George Wishart?'

Melville doesn't wait for a reply, but continues as though he is a preacher in the kirk delivering a disputation, such as the reforming priest Luther strongly advocates. Beaton, who had pulled himself upright in his chair, hoping Melville would release him, slumps again. He's bleeding freely from his slashed arms and chest, blood pooling on the flagstones at his feet.

'We are sent from God to revenge the death of his humble servant George Wishart. And here, before God, I protest, that neither the hatred of thy person, nor the love of thy riches, nor the fear of any trouble have moved me to strike you; but only because you have been and remain an obstinate enemy against Christ Jesus and his holy Evangel.'

The Cardinal shrinks further as Melville delivers a verdict on his wicked life, dwelling especially on the murder of innocents and his love of riches. Melville talks in loud sonorous tones, shouting as he reaches his crescendo. 'How are the mighty fallen. Wicked pride lies humbled. God is not mocked. Priest of wickedness, REPENT!'

Still Will is expecting the Cardinal to be chained and thrown into the castle's dank dungeon, to be tried later. He imagines Beaton being made to stand in front of them and plead his case as George Wishart did. Melville is too portentous, too full of his own righteousness and too dull to kill anyone. He can see that Beaton, although in considerable pain, is hopeful he will survive. They are both surprised when Melville, with the word repent still ringing around the chamber, takes his sword and runs Cardinal Beaton through.

He has no chance to even raise his arm in self-defence. He stares down at the sword protruding from his chest as Melville hauls it out and runs him through a second time. He falls forward over the sword and Melville has to press his foot into Beaton's chest to free it. He topples to the floor, more blood gushing from his mouth.

They all stare down at the crumpled body.

Nydie turns and vomits on the floor, splashing Will's legs with watery flux.

'Get him out,' instructs Melville, nodding towards Nydie.

Will takes James by the arm and leads him quickly away. Norman Leslie appears at the foot of the stairs, and glowers at them, for James's face is a sickly pallor and Will suspects his own is a similar hue.

'Is he dead?'

They nod.

'Hah, you lads have not the stomach for men's work,' Norman says derisively.

Will grimaces, thinking Leslie has no right to criticise, having stayed well away from the killing and left his Uncle John to oversee the foul deed. Will realises that Leslie knew Beaton would be killed and feels a flush of rage to have been led astray.

'I thought the Cardinal was to be tried?'

Norman Leslie ignores him, calling up to his fellows. 'The townsfolk have gathered outside and we should declare to all we are now in control of the castle.'

Will notices he doesn't climb the stairs, nor enter the room.

They all run up to the parapet to look down at the crowd below. Will hangs back. Hidden by the line of the roof rising steeply above, he peeps out watching the crowd far below. He doesn't want to be seen, doesn't want to be associated with the killing, is already ashamed of his part in it.

'The evil slayer of George Wishart is dead,' Norman Leslie shouts to the crowd.

There's silence and then a common intake of breath.

'Whaur's the body?' calls a fishwife and the crowd take up the call chanting, 'show us the body!'

Leslie stands back from the parapet and consults with his fellow leaders. Will can see Kirkcaldy speaking angrily and violently shaking his head, but it looks as if he's been over-ruled. Will ducks down in the doorway to make sure he's not commanded to carry the bloodied body of the Cardinal up all these stairs. Four men less quick on the uptake are sent and half drag, half carry the now naked Beaton. The blood runs from the wounds, leaving a trail of red, the colour of the Cardinal's robes, across the mellow sandstone. The body has been slashed many more times after Will left the chamber and the guts tumble from the belly. They hang it over the parapet by an arm and a leg, for all to see.

Norman Leslie addresses the crowd. 'He was Archbishop of St Andrews, the Pope's appointed leader in Scotland, Bishop of Mirepoix in France, Counsellor to James V and Chancellor to the young Queen's regency, yet all his grandiosity has not saved him from a well-deserved end. Take heed, for our Lord is not mocked.'

Will is watching, fists pressed into his cheeks, but worse is to come. Beaton's servant, that foul creature Guthrie, climbs upon the parapet and, fumbling in his breeches, he releases his stream upon the Cardinal's body, angling so as to fill the dead open mouth.

Part Two

Bethia

June to October 1546

Chapter Twelve

Gaining Entry

John is disappointed he missed it. He wants Bethia to tell him the story again and again: how the body was hung, how the blood fell, how the piss ran down the dead Cardinal's face and dripped into his mouth and how his shit-smeared legs dangled weak as a new born calf. Next day, as soon as Father leaves the house, John runs out to stare up at the castle but the body has gone; only a bright streak of red across the yellow stone marks where it hung. Bethia's relieved when John doesn't ask any more; it's all too grim to speak of, especially when she considers Will's involvement. She should've stopped him; oh, how she wishes she had.

'Do ye ken where's Will's gone?' Father asks, tugging at his beard.

'Nooo,' she answers but her eyes slide away. She's hoping he returns home soon, and his part can be hidden from both Father and the Queen's soldiers, who will no doubt quickly come to re-take the castle – and punish the perpetrators.

Father stares at her, rubbing at the back of his neck, but if she says aught she'll have to admit she saw all and did nothing.

'Aye well, he's probably away on some nonsense, as usual,' he says.

She picks at the skin around her thumb. They both know Will is a lad consumed by the right way to follow God's true word, and not much inclined to nonsense. The fear of what may happen to him scratches away inside her.

For the first few days, there's always a group of townsfolk gathered near the castle gate waiting for something to happen, but the soldiers expelled naked as newborns do not reappear to take back their dead Cardinal's palace. Loud laughter and carousing from within can be heard and soon some of the watchers are calling at the castle gate and asking to join the revellers. Everyone knows of the rich stores the Cardinal kept, why should they not join the celebration and partake of them? For did they not all suffer under his yoke?

Bethia goes to stand before the forbidding walls and closed gate. She stares up, willing her brother to look out and see her. Instead a group of men high above lean over the rampart calling down.

'Come on up my bonny lass and gie us all a wee cuddle.'

She thinks of asking for Will but doesn't want to be the town crier, letting everyone know he's inside. Their calls get louder, and more coarse, as she lingers. Then the men disappear and she hears the clatter as they run down the turnpike. She scoots away as the gate is flung open.

'Don't go, my wee lass. We're all lonely here,' they shout as she runs along the path that leads to the harbour. It's the path she came toiling up in search of John barely three months ago, only to witness the preacher, flesh shrivelling and slowly smoking to death. She shudders as she runs and then she's angry. She shouldn't have to spend her life taking care of her brothers, who live as though they've no responsibilities. She'd like one day of being indulged, as they have been all their lives, just one. Then she remembers the beatings John endures and the contempt with which Father treats Will; maybe life isn't easy for them after all.

She pauses by St Mary's on the Rock, her beloved chapel, says a quiet prayer to the Virgin to return Will safely home and bends to touch the stone with her lips. The harbour below is busy and Father's ship has come in. He's chatting to the captain as they watch the cargo of linen, furniture and coal being unloaded and taken to his warehouse. Father may be standing at ease, but he won't miss anything. Later he'll pass his scribbled notes for her to enter into the big accounting book. She should be home collecting carbon from the chimney to make up more ink, not spying on him, but she stays watching the bustle on the long wooden pier. There's been talk of building one of stone to hold strong against the winter storms, but this would be a big undertaking, which Father says won't happen, not in his lifetime.

A boat is being rowed out from the harbour. Curious, she retreats back along the path to watch, as it hugs close to the cliff. Both oarsmen are rowing strongly into the rising wind and a third man is sitting at his leisure in the stern, dark cloak wrapped tight around him. It's as well the tide is far enough out so they can see, and avoid, the rocks. They draw close to the castle, so close they may be fired upon, and she wonders why they're taking such a risk. Then the boat rounds the castle rock and disappears from view. She waits, holding onto her cap which the wind is tugging fiercely. Just when she thinks she must go home before Father returns, the boat re-appears, bobbing over the white caps, which the wind is frothing like Agnes beating eggs and sugar for a sweet pudding.

There are only the two oarsmen in it now. It is as she suspected: the cloaked figure will have entered the castle through the seaward postern – a gate through which she too might quietly gain entry. She needs a man with a small boat; a fisherman. She hurries home; if she can only get Agnes on side.

* * *

65

There are soldiers in front of the castle now, the Captain of the Guard has returned and found his men. They are clothed and booted and keep watch at a safe distance from musket shot or fired arrow although a well-aimed cannon might cause havoc. They are successful in preventing the garrison inside from coming and going freely as they have been doing up to now, and preventing those outside from joining them.

Father wonders where the captain found clothes and weapons for men who were expelled naked as squealing piglets. She's pleased to hear him laugh. It makes a change from pacing up and down worrying about Will.

'Why does he send no message?' she hears him mutter. 'Even a wee word to tell us he's safe.'

She thinks, that's what she should have done when she could, passed a note for Will through the gate, but when she remembers the leering men her heart fails her. It is wicked to leave Father in such an agony of not knowing, but she keeps expecting Will to return home, and if he does she'll have spoken unnecessarily. She gnaws at the skin around her finger nails; if he doesn't come soon then she must fetch him.

Mother says Father is fussing over nothing, and Will is off with young Nydie on some prank – which story she has fortunately shared with their neighbours. Father shakes his head, his expression grim. He guesses where Will is, Bethia thinks, but if he doesn't voice it then perhaps it won't be true.

Agnes has arranged the boat, but now Bethia must be brave and act. She doesn't know if she can do it and asks Agnes if her brother, Geordie the fisherman, would take a message to the castle instead. Agnes says he's a great gowk, who hasn't got the sense he was born with, and cannot be relied upon. Bethia tears some more at her skin and now her fingers are bleeding. May the Virgin grant her courage.

She rises before the first bells the next day and slips

down through the pends, passing the mill, its wheel turning and the miller already at work, through the Sea Yett and onto the quayside. Geordie, as arranged, is waiting on the pier. He bobs his head at her, climbs down the ladder and onto his boat. She stands on the edge and looks down at him looking up. It is a long drop to the boat below.

He frowns and beckons. She turns around and kneels on the pier then sits back on her haunches to suck out the splinter which has stabbed her, sharp as any needle.

'I haven't got all day. Are ye coming or no?'

Edging backwards, she gets her feet on the first step of the ladder fearful he can see up her skirts. Next time she'll borrow a pair of breeches from John – but there shouldn't be a next time. She fumbles to find the step, when a hand grips her foot placing it firmly on the rung and, by this method, she slowly descends until she's lifted and swung into the boat.

'Sit ye down,' he says and she does, sending the boat wildly rocking. Now the fear is of the unsteadiness of the small craft. She's only ever been on Father's ship, safely enclosed behind the rails on deck, and they never left the quay. She grips the sides tightly, knuckles white. They pull swiftly away, the wind pushing the boat along and whipping her hair out from under her cap and around her face. The tide is on its way out, and more of the shoals are exposed than when she watched the boat creep close to the base of the cliff at high tide yesterday. Agnes's brother swerves around the half-hidden rocks; he'll know this coastline, no doubt as well as the wrinkles on his wife's face.

They reach their destination sooner than she expects, bumping up against smooth rocks below the cliff, which form a jetty. Geordie leaps out and offers his hand to steady her as she follows him. The crumbling sandstone is soothing to the eye, but the castle rising above is grey and forbidding. She tips her head back and can see a small gate high above, but she can't see any way to reach it.

Geordie shouts and after a few moments a face peers through the bars of the yett. He sniffs, 'They must be thinking God is keeping watch for them, since they're no bothering.'

'Bethia Seton, what are you doing here?'

She sees James of Nydie's blonde head and frowning face looking down.

'Is there a way up, I need to speak with Will.'

'There is a ladder but it's not an easy climb.'

'I'll manage,' she calls, voice quivering.

A rope ladder is unravelled and hangs, swinging in the breeze. Geordie grabs the end of it and she goes to step on.

'Wait,' cries James and a rope comes slithering down. 'Tie it around you.'

Up she goes, the ladder swaying and banging off the cliff. She keeps her eyes fixed on the uneven rock close to her face, so close in places that her nose and knees bump off it, and her knuckles scrape over it. Her breathing is loud in her ears, fluttering and panicked, but she's grateful to James for the rope, doesn't think she could have done it otherwise.

'Ye'd better no be long,' Geordie shouts, as she's crawling through the gate. 'If the tide gets too far out the boat will be stuck till it rises again.'

She waves a hand in acknowledgement as James helps her up. Then she's passing through the yett and into darkness. The stone feels uneven beneath her feet, it must be the servants area, perhaps the cellars and store rooms. There's a doorway at the end; the door is ajar and a shaft of light illuminates the vaulted ceiling. They pass through into a large courtyard and, in front of her, is the portico.

The painter, Antonio, has talked of the porticos of his Firenze and of the graceful stone arches which are a walkway providing cool shelter from their hot sun. She is sure this one is as beautiful as any in Florence, although Antonio says in Scotland a castle portico only gives shelter from the rain. A pretty folly, he calls them, and perhaps he's right, as the rain, which had held off for her passage, is now splashing onto the cobbles.

Above the portico are tall windows rich with coloured glass, probably the chapel. She wonders if the Cardinal's body is laid out there, although it will stink by now. Perhaps they've preserved it in salt like Agnes does to keep the beef after the autumn killings. No, more likely they saved the precious salt, and tossed the Cardinal's remains into the sea.

There is a tug on her arm, and she's brought back to herself.

Chapter Thirteen

The Regent's Son

'Bethia, what brings you here? It's not safe.'

'Will, at last.' She touches his arm. 'Thanks be to Mary, you are safe,' she looks him over, 'and seem unharmed.'

He steps back. 'Of course I'm unharmed. We barely had to raise a sword and they were pissing themselves and begging to be let go. We made them strip and run out, naked as they came into the world.' He gives a bellow of laughter in the telling which sounds overloud to her ears.

'I saw,' she says, brushing the hair out of her eyes.

They move to shelter beneath the overhang of the great hall roof, for the rain is falling steadily now, like an old grey cloak. He stands with his feet wide apart, arms akimbo but he is such a boy that his beard is a fluff upon his chin.

'You must come home with me now, Father is angry.'

'So,' he shrugs.

'He's worried, so worried he paces night and day. You know how Father can pace.' She stutters over the words in her anxiety.

But Will's not to be mollified. 'I will stay with my friends,' he says, thrusting out his chest. 'I cannot creep away like a scared lassie.'

She steps back. 'The friends who murdered the Cardinal.'

He looks at the ground, shuffling his feet.

'Please tell me you had no part in his death.'

Before he can reply, two men appear at his side.

'Who's this, young Will?'

Will dips his head and introduces her. She recognises Norman Leslie, Master of Rothes, and the smaller and more handsome, who's named as Peter Carmichael, also looks familiar. Both men bow and she's forced to hold out her hand, conscious that the wind has made a wild tangle of her hair, for them to give their obeisance, which they do. Then she's angry with herself; she doesn't want killers kissing her hand. Yet she is relieved that they treat her courteously and not like the ruffians who shouted the other day – although she thinks Carmichael, who has his eyes fixed upon her chest, might have been among them. She pulls her jacket close around her.

''Tis better you leave here. Let me escort you to the gate,' offers the Master of Rothes.

She doesn't want to leave, not until she's had a chance to speak with Will some more – and she certainly doesn't want to leave by the main gate, for all the town to see, even if she didn't have a boat waiting.

'There's family business. I must speak with my brother,' she mumbles.

The man smiles and she can see understanding in his eyes.

'Then we will leave you.' Bowing, he turns and walks out into the rain with his companion by his side.

'They say it is Norman Leslie who murdered the Cardinal.'

'Then *they* are wrong,' says Will. 'Norman Leslie wasn't even there, although that puffed-up toad Carmichael was. Leslie is a great man, especially for one so young. It was Leslie's Uncle John who struck first...,' he stammers, '...or so they say.'

Her eyes widen. 'You saw it?'

Will looks around the courtyard and doesn't reply.

'Anyway, never mind that,' she says, for she's not here to argue about the killing, it's too late for that. She grasps his sleeve. 'Please come home. They'll send troops soon and you'll all be hung, or worse.' She feels the clench of fear, remembering Wishart's gentle face and the smell of burnt flesh. She hopes Will understands that she's not only here as their father's proxy, but also for love of him, her brother.

'Come, Bethia, let me show you. You'll see, we *Castilians* shall not be so easily got out.'

She hesitates. Agnes's brother won't wait long below, between the tide, and now the rain filling the boat, but curiosity gets the better of her. She's a merchant's daughter and, as such, is unlikely ever to see inside this bishop's palace again.

He takes her first to the Cardinal's apartments and she is left gasping: the cloying smell of perfumes in his armoires; his clothes of violet camlet; the yellow velvet cassock slashed and pulled out with white tinsel sarcenet; the ermine-lined tunics; the red damask sandals; his four poster bed hung with red taffeta; the French lace and Antwerp silver plate; the brightly painted panels far more ornate than anything Antonio has created for their home; the chairs with the Cardinal's coat of arms carved on their backs and the emblem of his house picked out in cross stitch on the seats.

'He even had an upholsterer in his employ,' Will says.

'He lived like a King,' she says, eyes big with wonder.

'Norman Leslie says he lived better than any King; that the Church is richer than the Crown.'

Will takes her everywhere, even to the stores.

'Fourteen barrels of eels from Loch Leven,' he says, standing among them, now opened and empty. He kicks as a rat runs over his foot. 'There were wines from Bordeaux,' he waves towards an empty wine rack, 'which we have much enjoyed.'

He smiles and she considers it a nasty, avaricious

smile. She turns to leave him and walks into a brace of wild fowl hanging from the rafters, knocking them out of her way; the flies rise, buzzing around her head.

'You'd better pluck and eat these quick, before they rot completely,' she says.

He shrugs. 'There's nae shortage of comestibles as you can see.'

'It depends how long you're planning on biding here, you and your fellow…,' she pauses, trying to recall the word Will had used.

'*Castilians*,' he says with a cheeky grin, and for a moment she sees again the little brother she loved to play with.

'We are "The Castilians".' He thrusts his hips out, folding his arms and flings his head back, so that his cap falls off.

She cannot help but laugh. 'But you'll soon run short of food.' She waves her arm around.

The smile fades from Will's face and he sniffs. 'Aye, ever the wee merchant, counting stock.'

'If you'd put the time into learning Father's trade you wouldn't be in this mess.'

'You think I want to spend my life bent over an abacus?' He bangs his hand down on an empty barrel. 'What will I say to St Peter at the Gates of Heaven, when he asks me to reflect on my life; that I counted and added and bought and sold? There must be something more, some higher purpose, and that's what we're working for here. The right way to live in God's true faith.'

'How is it that this whole escapade is about faith, and yet your fellows are running wild in our town? Our town, Will!'

All the fight goes from him and his shoulders droop. 'I do not leave the castle, I do not condone their actions.'

She notices how his wrists dangle from the too-short sleeves of his jerkin. He may be tall, but he's not yet come to manhood and, despite his broadening shoulders and beard growth, he can still sound like a lost boy.

'I know you would never attack the defenceless, but you belong to a group who do.' She reaches out and touches his arm.

'Enough.' He hits her hand away, and takes a deep breath, as though to calm himself. 'Come, you will see why Arran, for all that he's Regent of Scotland and must get us out, will tread cannily, very cannily.'

He leads her back to the portico. The rain has stopped, but the sun is obscured by cloud. She hopes the boat is waiting for her still.

They climb a turnpike, up and up, and come out in the gallery above the great hall. There are musical instruments lying here, which the Cardinal's minstrels must have left behind when they were expelled from the castle: a trumpet, viola and tabor. Will is tugging on her arm to come look over the edge of the gallery, but her eyes are drawn to an instrument tucked in the corner. It is a harp – she's never seen one before – and of such beauty it takes her breath away: the metal work of silver, the wood carved and painted with vermilion, a costly pigment; she well knows the price from father's accounting books. Somehow this harp brings home to her that the Cardinal truly did live better than any man in Scotland: the bed, the furnishings, the clothes and the food could be explained as a man who likes to have the best but they were at least necessary items. The harp is an indulgence, no doubt paid for by church tithes, tithes which should have gone to the poor. She thinks of the children she passed on the way to the harbour, huddled in corners and sleeping in their rags. It's such a familiar sight she barely notices, but shame upon Cardinal Beaton that he did so little to help the beggars living in the shadow of his great palace.

'Bethia,' hisses Will, beckoning.

She slips over to join him and peeps between the banisters. She doesn't know what she's looking at – is it

74

the tapestries hanging from the great walls, the long oak boards with benches down one side, the rugs upon the flagstones and the fire dwarfed by the huge fireplace within which it burns? She feels sick with all this richness now, like when she over-indulges on Agnes's marchpane.

He nudges her and points to the four boys sitting by the fire, who she judges to be no older than John. She looks curiously at him.

'See the one on the right, closest to the heat of the fire.'

She sees the boy is more finely dressed than the others, the colours purer, the ruching, the embroidery all pointing to the son of a wealthy man. Perhaps he is one of Beaton's children.

'He's Arran's son. Can you believe our luck, the Regent's son is here. We have him as a hostage!'

Will's voice has risen as he speaks. The boy flinches and turns to look up at the gallery. He's a comely lad; a comely lad with fear in his eyes.

'I must go,' she says.

Chapter Fourteen

Crown & Church

Bethia's so wet she may as well have fallen in the harbour, except it's as well that she did not, since she cannot swim. The rain grows heavier as they row away from the castle. Geordie picks up a bowl lying in the bottom of the boat and passes it to her. Her clothes cling to her hampering movement as she scoops as fast as she can, but the boat fills up faster. She's profoundly grateful when they reach the safety of land.

Mother's annoyed when she returns home dripping. Fortunately she's too preoccupied by the damage to Bethia's cap and the dye running off the gown, staining both Bethia and the floor, to ask where she's been.

'This is a new gown, a new gown which will be faded as an old rag now. Foolish girl!' She waves her hands chasing Bethia off to change.

Dry and garbed in her old gown, which is too short and skimming her ankles now she's full-grown, she finds Father staring at his books. She sits on the stool next to him. 'Can I help?'

He stares at her. 'Do you have aught to say to me, lass?'

She flushes, gazing at her hands.

'If you know anything of Will's whereabouts, please tell me.'

She looks him full in the face. Father doesn't ask, only commands. His gentleness is her undoing.

'He is in the castle.' She sighs. 'And he will not come out.'

Father slides his legs out from under the board and stands up, his face darkening with rage and something else, which she realises is an anguish of fear. 'This can never end well.'

'Will seems confident it may.'

'You've spoken with him?'

She nods. 'They have Regent Arran's son hostage. Will says that they can barter with Arran, that he'll not risk any harm to his son, and so cannot easily re-take the castle.'

'This has the sound of arrogant nonsense,'

'The son is there, he and some other boys, also the sons of noblemen, who were in the Cardinal's care for their studies. I saw them with my own eyes.'

Father sits down again, tapping his fingers on the board. 'If Will and they other conspirators think the Regent can sit on his hands and do nothing, they're fools. He must take action.'

She leans forward, 'But then why has he not come?'

'Provost Learmonth tells that Arran's trying to break the siege at Dumbarton Castle and will not turn his attention eastward till it's done.'

'Not even to rescue his own son?'

Father drums his fingers louder – she wishes he would stop. ''Tis more important to Arran to secure any advantage from Cardinal Beaton's death first. He'll be thinking of how he may benefit,' he pauses, 'as any wise man should for his family's sake. But make no mistake, he'll not leave the lairds strutting around the castle, and the town, for long.'

'How can it be to the Regent's advantage to have the Cardinal dead? I thought they were working together to keep Scotland safe?'

'Only when it suited them, but they were aye fighting for control. Arran had Beaton locked up in Blackness castle not two years ago. Beaton wanted to be Regent and Arran wanted the chancellery and the rich livings which were under Beaton's control. Now Regent Arran will be power broking to make sure his family and supporters get what was once the Cardinal's.'

He tugs his beard. 'The Church has vast revenues, greater than the Crown commands in many regions.' He gives a bark of laughter. 'I heard tell that King James thought to follow the path of his Uncle Henry and take all for himself, but the Pope suddenly granted him 50,000 gold crowns from church rents, claiming his motives to be entirely patriotic.'

'Why did King James not take the Church's all anyway, like the English king has?'

'Ach well, who knows. James may have feared for his immortal soul but with his wife a powerful French woman, and all they grants coming from France, he was unlikely to be turned from the true word – which was a wise choice now he's dead and can enter the kingdom of heaven.'

There's nothing more said, nothing more to say. Father sits down again and passes Bethia some notes on the usual grubby scraps of paper for her to record in the Day Book. *"Item"* she writes in her careful copperplate, and lists the transactions he's made including a supply of onion seed come from England, three cran of herring and, like the Cardinal, barrels of eel from Loch Leven.

Father mutters to himself as she carefully forms her letters. He rises abruptly. 'I will speak with Walter Wardlaw. He'll know what the Regent is planning, assuming the Provost is sharing the information with his own assistant, and also assuming I can get through the streets without being stopped at every turn by our townsfolk milking me for news. I swear no work's been done since the castle was took, for all any bugger wants to do is stand on the corner guessing what'll happen next.'

He goes to leave, but comes back moments later dressed in his cap, short cloak and boots, laying a heavy hand upon her shoulder. 'You did well this day, but you will not go into the castle again. You will obey me in this, Bethia.'

She twist her head to look up at him and nods. 'Yes, Father.'

'And you must tell no one, No One, where Will is. He's stayed out of sight thus far, so he's no entirely without sense. Perhaps we may still get him safely home.'

She frowns.

'What is it?'

'Isn't there is some support in the town for *The Castilians*, as they're styling themselves?'

He snorts.

'Might it be to our advantage to have it known Will is among them?'

'It is a consideration but I fear any support will be short-lived, especially if they continue to strut around the town as though they're our masters – and there's tales of them attacking women. No, better he stays hid.'

He gazes out the window, then pats her head. 'You're a guid lass.'

Tears come to her eyes to be so praised.

Chapter Fifteen

Proclamation

Father arrives home huffing and puffing. He says there's a proclamation come from the Parliament in Stirling, which has been posted at the Mercat Cross in Cupar, and is now to be delivered to they brutes within the castle. He refuses to call them by the name they've adopted – Castilians – for he says they're not worthy of such grandiosity. Bethia wonders if he's considered, in calling them brutes, that he's including his own son.

Provost Learmonth, ever to the fore, has determined he will read the proclamation aloud so all may know its content, and Bethia plans to sneak to the castle to listen. Father raises his bushy eyebrows and looks at her as though he's divined her thoughts.

'You winna go,' he says….'Unless it is with me.'

She hugs his arm and breathes in his familiar smell: wool, leather and sweat.

He looks pleased by this rare gesture of daughterly affection. 'Well now,' he says, 'enough of this.'

They go together and stand in the sunshine before the castle. The sea is a dazzling blue, but the wind whipping off it is chilly against the skin for June, and she wishes she'd worn her warm cloak. A small troop of soldiers march up in formation and the Castilians hang over the parapet jeering, upsetting the pigeons in the doocot in the roof of one of the towers. Father explained, when once she wondered why the Cardinal would want the stink of pigeons above him, that it can be useful in a siege to have fresh meat and eggs available. No doubt the garrison will now find it so, especially in view of the proclamation that Learmonth reads loudly to both them, and the townsfolk who've been commanded to gather and listen.

None are to sell, or gift, the garrison supplies of any kind under pain of forfeiture of their property and imprisonment. Furthermore Norman Leslie and his fellow lairds must come to Edinburgh and plead their case before the Crown within the next sixteen days. It is handed in at the castle gate, and a notice forbidding the sale, or gift, of any supplies is pinned to the Mercat Cross.

The soldiers march away, leaving her confused; one moment the castle's guarded, the next it's not. Father says Provost Learmonth is keeping a foot in both camps – his own sister is married to William Kirkcaldy of Grange who, along with most of the Grange extended family, is holed up in the castle. Learmonth will want the appearance of being on the side of the Queen's troops and Regent Arran, but who knows where his sympathies truly lie. Indeed, at one time, he was promoting the marriage of Prince Edward and the wee Queen Mary, but then so was Regent Arran. Father says it may be sensible for the Provost to operate this way, but it's not in the interests of the town, although Learmonth considers his interests and the town's to be indivisible.

A week later and Learmonth's assistant, Walter Wardlaw, comes to speak with Father, bringing his brother Fat Norman. Wardlaw stands although he's been invited to sit, legs splayed for all as if he's Henry the Eighth in the etching of the Holbein portrait which a pedlar recently showed to Mother. In a rare moment of unity, she and Mother had laughed at the pose but there's no doubt the English King is impressive – much as, in a lesser way, the beadle is. He assesses her, tongue flicking over fleshy lips, and she looks away.

His brother Fat Norman is a different matter, though he takes up more space than King Henry and the beadle joined together. He's chosen to sit on the settle rather than the proffered chair, no doubt for fear of getting stuck, and is gazing down at his hands. She heard tell he's on the prowl for a new wife after the previous one died of the pox. Whoever ends up with him had best ride astride, or else be crushed to death. He glances up at her and flushes when he sees her eyes upon him, and she blushes too, – at the impropriety of her thoughts.

Father sends her to fetch victuals and she forgets about Norman Wardlaw as she walks slowly from the room, listening to what's said. All is doom, for the lairds have refused to go to Edinburgh and plead their case. Furthermore, the proclamation on the sale of supplies is without teeth as the garrison still come and go freely. When she returns the provost's beadle is sitting in the proffered chair telling Father that the town must mount a stronger guard to keep the garrison inside the castle.

'And I thought what we wanted was to get them out,' Father says, grinning at his own wit.

Wardlaw huffs. 'It is a serious matter. We canna leave them to come and go any longer. Arran will be here soon, for word has it that he's close to kicking Henry Tudor's lackey, Lennox, out of Dumbarton Castle.'

'About time.'

'Aye, and we don't want Arran to arrive in St Andrews and find the town has done not a thing about the castle, and his own son held hostage within.'

Father nods. 'That makes sense.'

'Where is yon son of yours? He'd be a right one to help lead a troop of townsfolk?' Wardlaw leans forward and stares intently at Father.

Bethia's pouring the malmsey carefully into the best pewter cups and her hand shakes so much she spills some on the board.

'Take care,' growls Father, but she can see he's glad of the diversion.

'Will is frae home,' he says, 'gone to my sister Jennet's in Edinburgh.'

She gulps, she can feel the sweat running down her back even though there's no fire lit in the grate.

'In Edinburgh? Why so far when he's wanted?'

Father shrugs, 'I need him to learn his trade, none better than Jennet and her husband to teach him.'

She's surprised to hear such praise heaped upon her aunt and uncle; it's not how Father normally speaks of them.

'If we're to form a troop, then the town council must make a tax. All the burghers must contribute.'

Father grows red-faced. 'It's no time since I paid a tax for the planting of trees and now you're asking for more siller. I'm no giving it.'

They argue back and forth while Bethia lingers in the background. She catches Fat Norman's eye and he smiles at her, then, hunching his shoulders, he returns to gazing at his hands. She's thinking about how peculiarly sweet Norman's smile is, when she becomes aware that Walter Wardlaw is watching her while Father is talking; indeed he is stroking around his codpiece, while he stares. He's revolting, she thinks, and he should consider that wearing such a large codpiece looks ridiculous. He sees her watching and smirks but she looks away, head held high.

Eventually the Wardlaws leave having failed to get Father's agreement to pay out any of his hard-earned money. She almost feels sorry for Provost Learmonth – if all his burgesses respond as Father does, then there'll be no local militia. But perhaps that's what he wants, otherwise he'd have made it an order and not a request. She remembers the stories that run around the town: of how the Learmonths think the leadership of the council is theirs by right and not the elected post it's supposed to be; of how Learmonth's uncle is said to have arranged the murder of one of the previous incumbents to ensure the family held onto the provostship. Her mind drifts to Walter Wardlaw, although she would prefer not to think on him at all. He is a disgusting man, but Norman seems of a kindlier temperament. Nevertheless, she hopes he's not considering her as a replacement bride, and then she smiles at her foolishness. Father wouldn't marry her to him, and Mother would certainly never agree.

Father strides up and down while she reflects. He stops, looks at her and sighs. 'It's as weel done now,' he mutters and leaves the room. He's gone for less than the time between bells.

'I'm sorry lass,' he says, taking her chin in his hand and tilting her head to look up at him as she sits quietly upon the settle. 'I've tried myself but it will not work. I can think of no other way to do the thing discreetly.'

She waits for him to blurt it out.

'We must get Will out of the castle – he'll see sense when he knows Arran is coming with his troops – and we must do it before then. I cannot do it without all the town knowing that my boy's inside. And it is of much greater risk to our safety as a family for me to be seen entering the castle, even by boat, than you. You managed to quietly gain entry once, do you think you can do it again?'

'Yes, Father.' She feels her heart lift in excitement and has to stop herself from rushing out the door. Better to go in the early morning as before, but she hasn't accounted for the weather – and Agnes.

Chapter Sixteen

Searching

The rain hasn't stopped for days. People scurry around the town, heads bent doing the tasks they must, and then retreat inside. Fires are lit as though it is winter, not July, and the smoke hangs heavy in the thick damp air. Bethia, holed up in the house, goes frequently to Agnes asking, then pleading, for her to arrange the boat trip.

Agnes shakes her head. 'Don't be daft, you'll be half-drowned before you reach the castle. Anywise, Geordie's from home and his wife doesn't ken where he's gone.'

Bethia stares at her.

'Don't you glower at me, lassie. I've wiped your nose, and your arse, more often than you've had hot dinners.'

She looks down the wiped nose at Agnes and leaves the room, in what she hopes is a dignified silence.

'Cheeky besom,' Agnes mutters.

She turns in the doorway. 'I heard that. Maybe Mother's right, and it *is* time we had new servants.'

'Aye, and maybe it's time Grissel and me found ourselves a better position, one where our hard work is appreciated.'

'Oh, Agnes, 'I didn't mean it,' she says, putting her arms around Agnes's bony body.

'Get away with you,' says Agnes, but Bethia can see she's touched – and presses her advantage.

'Please help me, please.'

Agnes's face grows stern. 'Get out of my kitchen. I told you my brother's not home and I'll let you know when he returns.'

A further proclamation comes from Stirling declaring Norman Leslie, Master of Rothes, a traitor.

'Bloody fools,' says Father. 'That'll no get him to come out. The lairds will fight all the harder to hold the castle, and Wardlaw is also telling that Regent Arran's son is excluded from the royal succession while he's held hostage.'

'What do you mean?'

'He's second in line to the throne, after Arran, who's the grandson of James the Second's sister. Ach, these royals don't survive well and, although they produce a wheen of bastards, they're always short on legitimate heirs. Arran's laddie has a good chance of being king, between the frailty of infants, and the amount of warring his father's doing with they English butchers aye at our door. This'll take the wind out of the garrison's sails, for King Henry of England will no be so willing to rescue them if Arran's son is no longer such a prize.'

'Do you think King Henry will come to their aid?'

Father sniffs. 'If he sees an advantage – and getting his hands on Young Arran was that – but not so much now.'

The garrison of lairds have held the castle for six weeks and, no doubt supplies are running low after the extravagant feasting on the Cardinal's stores, and they are swaggering out ever more frequently, unhindered, in search of more. They roam widely taking what they want by force, destroying where they're resisted and sometimes where they're not. Regardless of the weather, no one wants to go about in case they meet a group of these men, who think they're entitled to whatever they can take.

'For all as though they command the town, as well as the castle,' says Walter Wardlaw, when he speaks to Father. This time he is demanding, not asking, for funds to raise a troop. 'It is foolish, many in the town sympathised after what the Cardinal did to Wishart, but no more. Regent Arran is still dragging his heels even though Dumbarton Castle is now taken – and we can look to France all we want, but word is that the Queen Mother is getting nae response to her appeals for aid. King Francois recently signed a peace treaty with England and is unwilling to breach it – though he had no qualms about breaking the long-held alliance with Scotland by cosying up to the English. There'll be no help coming from the French.'

Wardlaw pauses, and watching from the settle Bethia sees him considering whether to speak his mind, then he shrugs. 'Of course the provost and I were not without sympathy for the cause these Castilians espouse, but they've no respect for the town. We cannot stand by and let them bleed us.'

Father gives the funds, mindful of his ship and warehouse and how the garrison could plunder them, yet barely concealing his rage that his son is among the renegades. 'The Cardinal may have had the best of everything,' he says, 'but at least he paid for it – mostly.'

After Wardlaw leaves, he tells Bethia it's too dangerous for her to go into the castle now and forbids it. She nods meekly, but decides she will go regardless – if she can find a way.

The watch in the town is strengthened, and Father doesn't complain about the cost. He even employs a stout man to guard their beasts in the back yard, which is as well for they are awoken one night by a commotion. Father rushes out, cudgel in hand, while Mother and Bethia, Agnes and Grissel stand shivering in their nightclothes behind the locked back door, holding onto

John who is demanding to be let out.

They listen for Father's knock and also listen for any sounds he may be hurt or even killed. In the event the men are chased away without having captured even one hen. Next morning when she goes to look, yawning after her disturbed night, the garden is a sad mess. Agnes, arms folded and disregarding the rain running down her face, is gazing on the trampled beans, onions, leeks, lettuce, beets and cabbage. Even the physic garden has not escaped, with the new thyme and the coriander seedlings crushed; but there's one small satisfaction. Agnes points to the hawthorn hedge, planted to protect their orchard. A piece of cloth is caught in the thorns, hanging limply in the rain. Bethia walks along the pathway and spreads it wide. The cloth looks to be part of the sleeve of a doublet.

'The thorns will likely have torn the skin too,' says Agnes. 'I hope it gie'd a good deep rent to the flesh of that wicked varmint.'

The talk at the board is all of the garden and Father's success in fighting off the thieves until John interrupts telling of Kopernik, a man from Poland who claims the earth moves around the sun. His book, *The Commentariolus*, has arrived from Antwerp on Father's ship, and John is much taken by its ideas. She thinks Father should be well pleased, for John's finally eager to study his Latin by reading Kopernik's thesis. But Father and John shout at one another until Mother too raises her voice.

'All this noise and I care not what rotates where, as long as we may have relief from an argument which has a most tedious circularity of its own.'

Bethia watches John gasping like a dying fish at the suggestion that the science is of no moment, while Grissel thumps a trencher in front of him and retreats.

'Nooo,' says John and pushes it away.

'What's this?' says Father.

Mother sighs. 'A potion of ground hedgehog bones for the nocturnal emissions.'

Father stands over him glowering and John, face twisted, takes a sip 'Well laddie, if you will wet the bed at your age...,' he says, hurrying out of the room as John retches.

Mother bends to pick up her sewing and Bethia grabs the trencher from John and swaps it with her own.

'See, it is not so bad once you get used to it,' says Mother, as John finishes Bethia's ale.

Bethia winks at John and goes to find Agnes, hoping to arrange the boat trip to the castle, for it has finally stopped raining. Instead she finds Grissel in the yard, her hands deep in a rooster pulling its innards, feathers scattered all around and sticking to her clothes and sweat-soaked face. Grissel says she'll help find her Uncle Geordie, but it must wait until she's finished her duties. 'Or else my mother will leather me.'

Each time she returns, Grissel's in wilder disarray and redder in the face as she moves from yard to kitchen, keeping the fire embers glowing to spit-roast the fowl.

Elspeth's at the door but Bethia neither knows nor cares where the painter is when she inquires – probably at his lodgings, for Father refuses to have him board with them, saying a little exposure to the artist goes a long way. 'But he'll no doubt return soon, for the portrait is begun,' she says, assuming Antonio's absence is what's causing Elspeth to look dejected.

'It's not that. My father says I must marry.'

A shiver runs down Bethia's spine. 'But you're no older than me.'

'Well take care, no doubt your father has plans for you also.'

'Do you know who your match is with?'

'He is speaking to the Wardlaws.'

'No! Not Fat Norman.'

Elspeth nods.

'May the Virgin protect you. He was here not long ago

– he has a kindly face, but he does smell bad and he is soooo fat.'

'You give me much comfort.'

She touches Elspeth's shoulder. 'I am sorry.'

Elspeth smiles wearily. 'It doesn't matter, for I won't marry him.' She shakes her head. 'I won't. I'd rather a convent.'

'You wouldn't!' Bethia rubs her forehead, 'I'm not sure I would. Anyway your father has talked of making a match before, has he not, and nothing came of it.'

Elspeth brightens. 'Yes, and it is unlikely to be successful, for Norman Wardlaw is most wealthy and will look to do better.'

Bethia thinks this is likely true, for it would be a step down for the Wardlaws. Elspeth's father runs a shop and the family live above it, although she's the only surviving child and will inherit all. But still her dowry is likely small in comparison to the Wardlaw aspirations.

She hooks her arm through Elspeth's. 'Come and see the painter's allegory of love and peace, which caused so many arguments about how Mother and I were to pose.'

Elspeth chuckles. 'Did Antonio prevail?'

'Almost, except Mother refuses to look down fondly upon me. She says it does not display her face to advantage and…'

'Shows her wrinkles.'

'Not quite, she says it is not a good position for a woman in her thirties.'

They laugh as they enter the room but Elspeth is quickly absorbed, bending close to study it. 'Antonio has hid the pox marks on your mother's face very well. His brushwork is truly masterly.'

Bethia grows bored waiting for the examination to conclude, until John provides a diversion, dancing around the portrait on its stand, pulling faces so horrible that she warns him if the wind changes, his face will stay that way.

'Where is Master Bellissima anyways,' he asks, making a grand flourish which mimics the painter so well that both girls burst out laughing. Pleased with himself, John capers more, giving bows until one wild gesture sends the painting, and its easel, flying.

They rush to right it. There's a shared gasp; the paint is smeared across Mother's face making her nose, which she's already sensitive about, look more bulbous.

'Oh John,' Bethia says reproachfully.

But John doesn't care. He knows Father hates the painter and all his pretensions. He doesn't care that is, until she points out a repair will cost. Then his face grows red at the prospect of another beating and he rubs at Mother's nose with his sleeve. This is a mistake; the paint smudges further and now Mother's nose has blurred into her forehead.

Elspeth giggles. It's a quiet giggle but she knows her friend well. This giggle will become louder and louder until Elspeth is crying with laughter and the whole house and half the street will hear, and become curious. She hustles them both out of the room and down the stairs.

'Go to your studies, John,' she says. For once, he doesn't argue .

She chases Elspeth out into the street, tugging her down the close at the side of the house. Elspeth is breathless from running and laughing, and bends over double, resting one hand against the wall of the house to steady herself.

Grissel appears, having finally finished her work. It is evening now, the long Scottish summer's evening, and bright as though it were midday. Now they can search for Geordie.

Chapter Seventeen

Attacked

Grissel, although younger than Bethia, is a strapping lass. She walks behind the girls, as is proper for a servant. Bethia knows they may not look it, but together they're a formidable trio; especially Elspeth, who is smaller even than her, but can be fierce when roused. She smiles, remembering, when they were children how Elspeth once split a teasing boy's lip with a well-aimed punch.

The gulls are hanging noisily over the midden heaps: swooping and diving; tearing, snatching; fighting and screaming. The catches have been good so far this year, the stench of rotting fish pervades the town and the girls bat the flies away as they hurry past.

Uncle Geordie is not to be found outside his house with his neighbours, fixing nets and baiting the lines ready for the morn's morn. Instead they're directed to an alehouse by the harbour. Bethia's nervous; this alehouse sits between the sailor's hostel and the whorehouse and she doesn't know which of the three is worse.

She sends Grissel into the alehouse alone; it's her uncle after all. She and Elspeth stand close, gazing out over the water while they wait. The harbour is busy with ships, as is usual at this time of year. Grissel ducks under the doorway and re-emerges, blinking in the evening sunshine. A gust of wind blows her hair free and Bethia realises Grissel is pretty in a big bold Norse woman way, like the Valkyries she was reading of only this morning. She wishes she was back in the safety of the chamber at the top of the house, out of the wind and reading a book.

'What do we do now?' asks Elspeth.

They leave the cloud scudding sky and go up the hill, under cover of the pends. There are a few pilgrims coming through the abbey port, from the south. They walk, although many are likely to be wealthy, for it is part of the pilgrimage, and the penance, to walk at least some of the way. Even those coming from overseas by ship will have disembarked at Earlsferry or Garrbridge, some distance from St Andrews. She thinks of the wonder any pilgrim must feel when they first see her city's tall spires; it's right that St Andrews is called a second Rome.

The pilgrims walk slowly, long staffs in hand, the badges signifying their pilgrimage pinned to their caps. They are a large group, for it is the safest way to travel – she's made donations in the past to help pilgrims who've been robbed.

Last in the group is a young man of a hue so rich brown, and bonny with it, she can't help but stare at him. They pass close by, as the pilgrims head towards the cathedral, and the young man looks her full in the face and smiles. She ducks her head, unused to such frank appraisal. They both turn and watch the distance grow between them, until Elspeth gives her a sharp nudge in the ribs.

Grissel knows of another hostelry in a vennel by Mutties Wynd, where her uncle may be found. They enter the close cautiously, for the sun has finally dropped low in the sky and it is shadowy within the narrow confines.

There's a burst of laughter from behind. A group of men have followed them in and are blocking their way out. The girls draw close together but the vennel ends abruptly with a high wall; they cannot easily escape. The men come nearer and the girls shrink against the wall, but the rough stone cannot protect, only entrap.

The men stop, cocky smiles spreading over their faces.

'Well what have we here? Some wee lassies looking for a kiss,' one says, and the other three roar with laughter.

'Aye, but there's only three o' them. You'll have to do without your kiss, Tam,' says another, nudging the ring leader.

'Och no, they'll each give me a kiss. I've got enough spunk to take them all.' He clutches at his groin and thrusts.

They move closer to the girls and Bethia feels Grissel beside her, shaking. She's especially vulnerable, being clearly, by dress, a servant. Most men would have pause for thought before attacking her or Elspeth, but these men are from the castle, she realises, and they think the normal rules do not apply.

They are surrounding them now, jostling each other, showing off and waiting to see which among them will make the first move. She hopes it's all bravado. There's a fumbling next to her, and she looks down. Elspeth has a knife in her hand.

The men halt their advance. They too can see it, glinting in the falling light.

'Our wee kitten has a claw,' says the ring leader softly. 'Let's see if she kens how to use it.'

The solid bulk of Grissel slips away while all eyes are on Elspeth. The men close the circle; they reek of sweat and drink. The ring leader steps confidently forward, his sword still sheathed and hand outstretched, expecting Elspeth to give up the knife. He doesn't know Elspeth. She waits until the hand is near upon her wrist then, quick as any sword-master she slashes, laying his arm open, and steps back. The man stares at the blood running down his arm and dripping onto the ground.

'Run,' Elspeth cries and flees back down the close, towards the light.

But Bethia doesn't run. Suddenly she's furious. 'Vipers,' she cries. 'My brother is among you, a Castilian too. Shame on you to threaten defenceless girls. You'll never get the town on side with such efforts. What are you about?'

The men retreat in front of her rage. It feels good.

'Who is your brother?' asks Tam, holding his arm aloft to stop the blood, his face a shining white in the dim light.

'William, but he's known as Will.'

'There are many Williams in this world, even Wills.'

'He is very tall.'

'Ah, Will the Giant.' He steps back and makes his obeisance and the others follow his courtly lead. She's suddenly aware she's standing ankle deep in a puddle. She lifts one foot at a time, feeling the mud suckering her to the earth.

'A most doughty fellow. I did not know he has such a pretty sister. We shall take our leave and please accept our humble apologies for any distress we make have caused you, and your friend.'

She shakes her head. They turn to go. 'Wait,' she calls, 'give my brother a message.'

They look at her, waiting.

'Please,' she says reluctantly.

'We're waiting for the message.'

'Oh,' she says, flustered. She draws herself up to her full height, which is not tall. 'Tell him to meet me tomorrow in the castle gardens at first bell.'

Tam bows. 'We will make sure he knows.'

She's pleased, and she didn't need Agnes after all. By the blessed Mary, Mother of Jesu, her brother will be waiting tomorrow. If she can persuade him to come home then Father won't care that she disobeyed him.

There's a flurry of activity at the entrance to the close

and Elspeth, with Grissel alongside, comes rushing in with the young pilgrim following. Bethia's heart lifts; they had not deserted her – they'd gone for help.

The pilgrim rushes to bar the exit, holding his staff lengthwise. The four men pause.

'What's this?' says Tam. 'Come laddie, you do not expect to take us all with yon stick.'

The pilgrim doesn't move. The men step forward, the ring leader in the centre.

'Take care, Tam,' one says. 'You already had a wee lassie lay your arm open, I'm no sure the saints are with you today.'

'God's blood, Dod, do you no ken we are no longer for the saints? It's a Papist invention and not part of the true word of the Lord.'

'Oh aye, right.'

'Come on laddie, get out the way. We mean you no harm, nor any to the lassies,' says Tam.

'Yes,' says Bethia. 'Thank you kindly for your assistance, but they truly did me no harm.'

The pilgrim stands aside, turning to the girls, but as the men swagger past Dod gives him a whack across the back with the flat of his sword. He staggers, quickly regains his balance and, swinging around, wields his staff.

Dod is laid out on the ground, howling in pain. 'My arm is broke, I swear that son of Satan broke my arm.'

Bethia's mouth drops open. It was so fast she's not even sure how the pilgrim did it.

Dod's fellows gather round their fallen friend, while the pilgrim encourages the girls quickly away.

'Laddie,' Tam calls.

The young pilgrim turns.

'That was neatly done. Perhaps you should join us, and give some lessons,'

'I am thinking not.' He ushers the girls out into the broad street.

'Let me be escorting to your home,' he says.

Elspeth and Grissel lead the way and Bethia walks shyly next to the pilgrim, wondering where he's from – perhaps Amsterdam or maybe Antwerp. She's aware they're drawing curious glances from her neighbours. He's around her age she guesses, almost as tall as her brother but even broader of shoulder. He walks with a loose-limbed confidence, as though he's nothing to fear and no wonder when he can use his staff to such devastating effect.

He stays with them to her door and bows as he goes to leave.

'Wait,' she calls. 'I do not know your name,'

'Mainard, I am Mainard de Lange.'

'Thank you kindly, Mainard de Lange.'

'It is my pleasure.' Again he turns to leave.

'And Mainard…'

'Yes my lady?'

'Will you teach me how to use a staff?'

He laughs.

'I truly want to learn.'

'Oh,' he pauses. 'Tomorrow I return to see you fine ladies.' He bows again, his eyes sweeping over them all. Grissel giggles behind her hand with pleasure to be so included. 'Took no hurt from the adventure. We may discuss then.'

She gives a little wave. Elspeth nudges Grissel, and Bethia sweeps past them both into the house, shutting the door behind her – although she can hear the hoots of laughter from the other side.

Chapter Eighteen

The Bonny Pilgrim

Bethia is at the castle gardens before the first bell next morning. The castle walls rise high above to her right, but it is the stable block and no windows overlook the gardens. She walks up and down the paths, under the watery sun and dull sky. Cardinal Beaton once strolled here, perhaps communing with God but, if what Father says is true, most likely with a head full of machinations. He was a man hard pressed by foes; no wonder though, with such rich livings to keep a hold upon.

The woody smell of sage is strong as she brushes past the clump of plants edging a bed filled with tall spires of larkspur. She's tempted to gather the seed, for no one seems to be caring much for the beds which are weed-choked; the Cardinal's gardeners no doubt fled, along with the rest of his servants. In the next bed is a planting of many roses. She's never seen such beautiful roses and in such a profusion of pinks, reds and even orange. Catching the sides of her apron she ties a knot, forms a deep pocket and gathers the fallen petals to scent her linens.

She draws nearer to the castle walls and can hear the rising clamour as the garrison begin their day, but Will does not come. Perhaps he has no one to wake him from his slumbers. Hearing voices close by she drops down, crouching low to the ground and hiding behind the plants. The rose bushes catch her skirt, sleeve, cap and even the hair under it, but she doesn't dare move. The voices draw nearer and then recede.

She cannot linger, it seems that Will either hasn't got her message or has chosen not to come. She's upset that he might leave his own sister waiting, unprotected. She disentangles herself with difficulty; the roses seem to be controlled by some witchery to hold her here. Then hurries away, dropping a trail of rose petals behind her.

When she reaches home Father is out but has left a note with instructions for her to copy some documents. Head bent and tongue between her teeth, she is forming the letters when a knock comes at the door. Distracted, she lifts her head, a blob of ink dripping onto the copy book. She lays down her quill and rises shaking out her skirts and smoothing her hair.

Grissel's grinning face appears around the door. ''Tis yer bonny man.'

'Thank you, Grissel,' she says, folding her hands over her stomach.

Grissel giggles.

'Please call Mother,'

'Och, yer mother's from home,' says Grissel holding the door wide.

'Fetch us some malmsey.'

Grissel disappears down the hallway and Bethia runs up the stairs, pausing before the closed door to catch her breath.

He's standing by the window, his brown skin dazzling in the shafts of sunlight and his long curls a dark halo around his head. He turns and a slow smile spreads across his face, as though he can read her thoughts. She dips her head and blushes, holding out her hand, which he bows over, her skin tingling at his touch. There's a pause as they stand back from one another. She can't think what to say and he, for all his tall presence, seems equally tongue-tied.

'Where are you...'

'I trust you are...'

They laugh and draw together, jumping when the door bangs wide and Grissel crashes in, closely followed by a watchful Agnes. The madeira is served and they sit down. Grissel leaves the room but Agnes stays, first fiddling with the decanter on the board, and then loitering by the window. She doesn't speak, she is after all a servant, but Bethia wishes she would: either that or leave. She can feel the sweat pooling in her cleavage and under her arms, as she tries to think of something to say. She manages a few questions and learns that Mainard de Lange is staying at the Hospitum at St Leonards.

'You are nearby,' she comments, while Agnes's forehead wrinkles at the news. Soon the pilgrim rises to leave and she cannot blame him. Her heart sinks as he says his farewells; she's unlikely to see him again, except by chance – but he, she soon discovers, has other ideas.

She's working with Father the next day when Grissel sidles into the room. Glancing up, she finds Grissel making big eyes, twitching her head and generally behaving oddly. She lays down the quill and stares. Unfortunately Father also chooses that moment to look up, and gaze at Grissel's antics.

'God's bones lassie, what are ye about?'

Grissel's struck dumb, but only briefly.

'The mistress,' she rolls her eyes as though for inspiration, 'aye, that's right, the mistress wants Bethia.'

'Can it no wait? We're busy here.'

'No, no. The mistress says now.'

She follows Grissel out and soon returns. She has a note from Mainard de Lange tucked away safely in her apron pocket, and has given Grissel a flea in her ear about her lack of discretion.

There is a quiet corner behind St Leonards by the cathedral wall where no one goes, except perhaps to hide from prying eyes. It's unwise and could seriously affect her marriage prospects if it were ever known, but she goes anyway, arguing to herself that Mainard de Lange is clearly well born. It is evident from his clothes and address that he's an educated young man from a wealthy family, and somehow that makes their secret meeting seem not so wrong.

At first she's shy in his presence for he engenders strange and unfamiliar sensations in her. Fortunately he's less tongue-tied away from Agnes's eagle-eyed presence. He can speak French, although his command of English is reasonable and his Latin excellent: another sign of his pedigree. She can speak some French and they chat flowing freely between Latin, English and French. He has come prepared for activity; producing a short stave which he hands to her.

'For practice,' he says, 'if you want the learning still.'

She strokes the staff. It's newly made and finely sanded, smooth to the touch and fits well to the palm of her hand. She's pleased that he's taken her request seriously.

'My one is too long for you,' Mainard says, 'so the wood-turner, I ask him make you a special one.'

'Thank you.' She can feel herself flushing, and it's not only her face, but all around her body.

'The skirts, they a difficulty, but my sister can use the staff, for I show her. You need let the attacker come close, and to a woman he will come very close. Give one hard hit to cause great pain, then... ' he opens his hands wide and shrugs his shoulders, 'the fight it is over.'

First he shows her the grip, moving her hand further down the staff and tugging her thumb out from under her fingers. Her face grows hotter. She's sure it would burn to the touch.

'I see you do much writing,' he says, touching the ink stains on her middle finger.

She rubs at them with her thumb. 'I make notes for

101

my Father, he is a merchant.'

'Ah, like my father. It is good you learn the family business. But come, let us begin.'

It's awkward, she doesn't think she can do it, wished she'd never asked him... but as he shows her how to move, she forgets herself and concentrates on learning.

'You let it flow, not fight with it.'

'It's fighting with me, the way it keeps catching in my skirt.'

He laughs.

They pause for a rest, while she ties back her hair which has come loose, and she asks about his home. He talks of Antwerp and, although she has heard some of what he has to tell, for Father has been there, she listens without interrupting, enjoying the attention he bestows upon her, while resisting the temptation to reach out and touch his skin.

He says Antwerp means to throw a hand and embarks on a long story about a giant's hand being flung into a river which she fails to follow because she's distracted by his dark eyelashes; how tightly they curl and how they stroke his cheek as he blinks. She becomes aware that he's moved on and is now describing how ships have to travel fifty miles up river to reach the city. She stops him, certain she must have misheard.

'It is true.' He nods.

'It must be a very small port.' She tries to imagine ships being rowed up river, but is only able to picture the sand banks of the Eden estuary, 'and without tides?'

He laughs. 'The river, it is very deep and often we have as many as two hundred ships and more than two thousand of carts to bring the goods into the city. They come from the New World with much silver, sugar from the West Indies and from the East they bring spices, and we have the big trade in textiles. It is with the textile my father does the trading.'

His story has her full attention now, for trade is

become her area of interest. He tells of the riches passing through his city and the bankers and merchants, come from the exotic lands of Portugal, Spain and Venice, who control them. He describes the art they commission and the books produced by the myriad of printing houses which have sprung up. Soon she feels that her town, of which she is so proud, is a poor place by comparison. However, it is when he talks of education that she truly feels envy, for his sister has been treated little differently to him in her access to learning. Indeed she is at this moment, he assures her, attending a school for girls. She questions him, until he insists they must practise the staff some more although she suspects it is to avoid any further questions about what a girl might learn at school in Antwerp.

They're soon meeting whenever they can. He continues to pass notes via Grissel and she to reply. Grissel is savouring being part of the secret, but is forever whispering to ask if there's a message Bethia wants her to take. Indeed so much whispering goes on that Mother, who is determined to find a reason to be rid of Grissel, looks hopeful and demands to know what is afoot. Bethia makes up a story about messages from Will and, since Mother refuses to discuss where Will might be, she lets it go.

Bethia speaks sharply to Grissel, but still she cannot help but smile when yet another note comes from her pilgrim. And so they keep meeting secretly, even though she is ever fearful of being discovered.

Chapter Nineteen

Caught

Bethia quickly masters the initial strike and soon wants to know more and, within the limitation of skirts which seem designed for the purpose of tripping her up, she learns a few other moves. He encourages her to come at him, saying he needs the practice, although he blocks her with ease.

'Did your father bring you because you're good with the staff?' she asks one day, when they're catching their breath between bouts.

'Oh no, Papa is the master with the staff, and sword. He does not need me for protecting. He asked me come for I speak English better, but Father did not understand that the Scots tongue can be so much different from the English one.'

She laughs and, after a quizzical look, he laughs too. 'But your Scots I am understanding.'

There is a question in his voice. She doesn't want to tell it's because Mother, after a childhood spent mostly in England, considers the Scots tongue common and insists she speak the *proper* way. She shrugs. 'It is how my mother taught me.'

'Well, you speak Latin very good too, better than men, even ones going for the university.'

She smiles, pleased by the compliment. 'My young

brother is to enter university here soon and I try to study with him, when I can.'

'You have a tutor?'

'John did, and did not like him overmuch for his tutor considered generous use of the rod to be an excellent means of teaching. My father himself is not averse to delivering a whipping, but even he balked at John's torn flesh, especially when it was not matched by an improvement in his Latin.'

He sniffs. 'We have all suffered from the tutors, and their beatings. But now you are the teacher?'

She nods and is pleased when he gives a bow of respect.

'I like to learn, but being a woman...' Her voice trails away as she remembers how dismissive Father was when Will suggested she might teach John, saying, 'I know you were forever peering over Will's shoulder when he was a scholar at St. Salvators, but that does not mean you understand much. A woman's brain is not made for learning, better you stick to housewifery and needlework.' Will had snorted and even Father had to laugh then, for her poor needlework is a family jest. Father shrugged his shoulders, and so she was allowed to *try* and soon nothing further was said about finding John another tutor.

Mainard strokes his curly beard. 'I know is difficult for you, but we all have the cross we must carry.'

She stares. 'What difficulties have ever been placed in your path?'

He shuffles his feet, rolling a stone beneath his sandal. 'You cannot see?'

'No, you are clearly of a wealthy family, well educated, can wield a staff skilfully and, I would guess, are equally able with the sword. And...,' she hesitates.

'And?' he prompts.

'You're the bonniest man I've ever seen.'

He gives a bellow of laughter and reaches to take her hand.

'No, tell me. What is the difficulty in your life that you

105

so sigh about, for I can see none?'

'I will tell it to you, for a kiss.'

She steps back, but she's smiling. 'You are too bold, sir.'

'A kiss, only small one,' he says, stepping forward.

'Fine, you may have your small kiss. Upon my hand.'

He laughs again and she shushes him, fearful they'll be discovered in their hidden corner. Then he holds out his hand, inviting Bethia to place her hand in it, but she crosses her hands upon her chest. 'First you tell, then I will judge if you deserve your reward.'

The laughter fades from his face. He opens his mouth and closes it and she wonders what he was going to say. Instead he pulls up the sleeve of his silk doublet and shows his arm, twisting and turning it.

'You see?'

She has a sense he was going to tell her something important, that he's distracting her. She looks for a scar.

'I see an arm.'

'What is different about the arm?'

She reaches out to touch his skin with her fingertips. 'It is soft.'

'Bethia, concentrate. Look at your arm and tell what it is the difference.'

'The colour, your arm is a pretty colour.'

'Am I the first you see of this colour?'

'No, we have Moors living in Scotland, especially at the court. When Mary of Guise came to St Andrews to be wed, she brought Moors in her entourage, and the King disguised himself as a black knight in the tournaments held to celebrate the wedding. And we see pilgrims of many different hues.'

'It is not easy to be this difference.'

'There are many challenges in this world; being born a woman is one, but most of all to be poor. Is it really so difficult to be a golden boy?'

'Sometimes.'

She notices the sun is low in the sky. 'They'll wonder where I am, I must go.'

She hurries home, still with the feeling that his colour is not the true difficulty concerning him. He has something he'd rather not tell and it seems to have to do with his father.

When they meet again she probes as to why Master de Lange is on a pilgrimage. He's a merchant, like her own father, but from Mainard's description of their home, she knows it's a much wealthier one. She cannot imagine Father ever undertaking a pilgrimage and is curious why his father has.

'My father paid for an altar in the Holy Trinity,' she says, 'but a pilgrimage, I cannot see it. Your father must be very pious.'

'No, Papa is not the pious one.' He laughs, then grows serious. 'But why your father not give the altar to the great cathedral?'

'Holy Trinity Kirk is for the townsfolk. The cathedral is only for high days and holy days.'

'And it so beautiful, one of the finest I ever see.'

'I know aught about that but Father says 'tis the biggest in Scotland and probably England too; but we fear there is some malevolent spirit at work within.'

He looks shocked. 'You say it is a cursed place?'

She leans in close to whisper her answer. 'Twice since it was completed the towers were blown down, and once it was greatly damaged by fire. They tell in the town it is a sign. There's too much pride, too much vainglory and God is not pleased with the folly of our over-grand cathedral.'

She feels the fear low in her belly as she speaks. Mainard makes the sign of the cross to ward off evil, then takes her hand. She looks at the slim, dark hand with its fine long fingers resting on her bare skin; the hand of a rich man's son, and wonders again why he's truly in her town.

They are practising when she catches a movement out

107

of the corner of her eye. It is Father upon his horse, about to pass through the Abbey port heading out of town, no doubt off to Pittenweem where he has recently bought a warehouse, saying if things continue as they are in St Andrews they may have to move there. She shrinks back against the high cathedral wall, pulling Mainard with her.

'My father,' she hisses.

'I will speak with him,'

'No!' she grabs his sleeve. 'Stay here.'

He shakes his head, but doesn't move.

She peeps out from behind the buttress, hoping Father will be gone. But no, he's beckoning a boy who's loitering by the port. The boy seems reluctant but perks up after Father bends from the horse and passes him something. She is sure a coin has changed hands, for the boy sets off at speed.

'Why you not let me go? You are ashamed he see you with me?'

'No, I am not. But imagine it was your sister secretly meeting a man?'

He looks shocked.

'I must go,' she says, breathless as though she's already run a race and lost.

'I will say my papa to meet with your father,' he calls as she runs off.

Mother is waiting when she gets home. 'Your father has sent a message,' she says as soon as Bethia enters the room. 'You're to stay indoors biding his return tomorrow.'

So he did see us, she thinks.

Mother waits but Bethia says nothing. 'I hope you've brought no disgrace upon our house child. It's difficult enough holding Father back as it is, especially since Will's foolishness.'

She wonders what Mother's talking about.

But it is for another reason she disobeys father's

instructions. Early the next morning Grissel slides into Bethia's room and shakes her awake. Fortunately she's sleeping alone as Mother has returned to the marital bed while it is empty.

'A message come from Will,' Grissel says softly. 'You are to meet him now.'

Grissel helps her dress and then she's off across the yard, clambering over the back dyke and creeping through vennels to find Will.

Chapter Twenty

The Succession

'And Henry Tudor will send a relief force, mark my words,' says Will. They are standing on battlements gazing at the cannons that Cardinal Beaton recently had installed, in case of attack from England.

'Why would he, now you and all your great friends have done the deed and rid him of the Cardinal?' The rising sun lights up Will's countenance. Bethia sees a sheen of sweat upon his pale face.

'You're sick.'

'It is nothing.' He flaps her away. 'Anywise, you're wrong, help is coming. Norman Leslie will soon go to Henry's court and then he'll give us funds.'

She thinks Will is speaking to persuade himself as much as her. 'Why did you want to see me...and why didn't you come when I sent a message before? Did you get it? You know I waited and waited in the gardens, and it's not safe.'

He shrugs.

'Your fine friends were threatening me, me and Elspeth. Did they tell you that?'

'Elspeth, what does she have to do with it?'

She knew he was sweet on Elspeth, she just knew it. 'Elspeth was with me when they trapped us. If she hadn't pulled a knife, it could've gone very ill.' She decides not to mention the assistance Mainard rendered.

He smiles and she wants to slap him. All he can think on is Elspeth and her courage, not the danger his own sister was in, the danger he's placing his whole family in. She feels like a dam is bursting inside her, and all her frustrations come pouring out.

'Never mind Elspeth, what about me? What about Father and his business and John and even Mother? Do you not understand? We could lose everything if it's known you are here. They will confiscate all that Father has for aiding rebels.'

She's shouting in his face and he looks round, anxious not to be seen being scolded by a girl. She's losing him, indeed never had his attention apart from mention of Elspeth.

'Elspeth is to marry,' she says bluntly. Let him stew on that.

His face grows paler. 'Who's she to marry? When?'

'Her father is seeking a match with Norman Wardlaw, but it's you we must take care of.' She reaches up to touch his face, to call him to her, but he knocks her hand away.

'Dinna come here again Bethia. I'll not leave my fellows; we're in this to the end, whatever may happen. Look around, they will not easily dislodge us.'

A crow circles above them, a black witch cawing. She looks out upon the courtyard, no doubt once well kept. It's ankle deep in muck from rain, animal excreta and probably human too. A couple of rats are leaping across it.

She points to them. 'If the stocks of food run low, you'll not starve.'

Will rolls his eyes. 'Don't be so stupid.'

She shrugs. Even this high above, the stench scratches at the throat. Clearly they have no servants, or at least none willing to clean up. A man is capering over the muck trailing red satin and bowing low, his fellows chortling as he sweeps the cardinal's hat from his head.

111

She cannot imagine Cardinal Beaton, in all his grandeur, travelling with his own bed with its trap to let fresh air in, living amidst this stinking midden.

She wants to scream at Will for his foolishness but instead says, 'you Castilians must take charge of cleaning this place, or else you'll have pestilence among you.'

He tugs on his scraggly beard in a gesture reminiscent of Father.

'You already have sickness, don't you?'

'Only a couple of our lads, it is nothing, something they ate.'

'Well, I hope it wasn't the fish I saw rotting in the stanks while I was waiting and waiting for you yon day in the gardens.'

'Do ye think we're fools?' he shouts, but she can see from the way his eyes shift that she is not so wide of the mark.

He takes a breath and speaks quietly although his lips are drawn tight across his teeth. 'We are low on supplies now we cannot move so freely around the countryside, but we expect some to arrive any day.' He humphs. 'And, anyway, you know I hate fish.'

She refuses to be distracted. 'Oh Will, have the English been here? If Henry has sent a delegation, you'll have caught something from them; they say the sweating sickness is bad in England this summer. Please come home and we'll look after you.'

'Enough Bethia!' He pauses. 'Come and meet the Regent's son, he's a good lad.'

She knows he's trying to distract her but she's curious. 'You've spoken with him?'

'Of course. He's given us his surety he'll not try to escape, so we let him roam freely within the castle.'

'It's as well you have his bond, for his father is finally come and there are plans afoot.'

'I am sure there are.' He takes her by the arm as they walk, 'what can you tell me about the Regent's preparations; how does he plan to break the siege?'

She hesitates, one foot on the stairs, not sure she wants Will to know how little activity there has been so far. She runs down the turnpike to give herself time to form a reply.

'This way,' he points. The corridor is lined with fine paintings and she wants to stop and look, but Will has her by the arm again and is waiting for an answer.

'Troops are arriving all the time and he has huge cannon – but I am not in the Regent's confidence.'

This is a slight exaggeration, some troops have come, though Father says there is much havering amongst the Regent's supporters and little action, but she won't tell Will that. He'll never leave if he knows how chaotic the siege-breakers are; and how reluctant.

He screws up his face. 'You're only a girl, what would you know anyway.'

She glares at him. They're outside a heavy oak door, the wood badly scorched along its base. He knocks and enters. The boy sitting by the fire rises and smiles when he sees who it is.

'My Lord, this is my sister, Mistress Bethia.'

She smiles in response and makes her curtsey, and the young lord bows in return. There is a weary sadness about him, and she wants to give him a hug – just as she would if he were John.

'Is that a chess set I see?' she asks, nodding to the board.

'Aye, do you play?'

'Yes I do. I often beat my youngest brother.'

Young Arran grins. 'Unfortunately it's not a game this brother loves.'

'No, he's more the man of action.' She can see, out of the corner of her eye, that Will has puffed his chest out. At least she's said one thing today to please him.

'Play with me, my lady, if you will.'

He looks at her, appealing from under his fair brows

and, even though she wants to get home, she agrees. It may be better anyway to wait and leave under cover of darkness, there will be less chance of being seen – although greater chance of being attacked.

'I will be happy to oblige you.'

'There's a chess game in the gardens,' he says as he pulls up stools to the small table where the board sits. 'We used it regularly. It was fun to play with giant pieces. But I cannot go there now.'

'Oh yes, I noticed it the other day, while I was waiting…' She glances at Will, but he's suddenly absorbed in studying the arras tapestry of unicorns and knights.

'Are you really expecting England to send supplies?' she asks later as Will walks her along a passageway, lit only by the fading dusk.

He rubs his head. 'So we have been told.'

'You think that wily old king, who's beheaded two wives and disposed of two more that he judged unsatisfactory, cares whether you starve?'

'You don't know anything about it.'

She shakes her head. 'He wants something, doesn't he? What do you have to give him in return?'

'We haven't got anything he'd want,' says Will tugging on his beard.

'It's that laddie.' She knows from the way he won't meet her eyes that she's right. 'He wants you to give him that innocent wee laddie who's trapped here only because he's Regent Arran's son.'

'He's no so young as he looks, and no so innocent either. He's next in line to the throne, after all.'

'That's not his fault. He *is* an innocent. How can he help the frailty of infants should Queen Mary die, and that he is his father's son?'

'The sins of the father,' says Will.

She restrains herself from whacking his arm. 'Get me out of here. I'm ashamed to call you brother.'

They are half-walking, half-running towards the garden gate when she remembers. 'Young Arran isn't second in line to the throne, not anymore.'

'What are you blethering about, of course he is – the Regent Arran is next in line and then James, as his eldest son.'

'You haven't heard.'

'I'm shut up in this mouldering castle, how would I hear anything? I'm almost as much a prisoner as James Hamilton.'

'At least you're free to leave.'

'Aye, right.' Will stops and takes a deep breath. 'There must always be sacrifices for a true cause. I will never leave my fellows.'

He evidently thinks he's in some Chaucer's tale of brave knights. 'So you've mentioned, several times,' she says, her voice dry as well-seasoned hay.

'What's the information you have about the Regent's son?' he demands.

Now they are by a narrow gate, leading to the castle gardens, but the stout iron yett is closed. Next to it a young man stands guard, long pike in hand.

'Oh, you do have some guards,' she says.

'Don't be so daft, of course we do.'

'I thought everyone here was too important to take a turn at the common work.'

She can see he's ready to shake her, if they didn't have a witness. She doesn't know why she keeps provoking him, it won't achieve anything except his further estrangement, but she can't seem to stop herself.

She grabs his sleeve. 'Arran's son is no longer second in line to the throne.'

'Stop it.' He shakes her hand off.

'It's true, he's been excluded.'

'No, how can that be? You're telling lies to get me to leave.' Will folds his arms.

'For as long as he's imprisoned here, young Arran is excluded from the succession. He's not the great chess piece to play after all. And Norman Leslie must know this – he's not being so loyal!'

She can see doubt, and then the realisation she speaks true, race across his face.

'He's still Arran's son, and King Henry will want him for that reason alone.'

'You think.' She tosses her head.

'Let her out,' he shouts to the guard and stalks away.

The man looks flummoxed. 'But, but…,' he calls to Will's retreating back, '… I dinna hold the key.'

Chapter Twenty-One

The De Langes

Father looks grave when Bethia describes the state of the castle, and the state of Will. Indeed, so concerned is he, that he doesn't scold her for disobeying him. He paces up and down as she talks of Will's unswerving belief in the rightness of his actions, his intransigence and the poor wee hostage James Hamilton.

'This is bad, very bad,' he mutters.

He stops and stares at her under lowered brows, his sharp nose like a mouse peeping out from the wainscotting. Then he resumes his pacing.

'We need to do something and fast, otherwise it'll be too late.'

'Too late for what, Father?'

'Never you mind lass, never you mind. We'll have something sorted quick before word leaks out about Will's whereabouts. I must see Walter Wardlaw.' He flies out of the room calling for Grissel or Agnes or some bugger to bring his bonnet and cloak, and fast.

She's carefully writing out a contract ready for the notary to affix his mark to, when Father returns, slumping into the chair. She glances up, but he won't meet her eyes and she wonders what he has done to look so guilty about.

The next day the beadle comes to visit again, with his

fat brother in tow. He's telling how Regent Arran is demanding money from the monasteries to pay for the siege.

'Aye it's good to know that they rich friars must give up their siller, to the tune of six thousand pounds to recover the castle.' Father chortles long and loud, until he remembers his heir is inside.

She's sent to fetch them some of the claret that Father brought, in a recent shipment.

'The captain says the crossing of the Bay of Biscay was terrible,' Father tells the Wardlaws as she sets off on her errand, 'worse than ever he can remember, and in August, when all should be easy.'

When she returns with the silver salver bearing decanter and glasses, one of Mother's few dowry items, they fall silent. She has a feeling they've been talking about her. Everyone watches as she concentrates on reaching the board, the contents of her tray wobbling. She senses Father relaxing as she places the tray down and serves their drinks. They leave soon after, Walter Wardlaw staring at her as he goes. He makes her feel unclean and she doesn't know why he's staring anyway, since he already has a wife: a poor trauchled creature.

The painter is still busy about his work with Elspeth ever his devoted assistant, although Mother has already lost interest in her ceiling after Lady Merione pronounced it *a good effort.* Father however is pleased with the progress of the portrait, which thankfully Antonio managed to repair discretely, meriting John's respect.

Elspeth's come to have Bethia pluck her hair line, giving a raised brow like that of the Dowager Queen, ladies of the nobility and, of course, Mother too. Antonio insisted Bethia had her's plucked high for the mother and daughter portrait, and her eyebrows taken off. After the deed was done, she stared into the polished hand mirror Father once brought her as a gift from France, and a calm, assured lady gazed back. She assumes Elspeth has hopes that something may come of her time with the painter since she's enduring the tweezers again, but Elspeth says he's rushing the work now and will soon be finished.

'Why is he rushing, does he have another commission elsewhere?'

'No, he says St Andrews is no longer safe and 'tis better to leave while he can easily find a ship.' A tear runs down her cheek. 'It seems I am nothing to him.'

'Ach, things are not so bad and the siege must soon be over now Arran is come. Tell him not to worry, and Father is pleased and will no doubt recommend him.'

Elspeth wipes away the tears and sits up, while Bethia wields the tweezers. She frowns as she works, thinking, what did Elspeth expect? There could never be a future for her with the painter as he wanders the world following commissions, and he is used to, indeed needs to, charm women, with his snapping black eyes, sweet words and courtly manners. He couldn't take a wife and she doubts he would ever make a reliable husband or be a good provider. Now the bonny pilgrim – he's a different matter, and Bethia leaves Elspeth to her misery as her imagination wanders around the young man from Flanders. Father seems to have forgot all about him in his anxiety over Will and, as soon as the plucking is done to Elspeth's satisfaction, she plans to slip out and find him.

But Mother calls before Bethia can leave the house in search of Mainard, wanting her to sort yarn.

'You spend altogether too much time with your Father, and I need you to assist me – and on more maidenly tasks,' she says.

Bethia sits hunched over the tangled basket of wools, stifling a yawn, next to John, who's swinging his legs in boredom, his Latin primer spread before him. All is quiet and she wonders how much longer she'll have to sit here playing the dutiful daughter before she's released.

There's a knock on the front door below and she

119

quickly rises.

'Sit down,' says Mother. 'Grissel will answer.'

She huffs and drops back onto the stool.

'I heard that,' says Mother.

The knocking is renewed, more insistently. She's poised to go when they hear the door screeching open and Grissel's loud voice.

'Give us a moment, why can't ye.'

Mother sighs.

There's a murmur of voices, which Bethia strains to hear, and then the sound of more than one set of footsteps climbing the stairs. The door is flung wide by Grissel, behind her is Mainard, and following him the equally tall figure of Mainard's father. She drops the hank of yarn and covers her mouth.

Mother rises to greet them. 'You wish to see my husband, on business perhaps,' she says, then sharply to Grissel, 'fetch the master and bring us some malmsey.'

Grissel bangs out of the room, without a curtsy and Mother's lips grow thin.

Mainard smiles at Bethia and she hangs her head in embarrassment.

Both Mainard and his father make a courtly leg and bow low. Mother holds out her hand and first Master de Lange, and then Mainard, kisses it.

'Do take a seat,' says Mother, looking well pleased; handsome men are a rarity. Mainard's father begins to speak, but the door opens, and Father strides in. The de Langes stand up and Father stares at them from under bushy eyebrows.

Bethia shifts in her seat. 'Father, this is Master de Lange and his son, pilgrims come to St Andrews. Mainard helped me when I was troubled by Castilians.'

'I know who they are. Do ye think I don't keep an eye upon the doings of my own daughter?'

Mainard whispers a translation to his father.

'As well you should,' says Master de Lange smoothly,

making a bow.

Father nods and bows back, and they all sit down once more. They converse mostly in Latin with some Dutch, for Father has knowledge of both. It seems Master de Lange wants to discuss a trading partnership, and soon Father leads him to his room of business, while Mainard stays to charm Mother. Bethia doesn't know what to make of it, but Father is well pleased when he returns, and they leave amidst more courtly bowing.

'This could be a suitable connection,' he says rubbing his hands together. 'Very suitable, we need contacts in the Low Countries. And although they are of the brownish hue, a touch of the blackamoor there I think, the son may well do, if our partnership prospers. We'll give it a little more time, for it may be a better choice for you than the Wardlaws.'

He stares at Bethia and she blushes rosy pink and drops her gaze. She wonders what Master de Lange has been saying, and hopes Father doesn't mean what she thinks about a "better choice than the Wardlaws". And anyway, Fat Norman is seeking a match with Elspeth and Walter Wardlaw already has a wife.

Chapter Twenty-Two

Heartsore

The next day Bethia wakes early. She lies half asleep, puzzled by what has awoken her. There it is again – the rattle of a pebble hitting the shutter. Slipping out of bed she tucks the curtains tight around so's not to disturb mother, before opening the casement and peering out. Below, in the grey light, face turned up and wrapped in his cloak is Mainard. He gestures at her to come down. She waves understanding, pulls on her skirt and wraps her shawl around her.

The front door, wood swollen by last night's heavy rain, sticks and she struggles to tug it open until he lends his weight on the other side. Stepping outside she takes his hand and leads him down the close and into the shelter of the byre. Anyone who's abroad so early will be hurrying for cover before it rains again, but it's better to be discrete, and dry.

Inside the beasts exude calm, but her breathing stays rapid and she cannot seem to make it slow to match their steady rhythm.

'How did you know that was my window?'

'Grissel told me, many days ago.'

Bethia shakes her head; Grissel and her love of intrigue.

'I am sorry, my Bethia, but we are departing. Father

receive an urgent message from a ship newly come and we go now.'

He looks down into her eyes and she waits for him to say more. After what feels like a long silence she asks, 'will you come back, ever?' in a small voice.

'I promise, I will return. But it is, how shall we say, complicated.'

Again she waits, light-headed with anticipation.

'I do not have long, Papa is waiting, and it is not quick to make the explanation.'

''Tis a pity you did not give it sooner, then.'

He blinks, but continues. 'You remember I tell there are merchants from Spain and Portugal living in my city?'

She nods, wondering why he is repeating himself if they have so little time.

'My family come from Spain, and long ago from a country further south.'

She nods rapidly. Does he truly want to spend their last moments together giving a family history?

'My grandparents, they were Jews and convert to Christianity but still it was not so safe for us in Spain. Then they come to Antwerp where many different peoples reside all together. It was good decision and the family businesses do very well, but our difference is clear to all.' He pauses and taps the skin on his left hand. 'And now, with the talk of reforming, life is difficult again. You understand?'

'No, not really.' She shifts her weight from one foot to the other. The cows too, heavy with milk, begin to shift restlessly in their stalls. Their calves, in a separate pen, call plaintively, but they must wait until Grissel's done the milking and taken the family's share.

He screws up his eyes and his forehead wrinkles. 'There is group of Jews live in Antwerp. They get angry because we convert.' He sighs. 'Even though was long time ago. We can be citizens and trade freely, and the Jews cannot. We are good Catholics, yet it is always difficult to be accepted. Many of the Catholic peoples we do business with, they do not like it because once we were Jews. Now some are no longer sure they are good Catholics, and want the church reform. We do not want more change, we only want to do our work and live the peaceful lives.'

She wonders why he's telling her all this. A jolt runs through her, perhaps he *does* mean to ask for her hand; he'd better be quick if he's to get Father's permission before he leaves. She can't stop herself from shaking. He's telling her this because he wants her to understand what she will be going to. She doesn't care, she'd follow him anywhere.

'Papa was much troubled and one night he is stopped by men coming from a hostelry who are angry. He did not want to speak with them and they attack. I tell to you before, he can use the staff better than I, and he defend himself from the attack. One man fall and hit his head hard, and he dies. Papa is called the murderer but in the end his sentence is commuted, thanks be to his true friends and our good Lord. Instead he must pay the man's family much money and do the pilgrimage.' He bites his lips. 'Now you know all.'

She looks up into his eyes, but doesn't know what to say.

'I know what I tell is bad. I should tell you before, but our time together was a happy one and…,' he spreads his arms wide.

She nods in understanding and he, taking it as a sign, reaches for her hand. She allows it but all she can think is, his father is a murderer, and she knows, even if she can overlook it, her own father may not.

He gives her hand a shake to get her attention again. 'I cannot wait Bethia. I am sorry, I thought we have more time. Papa has news from home – there are attacks. He say we will go now quickly for we must protect our family and property. There are people who say my father

124

must be punished more and they will take this time of disturbance, when he is from home, to attack, steal and destroy what we have. Already Papa is on the ship waiting and I stay too long, we must get the tide.'

He bends and kisses the back of each hand, and then he turns her hand and kisses each palm, light as a thistledown. He lets go gently and opens the byre door. 'I will write you,' he says, 'and I *will* come back.' Then he is gone.

She takes a hold of the post next to her, for her world is spinning. The tears fall slowly to begin with, but then they flow like a river, and she sobs and sobs while the rain starts up again, battering down on the roof and bouncing off the timbers above her head.

Chapter Twenty-Three

Cannon Fire

The noise begins as they sit down to their midday meal. Father is from home but Bethia, Mother and John all leap to their feet rattling the board so that the broth slops across the wood, dripping over the edge onto the flagstones, and the collops of bacon look to come sliding after.

'Mercy me!' shrieks Agnes, dropping a bowl full of fresh picked brambles.

They run out into the street along with nearly all the people of St. Andrews, covering their ears with each ground–shaking boom. The sound even overpowers the church bells and Bethia cowers down clutching her head when the blast comes again.

At first the family look in consternation at their neighbours, then people begin to move towards the Swallowgait and the castle. Bethia realises John is gone, no doubt at the head of the crowd, which is moving fast now. She picks up her skirts and runs, soon overtaking Mother and Agnes, and even outstripping Grissel.

The townsfolk back up in Ladyheid, and she pushes forward but finds her way blocked. She can see the steel helmets of soldiers bobbing above the crowd ahead, but she can't get any nearer – no doubt John is among them already. She turns and fights her way back. She'll try going down Northgait and gain the Swallowgait by its port. She can't believe that once more she's running into danger to rescue John – and yet a small part of her finds it arousing. She squashes the thought, although it is a welcome distraction from her aching heart.

But before she can put her plan into effect, the crowd turns screaming, with those at the front scrambling over those slower to react. A cannon ball has landed in their midst, as the Castilians return fire. She presses herself as close to the wall of the nearest house as she can. Lucky it's newly built of stone; if it was one of the older wooden houses the pressure of people would likely have collapsed the walls.

A woman with her baby in the plaid wrapped tight around her, one arm supporting the child, trips as she is carried past. Bethia catches the woman's free arm, holding her upright. Her own arm is tugged, the pain in the shoulder socket excruciating, but she hangs on. The woman squeals, but regains her balance, jerks her arm free and flees.

The crowd is thinning now and she sees a few people lying on the ground. She goes to help an old man up, blood dripping from a scrape on his bald head and what looks like a bootprint scoring his cheek. He's dressed in hessian, tied around his middle by a length of rope and smells strongly of urine. She decides not to offer him her handkerchief to clean the blood off his face. It's of the softest Flanders linen after all, and was a gift from Aunt Jennet; he'd probably sell it.

Instead she steadies him, breathing through her mouth and trying not to gag, and once he's upright, judges he can make his way back to the safety of the Mercatgait unaided, assuming the garrison doesn't start firing into the town centre.

There's a lull. It's no doubt hot and heavy work loading, aiming and firing cannons. Hugging the wall, she creeps towards the soldiers who are running back and forward where the street opens onto Swallowgait, the castle towering behind them. The drifting smoke makes her cough and there's lots of shouting from directly in front of her and more distantly from inside the castle. She reaches the end of the street and peers around the corner. There are soldiers dragging a cannon away from the castle while the Castilians shout insults from above. She's grabbed by the arm and swung around.

'Must I always find you where you should not be, my lady?'

She jumps.

'Wheesht, I didn't mean to frighten you.'

She looks into the scarred face and kindly green eyes of the officer from the day of Wishart's burning. 'Oh it's you.'

Before she can say anything further, there's more shouting and bustle from the mouth of the street. He looks around and pulls her into the relative darkness of the close between two houses.

'Stay there,' he commands and leaves her.

She misses him, which she knows makes no sense; he was at her side so briefly – it's something about the way he looked at her that reminds her of Mainard. There's a loud rattling over the cobblestones and she glimpses soldiers heaving on ropes, heads hung like half-starved ponies. The captain runs alongside encouraging them.

'Pull lads, pull. Let's get our Deaf Meg to safety. We'll find a sweet spot from which we can pulverise those protesting bastards, I promise you.'

The soldiers heave and grunt, heave and grunt until the cannon wheels get stuck in the mud when they heave and swear. Eventually they stop halfway down the wynd. She realises she's trapped. If she comes out of hiding, she'll either have to run the gauntlet past the cannon heavers or, if she escapes the other way, it'll be past those braying dogs hanging over the castle parapet.

The soldiers are resting against the cannon now,

wiping sweat off their grimy faces, and she can't see their captain anywhere. She slides down the wall and sits on her heels, not caring that her skirts are dipping in the muck. There's a rush of air followed by a crash and splinters of wood flying. She curls in on herself as something brushes the top of her head and clatters down behind her.

She stays still, coughing in the dust. Across from the vennel where she's crouching, a door opens to reveal a family of fisherfolk; mother with her bairns crowded around her, man beside her in his sealskin boots. They're staring down at the empty space, where once their fore-stair was. A child is lowered clinging to an old fishing net, quickly followed by the rest of the family.

The captain returns and bows, proffering his arm. 'Let me escort you home, my lady,' he says, eliciting curious looks from the fisher family and their neighbours, and a giggle from Bethia. She knows there's nothing to laugh about, but his mockery seems so kindly meant she cannot help herself.

'But we have not been properly introduced, sir.'

'That is easily rectified. I am Gilbert Logie.'

She starts. 'Of Clatto?'

He nods. 'You know of my family?'

'I think my mother and your mother have met.' She had been going to say, are friends, but suspects the friendship may all be on her mother's side. But she doesn't regret claiming some relationship between their two families; he should know she's not just any wench wandering the streets.

'Ah, and you are?'

'My name is Bethia.'

He offers his arm. 'Well Bethia of the quiet confidence, and blue eyes that are so appealing, lead the way.'

'Thank you kindly, my lord.' She dips a curtsy, enjoying the mild flirtation, despite the soldiers smirking and nudging one another.

Chapter Twenty-Four

Elspeth

Drifting to the work room, and hoping Father has lots for her to do, for she needs the distraction, she hears a knock on the door. She hurries to answer, hoping it might be Gilbert, but blocking out the low afternoon light are Walter Wardlaw and his brother. Wardlaw pushes past her although Norman, who shifts uncomfortably – is he looking apologetic? – bows and stutters a good day.

She welcomes him in return and he lumbers over the door step saying, 'I have b-b-b-brought you a-a b-b-book, my lady, which I thought you m-m-might like for I under-r-r-s-s-stand you are quite the s-s-scholar.'

Bethia, touched by his thoughtfulness, follows him up to the chamber, where Father is. Norman sits down and fumbles in his bag. She holds out her hand for the book he's clutching, but he looks up, shoulders hunching, and mumbles, 'I thought we m-m-m-might read the b-b-book together and I c-c-can explain it to you.'

She bites her lip, holding in a sigh, but it's hard to reject the appeal in his eyes. He looks like a dog that expects to be kicked, and yet Father says he is not a man to cross in business. 'What is the title of your book?' she asks, swallowing a yawn.

'It is called *Historia Gentis Scotorum*,' says Norman, enunciating each letter and struggling to get past the sco of *Scotorum.*

'Oh yes, Hector Boece's *History of the Scottish People.* I have already read…'

'Sit down, Bethia, and look at the book with Norman,' says Father, while Walter Wardlaw frowns beside him.

She tucks herself into the small space on the settle that is free of Norman's bulk and he unclasps the book, spreading it open over her lap. Aware that Father is watching, she grits her teeth and allows it. Norman asks if he should translate but she reads aloud, translating as she goes.

Norman looks surprised, 'that is ve-ve-very good.' He nods to Father, 'you have a learned one h-here, Master Seton.'

'She's not so bad with the Latin,' says Father, 'but more usefully she writes a good hand, can keep the day-book up to date and her figuring is improving.'

'Those are indeed useful attributes, especially in a wife,' says Walter Wardlaw.

Why does he stare at her so? She looks from one man to the other to the other. Father avoids her gaze – what is happening here?

'But a w-w-woman who can read with such ease is indeed a w-wonder,' says Norman to the men, then smiles at her.

She knows it's unusual to find a man unfazed by learning in a woman but she wishes he would not look at her so, and his breath smells of onions. The Wardlaws leave soon after, Father glowering when she insists on returning the book, which Norman reluctantly takes.

Wrapping herself in her cloak, she slips out the back door while Father is saying farewells at the front. She wants to speak with Elspeth and find out how things stand, even though the last time they spoke of it, Elspeth was still determined she would never marry Norman Wardlaw, saying, 'I'd rather a nunnery than be squashed under that weight.'

Bethia thinks on it as she walks; would she rather a nunnery than Norman? On balance, she thinks she'd tolerate the husband better than the cloisters, but then she's not having to make such a choice... she hopes. She tugs her cloak more closely around her. They had the first frost last night and Father says that an early frost betokens a hard winter – maybe that'll drive Will out the castle and home. At least the cold weather means the town won't smell as bad; it's been worse than usual recently with all the soldiers here.

She's knocking on Elspeth's door when she notices three carts hauled by oxen and heaped with rubble. There are men either side of each cart pushing, as the oxen strain to get the carts over the cobbles. She wonders why they are removing it when it is near dark and the gaits will soon be closed. The door is flung open and she forgets about the carts. Elspeth's father stands before her, eyes bulging.

Bethia reaches home ahead of Elspeth's father and bursts into the workroom.

'Master Niven is coming,' she pants, bending over to catch her breath.

Father frowns at the interruption but before she can say anything further Elspeth's father is among them, shouting.

He points at Father. 'You, you, Judas! Giving houseroom to a son of Satan.'

Father leaps up. 'What did you say?'

Niven thrusts his face into Father's. 'You heard me!'

She tugs on Father's sleeve. 'Elspeth has gone.'

'Gone, gone where?'

Niven collapses onto the settle and covers his face with his hands. 'My child, my child,' he cries.

Father looks from Bethia to Niven. 'I am very sorry your daughter is gone, but what has this to do with me?'

132

Niven lifts his head and points to where Mother, Agnes, Grissel, and John too, are crowded in the doorway. 'Ask your wife.'

'Me! What would I have to do with your daughter?'

'Mary, come in and close the door behind you.'

Mother stands in the centre of the room, shoulders back and hands crossed over her stomach, ignoring Elspeth's father.

He leaps up and stabs his finger at her. 'It's your fault, you and all your pretensions. Thinking you're better than everyone with yon airs and graces. You brought the poncy Italian here and he's stolen my daughter.' He drops back onto the settle and wipes his eyes with his sleeve. 'I thought Elspeth was safe in your home. My only child, and she's lost to me.'

'When did you last see Elspeth?' Father demands of Bethia.

'Yesterday, no, it's two days since but this... this doesn't sound like Elspeth. Are you sure?'

'Do you think I'd be here if I was not. Her clothes are gone, and the painter too. I went to his lodgings.'

'You were to chaperone the lassies,' Father says to Mother. 'How could this happen?'

'I am not Elspeth Niven's nurse. Let her parents look to themselves. She was here at all hours, when she had no business to be.'

'You knew she was here?'

'I knew nothing, she's not my responsibility It was her parents' responsibility to teach proper behaviour.' And Mother sweeps out of the room, pushing past Agnes and Grissel listening outside the door.

'It's not what you're thinking. She only ever assisted; she loves the art, not the artist,' pleads Bethia.

'Pure she may still be, but no man will take her now.' Master Niven pauses and then looks piercingly at her. 'You aided her because you want Norman Wardlaw for yourself.'

'I knew no more than you, and I would never want to

marry that man, any more than Elspeth did,' she shouts.

She looks at Father, who is tugging on his beard.

'But this will not get my daughter back. Can you help me?'

Father shifts from one foot to the other. 'Let me see what I can do.'

Master Niven shakes his head as he shuffles from the room. Bethia follows him and lays a hand on his arm when he opens the front door.

'Elspeth is a good girl.'

'That as may be, but it will not help her now.'

Chapter Twenty-Five

Gilbert Logie

Bethia watches Master Niven walk away, head bowed. He passes Gilbert Logie, who turns to look at him, then turns back to nod and smile at Bethia. She dips her head but waits with the door open. It is not the first time he has come, since he returned her home after the cannon fire. Father likes him, saying Logie's a fine, sensible fellow and Regent Arran is fortunate to have him as an aide.

She can see Gilbert's curious as to what's taken place but, as befits a well–mannered man, he does not ask. Father is burning some papers when she leads Gilbert into the workroom. He drops the poker and rubs his face, offers Gilbert the chair and sits down next to Bethia on the settle opposite, inquiring how the plans to break the siege are progressing.

Gilbert leans forward and plants his hands on his knees. She finds it an odd gesture, like something a much older man would do. 'Finally we have enough troops and the castle tightly besieged so none may easily leave, including by sea. You will no doubt have noticed the two ships patrolling in the bay.'

Father nods.

'They have destroyed the boat which the garrison had secured below the castle.' Logie leans back, stroking the scar puckering the side of his face. 'It's much more difficult for them to get provisions now. Soon they'll be hungry and cold – as long as we maintain the stranglehold.'

She flinches and Gilbert gazes at her. He, of course, has no idea that Will is inside; a Castilian, and a traitor. She drops her eyes to the hands resting on her lap, thankful that Will had the presence of mind to remain unseen from the beginning, protecting his family and their good name – so far.

Gilbert leans back in the chair. 'We know they'll not easily give up, but we have plans underway that *will* flush them out.'

She can feel Father next to her, drumming his fingers, and leans forward herself. 'Do the carts of rubble I saw being taken out of the city, earlier this evening, have anything to do with those plans?'

Gilbert stares at her and then at the floor. 'I know nothing about carts,' he says. 'Perhaps it's some building repairs after the damage done during the bombardment.'

'Most probably,' says Father, raising his eyebrows at her. 'On another matter, Logie, you may be able to render some assistance, if you will. The ship the Bonny Meg left harbour yesterday bound for Antwerp, but first will dock in Leith.'

'I know, a couple of my men are on it; they have duties at Holyrood.'

Father stands up to straighten the portrait of Mother and Bethia, which he was pleased enough with to hang on his workroom wall. 'The painter, Antonio, who I employed here, was also on board. If you could find out whether he travelled alone it would be most helpful to me. He may have taken a young girl on the journey.'

'I will get a courier off to Edinburgh and find out what I can.'

'Mind you, be discrete. She is of good family.'

'Of course,' says Gilbert. He rises.

'Thank you.' Father places his arm around Gilbert's

shoulders. 'Come again, son.'

She shows Gilbert out, pondering what she's heard, and goes to close the door behind him, when he calls out to her.

'Should you ever have need of me send a message to my lodgings, the house by Greyfriars, and I will come.'

'Thank you,' she says, but she cannot imagine what that need might be; the only need she has is of Mainard, and Gilbert can't do aught about that. It's two months since he left, and she knows he returned safely for Father has had much communication from Master de Lange. She has read the letters, they are about the trade they agreed – Flanders linen for Scottish hides is to be its beginning – but there has never been any letter, message or word for her included. She thought Mainard had more honour and, even if he no longer cares, that he would write and tell her, not leave her in this misery of uncertainty.

Father's smile has gone when she returns to the work room. 'This is bad, very bad,' he mutters, ringing his hands.

'Do you not think Gilbert can get her back?'

'What ... oh I'm not thinking of Elspeth, though 'tis a shame for the lass, and her father.' He bends his head and rubs at the bald spot which Bethia notices is getting bigger. 'No, it's Will I'm thinking of.' He lifts his eyebrows and nods to her. 'That was well spotted, my lass, and a clever question.'

She raises her own eyebrows. She's no idea what he's talking about.

'The carts,' he says, 'the carts taking away rubble.'

'Yes?'

'Arran's troops may well be trying to dig their way into the castle, and, if so, the siege might quickly be over. I do not think we can get Will out now, even if he would come, and that leaves us in a dangerous place. I am sorry, lass, I know it is not to your liking, although we can be confident Norman is eager, but I think we must have an

137

alliance with the Wardlaws.'

Her mouth is so dry she can barely form the words. 'What sort of alliance?'

'A marriage settlement, of course.'

'No, Father, please no.' She reaches her hands out to him.

He steps back, holding his hands up, palms outwards. 'If we tarry, it may be too late; there are many who would be happy for a reason to strip us of our wealth and property. I will speak with Norman Wardlaw tomorrow and get things moving.'

Bethia drops onto the settle. She feels as though all the breath has been squeezed from her.

Part Three

Will

October 1546 to April 1547

Chapter Twenty-Six

Siege Tunnel

Will lies on the straw pallet he's been allocated in the Sea Tower on the other side of the courtyard from the portico and the comfort of the Cardinal's old rooms. The Cardinal haunts his dreams, blood-dripped arms reaching out to be saved. He wishes they'd given up the body when his concubine, Marion Ogilvy, came to the gate again last week. He thinks on how she was kept waiting just inside, head bent, the garrison watching while Norman Leslie strode over. She held her hands out as though beseeching him, but Leslie shook his head and she dropped to her knees before him. Despite his refusal, he helped her up with every appearance of gentleness and led her back to the gate. Will wonders what it must have taken for her to plead for her paramour's body with the man who was formerly the Cardinal's friend and, for all she knows, his killer.

'A pox on you and your bastards,' someone called, as she stumbled away.

Marion straightened her back, lifted her head and cried, 'shame on you all.' Then Leslie slapped and cursed the fellow, and Will considers he was right to do so.

Eventually he falls back into an uneasy sleep. He's awoken by his stomach cramping. His witch of a sister was right, they did get sick; five of the Castilians have perished of the plague, and his good friend James of Nydie has been near death. His fellows are saying the besiegers somehow placed a dead sheep in their water to poison them all, but Will doesn't see how that can be. The well is dug straight down deep, through the rock on which the castle is built. It's more likely they got sick eating rotten food, probably the dead pigeons which were all that was left in the pigeon loft. But things should be better now, for Henry Tudor has, at least, sent a supply ship, which successfully evaded ships on patrol from the Scottish fleet.

Henry Balnaves, one of the original conspirators, who had remained on the outside, joined them as the supply ship arrived – which is as well for he's a man, it seems, who likes to organise. He willingly, and determinedly, takes charge of the arrangements inside the castle. He prevents any pillaging or waste as happened before with the Cardinal's rich stores – two miscreants caught stealing wine were whipped – and has overseen the cleaning of the courtyard, directing the dung heap shovelled into the sea.

Will can hear the waves crashing against the rocks below; he was never so aware of the sea, and all its moods, till he came to live in the castle. The wind howls through the broken windows behind him and he buries his head beneath the blanket. Why did his co-conspirators break so many windows? He knows why. They did not expect to be here still. Henry of England was to send troops, as well as stores. Kirkcaldy and the Leslies said from the beginning that he would seize the opportunity to invade, that they would be rescued. Much as he's reluctant to admit it, his father was right. The old wind-bag said King Henry was ower wily to get drawn in, and where is the benefit for him now Beaton, may God have guided his steps to hell, is dead? Instead the message from the English king demanded they give up their greatest bargaining tool and send him Arran's son.

He thinks what it must be like to be James Hamilton, son of the Regent and second in line to the throne, a pawn in everyone's game. Sometimes he's grateful to be only the son of a merchant, and not much worthy of anyone's attention.

'Get up!'

Will jumps.

Carmichael kicks at his feet. 'I said get up, you lazy stinkfart.'

Will leaps off his pallet and stands, fists raised.

'Oh ho,' Carmichael crows, holding up his hands in pretend dismay. 'Our wee boy thinks he's a man.' He steps forward, swings high and clouts Will around the head. 'Take that as a warning, I'll tolerate no kail-headed coddroch threatening me. Now get down to the courtyard and fast, Arran's soldiers are bent on the Devil's work and we must stop them.'

Will rubs his burning ear muttering, 'a pox on you, you horse penis,' at Carmichael's retreating back.

'I heard that, you useless giant bairn,' Carmichael roars.

He strides over to where Will is standing, eyes on the ground, and punches him in the stomach. Will bends double clutching his belly and gasping for breath. Carmichael kicks him in the arse, so hard it is as though Carmichael's boot will come out the other end.

Groaning he drops to his knees, then topples onto his side, curling up as small as his tall frame will allow. He can feel Carmichael standing above him but he keeps his eyes closed.

'I'm not finished with you yet, Will Seton.' He hawks and gobs.

Will feels the damp spittle landing on his hand, which is shielding his face.

He lies still as he can, in a body which is exploding with pain. When he hears Carmichael's footsteps going down the stairs, he allows himself to whimper. What did he ever do to be so hated and despised by another man? And why didn't he, at least try, to defend himself. What's wrong with him; a dying mouse has more spirit.

He lies there for a long time, but Carmichael doesn't return. Eventually he rolls onto his hands and knees, and, using the rough stone wall for support, gets to his feet. Leaning against the wall, he makes a vow: I will not allow Carmichael, or any man, to attack me again. He repeats it, aloud this time. Never again, not without putting up some sort of fight. The humiliation of defeat, without even an attempt to resist, is far worse than the pain of any beating.

When he eventually clatters into the courtyard he's told to hush his infernal racket. They're all there, standing still and listening, apart from Nydie, who's shakily drawing water from the well. Taking the bucket out of James's hand he winces as it swings into his aching belly. James looks curiously at him.

He's directed to pour the water into a range of wooden bowls, which are dotted around the edge of the courtyard and in the gateway. A man is stationed by each bowl, staring down into it.

He looks to Nydie. 'What's going on?'

'We think our besiegers may be trying something different – a mine.'

'And the bowls of water, what do they tell us?'

'If the water ripples then it'll be from vibrations in the ground.'

'From them digging?'

Nydie nods.

He is silent, absorbing the information. 'Can we do anything to stop them?'

'Oh yes, laddie,' says Carmichael strolling over with a smirk on his face. 'Our baby boy is going to be getting his hands dirty; very dirty and very sore.'

They start in the guard-room. The plan is to dig straight down, halting often to listen. They don't know for certain if a siege tunnel has been started by Arran, but Richard Lee says it's as well to be prepared. Lee came with the stores that King Henry sent, and may be of use in ending the siege, for he's a clever man who understands siege warfare and has already made improvements to the garrison's defences.

Will holds the pick ready in his hands. He's never used a pick-axe before, but how difficult can it be? It's just hitting the ground.

He raises it high above his head and whacks it down with all his might. His whole body reverberates. He drops the pick, hands stinging, tucking them in his oxters and bending double to contain the pain. It hurts so much he doesn't care that Carmichael is roaring with laughter.

Richard Lee and Norman Leslie consult with one another.

'Where does Lee come from?' Will whispers to Nydie, as they wait. 'He twists his words so I can barely understand him.'

'His speech is most strange. He's not from London. Perhaps Yorkshire or maybe Hereford – and he is of common folk, I heard tell.'

'Do we have no sappers among us?' Will hears Lee say, 'Or at least a man, who knows how to use a pick in all the hundred within?'

Leslie shifts from one foot to the other. 'I fear not. Seton here's a merchant's son and I doubt he ever dug a hole in his life unless to make a mud puddle.'

Will hopes Leslie and Lee can't see him colour in the dim light.

'He is but a scrawny chapman,' says Lee. 'And no more than a boy, despite his great height. You there,' he points at Carmichael, 'let's see what you're made of.'

Will sniggers at Carmichael's expression.

'But my father is…,' he stutters.

'It matters not whose son you are. There are too many fine fellows within this palace and not enough foot

145

soldiers. We must all take our turn. And you,' says Lee to Nydie. 'I need every person here gathered in the courtyard now. Seton, is that your name?'

Will nods.

'Go and help him.'

They rush out of the guardroom, remembering to duck their heads under the low arch and then stop for a quick consultation. Should they go together, it'll be quicker to split up, but will people listen to them? They hear voices from behind and shoot off in opposite directions.

Deciding aggression is the best approach, Will roars and points herding all before him. He's pleased with the effect he's having, as servants and hangers-on rush down the turnpike and out the wooden stairs. He must remember the feeling and build on it, learn to be a man of power.

Richard Lee selects the strongest looking among them and pulls them off into one group. Neither Will nor James are part of it; Will because he's already failed and James because he's still weak from his illness.

'We must have men who know how to mine,' says Lee. 'Surely somewhere in this godforsaken land you mine for coal, or at least quarry for stone.'

Nydie drops the bucket he's carrying. 'My father,' he says breathlessly, 'Hugh of Nydie, has men who excavate, for we dig much stone from our land. The abbey at Balmerino was built from our sandstone.'

'Well, we do not care for abbeys, but miners we must have,' says Lee. 'Leslie, can you find some way to get these men here, and any others from the lands of the many lairds herein, who may have mines or quarries. In the meantime we must somehow manage with who we have.'

Lee seizes the pick-axe and demonstrates how to swing it. It's plain that most of those he's selected are both unskilled and unwilling, but there are a few who know what they're about. He sets to with a will and the others follow reluctantly. Soon there's a small hole and he tasks James and Will with clearing the rubble. They're to collect it in baskets, lift them onto their backs and dump it in the corner of the courtyard. The baskets are heavy, and after lifting only a few they're sweating freely. The digging is to go on night and day until they establish where, and if, the besiegers are mining. Will doesn't know how he'll find the strength to keep going and is even more concerned about Nydie, who has gone pale as marble. But somehow they must.

Chapter Twenty-Seven

Whiffle-Whaffle

Will works away clearing rubble but puzzling over what they're doing.

'Why do we not wait for our attackers to break through and then pick them off as they emerge? Then we would not have to expend effort digging, and surely it is better than both attackers and defenders meeting underground,' he whispers to an equally baffled Nydie.

'It would not,' sighs Lee who has overheard them. He stops to speak and Will suspects it's preferable, even for Richard Lee, to stand outside by their rubble pile than inside in the creeping dark, coughing on the soot from the smoking torches and watching a bunch of incompetents.

'Arran's intent is not to gain entry; the purpose of a siege tunnel is to undermine the castle defences and that is why we call it *a mine*. Our attackers will begin at a safe distance from the castle so they cannot be seen or fired upon, which is how we cannot yet be sure they are digging.'

'How will it cause the castle walls to collapse, unless they mine close beneath the surface?' Nydie asks.

'No, that would not be wise – else they would find themselves buried alive if the wall collapsed unexpectedly. Once they believe themselves to be underneath the castle walls they'll hollow out an area, which is supported by timber props to keep those digging safe, until all is ready. Then explosives will be laid and fires set below each prop and, when the miners are confident the fire has taken hold, they'll flee out of the mine to safety. The conflagration will cause the tunnel to cave in and, if they've done their work well, the defensive wall above the tunnel will tumble down and the besiegers can take the castle.'

Will ponders Lee's explanation. 'But ...,' he says and stops as Nydie gives him a nudge.

'What is unclear for you, young Seton?' Lee asks rubbing his forehead. 'Spit it out, for I would not have someone as important as you confused.'

He ignores the slight, for he very much wants to understand. 'How will us tunnelling out stop them from tunnelling in? We will simply create a route for all to access the castle.'

'Ah, not such a stupid question. It is down to the skill of the siege engineer, and you are fortunate in having a greatly experienced one before you.' Lee makes Will a courtly bow. 'It is vital that we countermine with all possible speed for we must reach them before they are beneath our walls, which means we must go to work – harder and faster. Though I could wish it was not rock we had to dig through, for I do not know how successful we can be,' he mutters to himself as he turns, swerving to avoid Balnaves who has come to listen.

'We must remember,' Balnaves says, his voice booming around the courtyard, 'that Arran is a whiffle-whaffle. I never saw a man who has so much difficulty in making up his mind; if he agrees with you at dinner, he'll be agin you by nightfall. We must not dig blindly, but frequently stop and listen to ascertain if his men are indeed at work.'

Lee raises his eyebrows. 'Naturally,' he says. 'Now, Balnaves , you must excuse me for I have not the time for idle chatter.'

Will and Nydie glance at one another, smothering smiles, but it's the last time for many days they have anything to smile about.

The work is relentless. They dig straight down for around twenty feet, occasionally using small amounts of explosive to help them along, and then Lee announces they are in the wrong place. He moves them only a short distance inside the guardroom, and they start again, still by no means certain it's the right place to intercept their attackers – or that they have even begun a siege tunnel. Nevertheless Lee will brook no rest.

Will knows he has it easy in comparison to the miners, but his hands are cracked, the skin tight and claw-like making it difficult, as well as painful, to lift the buckets full of rubble, and all made worse by his aching body from the kicking he took. They break only for a short daily service, gathering to stand in the courtyard, for the chapel is too small to contain them all. Their preacher John Rough was, by a strange twist of fate, recently private priest to Regent Arran – when Arran had his godly fit and leaned towards Protestantism and reform. As soon as Cardinal Beaton held his inquisition and turned Arran back to the Papists, Rough had to flee. Will, standing at the back, sways then jerks awake, thinking it's no wonder Arran didn't continue down the Protestant path, with Rough as his guide. He may be an earnest, right-thinking man, but his grasp of doctrine is woolly.

He detaches himself from the group, and slinks into the chapel instead. It's a peaceful place, although considerably barer now the rich hangings have been removed. He sits on the massive chair that would once, no doubt, have been the Cardinal's, head resting in his hands. The sound of voices comes from outside, the service must be finished and he cannot tarry. He spits on his hands, hauls up his breeches and goes back out, wondering how much longer he can keep this up.

Chapter Twenty-Eight

Moonstruck

Will and Nydie are called away from their work to speak with Balnaves and Leslie. Will scrubs his face, the water stinging the cuts in his hands, before they climb the stairs to the Cardinal's chamber like old men, hands pressed to their lower backs.

'Lee wants the stone cutters brought from your father's lands,' says Leslie to James.

'Although we still have no certainty Arran *is* tunnelling,' says Balnaves, gazing out of the window.

Leslie sighs. Will and James wait, eyes on the floor.

'Nydie lands border the River Eden, do they not?' Leslie asks.

James nods.

'Then it is best to go by boat.'

'Aye, and that may prove difficult since our boat was destroyed,' says Balnaves turning from the window.

'And if you went by a boat,' says Leslie, as though Balnaves had not spoken, 'which we *will* acquire, and into the Eden Estuary, you may also go to Erlishall Castle, and get supplies.'

'That is assuming the Mountquhanys have supplies and at least one more boat in which to carry them. It is wild lands at Tents Muir, caught as they are between the Eden and the Tay.'

'I think you've swallowed a bucket of gloom today, Balnaves,' says Leslie.

Will can't help but grin, although it disappears when Leslie turns those protruding eyes on him.

'You must know the harbour here well.'

Will gulps, Bethia knows the harbour far better than he. One of the many reasons he's reluctant to go to his father's warehouse, is the permanent stench of fish around the harbour – and he avoids Fishergate, with its stinking middens full of rotting fish guts, as much as is possible.

Leslie doesn't wait for an answer. 'You must get a boat from the harbour and bring it here.'

Will's mouth falls open.

'You may need to swim to get to there, for you'll need to leave by the sea yett. We are too well watched to get out through the gates, and Arran's troops patrol the gardens now too.'

'Well, if do this we must,' says Balnaves, 'although I still have my doubts about the need for miners, and it means more mouths to feed, then send this lad alone – he's less likely to be noticed. Young Nydie here can save his strength for the trip to his family's lands, once we have a boat.'

Leslie rubs his chin, mouth pursed. Will is more than willing to be of a party for he desperately wants a break from mining, to get out of the crowded castle and breath some clean air, and especially to get away from Carmichael, but he doesn't want to go by himself – and he can only swim a few strokes before he sinks.

'Aye, that is a good plan.'

'But, but…'

They stare at Will.

'There's a storm.'

Leslie and Balnaves laugh and James rests his hand on Will's arm.

'Of course we will wait until it has passed,' says

Leslie. 'Unless you want to take your chances now – and likely be battered to death on the rocks, if you're not swept out to sea.'

By the next night, the storm has worn itself out but the moon is obscured by cloud and Will tells Leslie he must have a moon. 'Else how can I find my way?'

Leslie frowns, but agrees.

'I must have a low tide,' says Will when Leslie summons him the following evening.

'It'll be Yule in the year of our Lord 1600 before there's the perfect conjunction of moon, weather and tide. You will take your chance tonight, lad, and make the best of it.'

The moon has risen, late in the night, when he's let out. He sees the white of James's face above as he climbs down the rope ladder, the clang of the yett closing, after they've hauled the ladder up, loud in the stillness. He strides over the rocks, keen to get to the harbour and be done with this task. His feet go from under him and feels the air beneath him, then he's on his back, head thumping off the ground. He lies still for a moment on the slimy seaweed before rolling onto his knees and getting up, the breeze chill against his damp back. The moon is casting long shadows making it difficult to work out where to place his feet safely. He picks his way carefully, sinking into the fronds of seaweed, long and thick as a mermaid's hair, which tangle around his ankles. He slips again, nearly falling into the deep gully between two shoals, the water glistening below him. He can hear the soft shush of waves touching the edge of the long fingers of rock nearby – the tide must be further in than he'd hoped.

Will clambers around the rocky promontory until he's below the palace chapel. There's the yellow light of a candle shining from its windows and he wonders who is at prayers so early. He stays close to the cliffs, slipping and sliding sometimes over seaweed and sometimes over a green moss covering the rocks, which glows in the moonlight. It looks dry and safe to walk on but is as treacherous as the seaweed. He's glad he'll be returning by boat, would not wish this way on anyone and wonders why there is so much seaweed about when normally it's collected for the fields. But then no one, he supposes, will feel safe on this shore at the moment.

There is a break in the rocks and the sea ripples ghostly before him. His heart thumps in his chest but he steadies when the first wave breaks over his foot. He looks out over the water lit by the moon: a pathway to heaven; may the saints aid him and keep him safe. He sits down on the rocks chiding himself, for what is he thinking to invoke the saints who are naught but Papist flummery. Sighing he slides into the sea, which is the only way to reach the next shoal. Fortunately the water is only thigh high and he makes progress until he trips, arms flailing to keep his balance.

A pox on Leslie and his big idea, he mutters as he clambers onto the rocks, the barnacles scratching his skin. He's glad none of the company can see him stumbling around, especially that fat slug Carmichael. He shivers, his wet breeches sticking chill against his skin. He can see the dark line of the pier jutting into the sea – not far to go. The sun is sending its first rays over the horizon when he finally stands on its secure footing. Now to find oars and a boat.

He hears voices, and, instead, he's looking for a place to hide. He climbs down a ladder and onto the supporting struts of the wooden pier, sinking his head into his shoulders. He's been too slow, left it too late and with the sun rising on a calm sea, the fishermen will be taking to their boats. He'll be caught if he tries to steal one.

Hanging there, without much idea of what to do, he realises this is his chance to escape the foul castle and muck-spouts like Carmichael and John Leslie – when he remembers their attack on Beaton he shudders still. He could slip from the harbour back to his home right now, with no one to stop him. Nydie has whispered more than once that he doesn't trust either Leslie and their whole escapade is more about the Leslies' revenge on Cardinal Beaton for appropriating lands they considered theirs, than any true belief in the need for the church to reform. Why should he suffer for them? He reminds himself that the Leslies can conspire all they want, but there are some among the Castilians who are honest and faithful. No, it is tempting, but he will never leave men the like of James Melville and William Kirkcaldy of Grange, not to mention his friend James of Nydie – he will stay true. And he would not have Carmichael still unchallenged; their business is not yet done. Now, he must find some oars, steal a boat and get away from here, quick as he can.

Before he can move, the voices draw close. A rope is being tugged, hauling a boat alongside the quay. He sees a pair of legs, someone is descending the ladder. Will buries his face in his arm and holds his breath, praying he goes undiscovered. His prayer is answered, and the man passes him. He hears the thump of feet on boat and risks a peek, straight into Bethia's startled face.

'You're wearing breeches,' he says.

She has the grace to blush. 'I was coming to you.'

'I need to take the boat.'

She raises her eyebrows and continues her descent.

He watches from above as Grissel's uncle holds out his hand to steady her. He can't help but notice her confidence. There's something about wearing breeches that seems to have freed her – when it should shame her.

She settles herself and looks up at him. 'Geordie and I are ready to go, are you coming, or would you prefer to hang there?'

He's furious. God's blood, she's a girl, how dare she look at him with those straight blue eyes. He climbs out from the struts and onto the ladder, which he descends rapidly, and readies himself to jump.

'Whoah,' says Geordie, 'take care or you'll have us tippet-ower.'

He lowers his leg and feels Bethia's small hand grab it, placing his foot on the seat; his sister thinks herself very important. He sits down in the front of the boat and they cast off, pulling strongly away, hugging the cliffs that he's just scrambled over to the detriment of his knees, hands and clothes.

'I was coming to the bishop's palace because…,' Bethia begins.

He raises his hand. Let her come. She's so busy with her own concerns she doesn't ask about his, about why he should risk life and limb to get to the harbour. Let her come, and once they reach the castle he'll take the boat, and Geordie to row it. Let her find her own way back to the comfort of their home. If she's going to adopt the dress and mannerisms of a man, let her find out what it means to be one and to have to look out for herself, instead of expecting others to take care of her frailties.

Chapter Twenty-Nine

Tents Muir

Other fishing boats are taking to the water as they pull away. The ships patrolling are standing well out to sea, obviously more watchful for anything coming from the South and England than from the harbour, and Will thinks they'll gain the castle safely, especially now the tide is well in.

Bethia tries to speak, but he holds his hand up and shakes his head each time. What can she possibly have to tell him, apart from more pleas for his return home, and he will not go. His decision was made once and for all as he hung under the quay just now.

She folds her hands in her lap and he's left with his thoughts; the only sound is the oars dipping in the sea and the cry of a lone seagull floating on the wing above. If he wasn't so furious he would enjoy the stillness but, in the face of Bethia's serenity, he cannot. He's sure she's pretending – she used to do this when they fought as children; the angrier he got, the calmer she became, which made him even angrier. He grinds his teeth, loud as Father, at the memory.

They near the castle. Will has not seen it from the sea before; it is a forbidding sight, although the brown smears down the walls below the privy chutes show its occupants' frailties. Bethia fumbles with a bundle in her lap and drops her skirts over her head, tying the strings tightly at her waist. He's relieved she's not entirely lost to modesty, and more relieved yet that he'll not have to defend her honour from the leers and asides if she entered the castle wearing breeches. She makes no further attempt to tell him why she is come. And, as he follows her out of the boat, over the rocks, and up the ladder he still chooses not to ask.

'It is said you have a siege engineer within, sent by King Henry,' she says, as they pass through the open postern.

He doesn't reply but Nydie, who's unbarred the gate, says indeed they do. She turns and looks at Will, but he stares at the ground.

'Please take me to him. I've some information he may find useful.'

He feels his face redden: how dare she issue orders.

They pass the kitchens and he can see a puny fire is burning in the centre of the huge fireplace with a pot hanging over it. Getting the fixings to light fires is increasingly difficult. They have long since used up the Cardinal's store of coal and wood; indeed they are now burning his furniture and books.

They enter the courtyard. Nydie rushes ahead, presumably to let Richard Lee know he has a visitor. Bethia lifts her feet, and, as he draws abreast of her, he sees her face wrinkle in disgust at what's sticking to them. The stench is throat-clogging after breathing sea air – even with Balnaves's clean ups.

Suddenly she grabs his arm. 'Will, you must come home. If you do not, Father will make me wed Norman Wardlaw.'

'Who?'

'You know, Fat Norman,'

'Oh, him. Why?'

'Because Father says our reputation will be as nothing once it is known you are among the Castilians, and we will be punished for it.'

'That makes no sense. Why it's more likely to be of advantage to have me as part of the garrison.' He knows this isn't so, even as he speaks, for his fellows have alienated the townsfolk.

She shakes her head. 'You cannot prevail. I have it on good authority, from one of his officers, that Arran's now determined to end this siege quickly. Oh Will, please come home.'

Before he can answer, Carmichael strolls out from under the portico, that supercilious smirk on his face which Will wants to smash each time he sees it.

'Well, boy, what have we here? Have you brought your wee sister to look after you?'

She behaves as though Carmichael doesn't exist, looking past him to Melville following behind. He's proud of her, especially when he notices Carmichael's face flush.

'Don't ignore me, you puffed up hussy,' he says, reaching out to grab her by the shoulder. Melville knocks Carmichael's hand away before Will can react, offering his arm to Bethia

'Come, my lady,' he says, 'let me escort you. I hear you wish to speak with Master Lee.'

Will knows Melville to be an honest if dour man, and is surprised to see him behave with such courtliness. But then Melville does surprise. He can never look at him without remembering the calm delivery of the killing blow, as he listed the Cardinal's evil doings.

They stride towards the guard-room. Carmichael sticks his foot out as Will passes, but he sees in time, leaps over, keeps going and doesn't give Carmichael the satisfaction of reacting; now is not the time, and he's discovering a certain pleasure can be had from it.

Richard Lee is leaning over the second pit they've started, calling down to the miners to put their backs into it. If Lee took up the pick-axe himself more often, he'd be more understanding of how painful it is to wield for a prolonged period, indeed, for any period.

Melville introduces Bethia to Lee, and he looks her up and down. Will bristles at this treatment of his sister, but the next moment he's back to wanting to give her a skelp. She's saying the Castilians are digging in the wrong place, she knows that Arran's troops are mining, and where. Why could she not have told him what she was here for, and why is he only hearing it now? If she'd shared the information, he'd have told his fellow conspirators and been the hero, which would make a welcome change from feeling the dunce.

Lee's all courtesy and consideration now: taking Bethia by the elbow; leading her above to the Cardinal's rooms; introducing her to Young Arran. Will notices Bethia doesn't admit to already having met James Hamilton. Lee calls for some wine for the lady. He glares at Will hovering in the doorway asking what he wants, and if it is nothing of import to get back to work.

'This is my sister.'

Lee looks surprised. 'Ah, so there is one useful member of the family.'

Will bites his lip. His mind churns back through all his wrongs; he risks his life daily here just like them, he works hard, his behaviour is more godly than most, and he has his sister as a spy. He frowns – Bethia has no Protestant sympathies, so far as he's aware; why would she bring them information?

Lee is laying out parchment and a quill upon the board. 'Tell me how the street looks wherein they dig.'

She speaks and Lee draws. Will is intrigued to see Lee's chorography emerge and Bethia, glancing over Lee's head mouths "John", and Will nods, knowing how much their young brother would enjoy seeing this drawing of their town's streets emerge.

He notices how respectful Lee is towards Bethia, now he's spoken with her. Men like his sister, and it's not only because she's prettyish. He studies her. It's something about how direct, and yet how unselfconscious, she is.

The servant comes with the wine and bowls of porridge, and goes to lay them by the drawing.

'Take care, man,' Lee says, waving his hand and coming close to knocking over the wine himself.

The servant hovers, uncertain what to do.

'Put it on the kist, you mouldiewarp,' Lee mutters.

Bethia is bent over the plan, absorbed and Will draws closer to see.

'Move your fat head,' says Lee.

'My brother has greater knowledge of the town than I do. He can help plot the exact place.'

He knows he should be grateful to her for including him, but he is not. Nevertheless they bend over the chorography together.

'The entry point is at the back of a house in Northgait. I believe they are digging from within the byre to stay hid.'

Will can see she knows perfectly well where that should be placed but is holding back, allowing him to show Lee and rather than mollifying, it incenses. Who is she, for all that she seems to charm every man in her sphere, including their father, to so patronise her own brother?

'Well,' says Lee. 'Would someone care to show me the correct positioning of this byre.'

In the end it is a success for him. Between them, he and Richard Lee work out where Arran's sappers are mining, with some help from Bethia, but it is he and Richard who agree the placement. Norman Leslie, who's joined them, even pats Will on the back.

Then it's decided that he and Nydie will take Bethia's boat to fetch the miners. Even better they do not have to row because Geordie is here; indeed he has tied up his boat and followed Bethia into the castle.

'I'm no taking you anywhere, laddie,' he says when

161

Will tries to give him his orders. 'I'll return your sister to the harbour and then I hae my fishing to go to. I've wasted enough time already the day.'

'You'll do as you're told,' says Will, aware the disagreement is attracting attention.

Geordie raises his fists. 'I'm no your servant and I'll do as I choose with my ane boat.'

Will draws his knife. 'I'll slice your nose open, you old fool, if you argue any more,'

'Stop it, Will,' says Bethia. She tries to restrain him and he shakes her hand off. 'Why must you always be such a fopdoodle?' she cries.

He turns, ready to slice her whole body open, roaring. 'And why must you always be such a fustylugs?'

'Calm down, both of you,' says Nydie stepping between them.

Will lowers his knife, and becomes aware of Carmichael, bent double with laughter, and muttering fopdoodle over and over to himself.

Bethia again lays a hand on Will's arm but he flings it off.

'Come,' says Leslie, 'there's no time for this. You must to Tents Muir and back while the weather remains calm, for the wind may get up at any moment.' He stares at Geordie, who hangs his head.

They go through the postern, climb down the ladder and into the boat, leaving Bethia in Leslie's care. All goes smoothly from then on. Geordie glowers at him for the whole trip, muttering under his breath, but Will doesn't care. He and Nydie talk and laugh and breathe the good air. Will has forgot his early morning escapade, has forgot about the painful scrambling, has forgot that he ever considered deserting his fellows.

They collect two miners, Hugh Forsyth hurrying them down the hill to the river once he understands what is wanted. Then they go to Erlishall, the nearly completed castle on the far side of the Eden. Nydie says it's sad the old hunting lodge was knocked down to build it, but such is progress. There are provisions made ready for them and more boats sent to Nydie's lands to collect the rest of the miners.

Even Geordie cheers up when a bonny servant asks. 'Are ye hungry?'

Nydie nudges Will and Geordie shuffles his feet and stares at the ground.

'Och well,' she grins. 'There's been a slaughtering of beasts for the winter and I have blood pudding ready to eat and a fine mug of ale to go with it – but I see you're no interested.'

Geordie barrels past Will and follows her into the cookhouse.

The lord and lady of the house treat Nydie and Will right good well, and even though Will knows it's because Nydie is who he is, he doesn't allow it to mar the time, which is all too short. They leave by late afternoon – already it's growing dark – with full bellies, and boats equally full of men and supplies.

The wind begins to rise, whirling across the sea and chopping up the waves but they are near the castle now. Bethia is waiting and climbs down to the boat, although Will's less than pleased to see the breeches have been donned once more.

She stops in front of him. 'Please, Will, you must help me.'

But he won't answer her, won't even look at her. What is there to say? He will not leave his fellows, and especially his good friend Nydie. He does not believe her story about being forced into a marriage with Fat Norman. It's a ruse to get him home. Father would not propose such a match, not for a bonny girl like Bethia and with a good dowry forby. There is, however, one thing he wants to know before she departs.

'Why did you tell Lee where Arran's men are mining?'

'We must go,' calls Geordie over the rising wind.

Will waves a hand at him to wait.

'If they take the castle by force then you may be hurt, or worse.'

'Thank you for looking out for me. You are a good sister, even if you can be annoying,' he says, and squeezes her arm.

Geordie shouts again. She opens her mouth to speak, sighs instead, pats his hand and leaves.

The fellows lower ropes to haul up the supplies and soon he is occupied with them and forgets about Bethia. There's some grumbling about the paucity of provisions, until Will tells them to look in the boats following. He feels better for his day out. Now he just needs to sort Carmichael out, once and for all.

Chapter Thirty

Countermine

Will and Nydie are much lauded for bringing the miners. Although there are only eight of them, they can do the work of many more Castilians, being used to tunnelling into hillsides to extract stone, and they counter-mine with such speed that Will's team have to enlist more help to keep pace with the rubble removal.

A further delivery of food comes, as promised, the next night, but by day three they no longer want provisions from Erlishall because Melville is sick and thirty others besides. It is said the Mountquhanys deliberately tried to poison the garrison but he's not so sure if the cause is the food from Tents Muir since he ate plenty of it, and he's not sick. The fish on the other hand he didn't eat – he shudders at the thought. It looked long caught with the eyes cloudy and gills slimy. He'd said as much to Nydie, but Nydie shrugged, saying they've eaten worse, and anyways what did Will know of fish when he can't bear to touch, never mind eat, them. But he does know how to size the quality of goods; learnt that at least from Father. And now Nydie is sick again, and James Hamilton too. They'd lose a great deal if the Regent's son should die, but more than that, he likes young Arran, feels protective of him after what he's endured as a hostage, always with politeness.

Richard Lee unfortunately is not sick. The new, and hopefully final, tunnel is begun outside the fore-tower, based on the information Bethia provided. Lee is driving his reduced workforce harder than ever – even the miners do not go fast enough to satisfy him. The one benefit, Will thinks wryly, is that he himself has strong muscles now and his shoulders have broadened, although his jerkin is tight across his back. No one can call him a gawky lad anymore – or push him around.

They pause often in their work to listen, and increasingly there are sounds to be heard. Lee is now convinced the besiegers are at work making their way steadily underground towards the castle walls – and Will notices that Balnaves no longer complains about the countermining.

He awakens one morning, shivering. The wind is whistling through the vents, and, although the air may be fresh, he'd rather have warmth even if it does make the stink worse. He's slept in all his clothes as usual. If Agnes were here she would likely take them off him by force and throw on the midden. God's good heart how he wishes she were here. He sighs at the memory of her comforting presence, her pies and her warm kitchen. But there's no time to get maudlin over Agnes and clean clothes. Walter Melville, James Melville's brother, died yesterday, and five others the day before: twenty in all from bad fish.

Will gets up and goes to tend Nydie who has soiled himself again. When he's fetched water from the well, he cleans and settles James with a sip of ale.

Nydie grasps his arm, as strongly as someone with no strength can, after all the vomiting he's done, and whispers, 'you are my good friend, my very good friend.'

Will tries to smile but it's more of a grimace. He wishes Bethia had not gone, for she could minister to the sick. He hates mining but he'd rather have blistered hands than ones reeking of vomit and shit. It's only because James of Nydie is his good friend that he tolerates it. He rubs his hands down his breeches, nods to Nydie and hurries down the turnpike to the mine, before Lee comes bellowing for him.

Night and day they work bent double, countermining with all possible speed. They're helped by more miners, brought from Kirkcaldy's lands this time. The tunnel is dug wide enough for one man to move down it at a time, crouched low, and no effort is to be wasted enlarging. For both diggers and those clearing behind them, all movement has to be planned, for they must turn sideways to pass one another. Will remembers Bethia screaming, and screaming, when he once shut her in an empty kist. He thinks how much she'd hate this. He doesn't much like it himself, especially as the longer the tunnel gets, the harder it is to breathe. Mining, it seems, is only about reaching their attackers and chasing them away, not about creating ease of ingress and egress – or sufficient air vents.

The further they hollow through the rock, the louder the sound of their enemies working near. Lee tells them they must work silently, and they muffle their implements as best they can, but it's hard to break through rock without making some noise. It helps that their attackers grow silent during the deepest hours of the night, when Lee has all his sappers at work, insisting all must lend a hand and even the lairds' sons take their turn.

For the last section they grow even more careful; they can hear voices close through the rock beneath their feet. Will is there, his aching back all forgot as he leans over to listen. He can feel that the good Lord is with them, wants the Castilians to succeed. They chip, quietly and steadily, quietly and steadily. The voices seem close, close enough to touch the speakers.

Chapter Thirty-One

Breaking Through

They hear sounds of alarm; it seems they are discovered. Any attempt to stay quiet is given up and they excavate as hard and fast as they can. Someone has fetched Richard Lee and he squeezes past Will, directing them to attack the ground beneath, and not before them.

'We must be quick,' he hisses, 'else they'll have time to set explosives and blow us into eternity.'

Will shovels the rubble behind him to keep the area clear for the miners to work – there's no time to scuttle back up the passageway with it now. A hole has appeared in the floor of the tunnel. Lee has a man shield the candles, whispering that he needs it dark to see if there's torchlight shining through from below.

Will, Lee and the two miners all squeezed tight together nudge one another; light is shining through from below. They enlarge the hole, cries beneath them growing loud, then fading. Lee kneels at the edge, and sticks his head through. Will can feel Lee's body tense, ready to jerk his head out if necessary; he is a brave man. They wait, then Lee lifts his head out and smiles.

'It could not be more perfect.'

They all shove their heads through in turn. Young Morrison, who's crept along the tunnel to join them, wants to climb down and explore, but Lee forbids it. When it's

Will's turn to look, he sees they've broken through more than the height of a man above their attackers. The tunnel beneath is spacious enough for six men to stand abreast and room to bring in horses, or ponies at least. He thinks how easy his task might have been if he'd had a pony and cart – and the space to use one.

'There is nothing Regent Arran's men can do,' says Lee rubbing his hands. 'You two,' he nods to the miners, 'stay here until I send down armed men to keep watch.'

When they emerge Balnaves, the Leslies and Kirkcaldy of Grange come running and cluster around Lee to hear the news.

'Their tunnel is made worthless – we can fire down upon them, or tip cauldrons of boiling water or even just a loud halloo will send them fleeing; they can excavate no further,' Lee says.

Balnaves claps his hands, Kirkcaldy claps Lee on the back and the Leslies cheer.

Then Balnaves is tugging on Lee's arm, and Will sees Lee frown. 'But surely they can still set explosives,' Balnaves says.

'They surely can, and light a fire under their wooden props too,' says Lee disengaging his arm. 'And it will cause the tunnel to collapse; but they never got far enough to reach beneath the castle walls, so only the ground before the castle would be brought down. Indeed it would be to our advantage if they did set explosives, for troops cannot easily storm the castle if the foreground is all broken up; it would be too treacherous.'

Richard Lee's plan has worked perfectly and their attackers have failed. For once *Dour Will*, as his fellows have named him, is as jubilant as the rest, albeit exhausted. They pat one another on the back and declare that Lee is truly the king of siege engineers.

Even Nydie rises from his sickbed to join the celebrations, leaning on Will, while James Hamilton looks on, his face ashen. Regent's son or no, he is smiling but then Will, and others, have taken the opportunity of his incarceration to teach him the new doctrine and the importance of reading the Bible.

Arran responds quickly after the failure of his plan, sending emissaries to the gate with a message offering terms if the Castilians will leave the castle, and release his son. They'll be taken to Blackness Castle and held there, at least the lairds will. As the son of a merchant, Will reflects, he'll probably be given more lowly imprisonment than a chamber at Blackness.

Far from seriously considering Arran's offer, the garrison is gleeful. It's yet another sign the Lord must be on their side, otherwise their besiegers would have got them out. The lairds send Arran's emissary back with an instant refusal. In response Arran rolls the big guns out again, Crook-mow and Deaf Meg, and stations them by the trenches, aiming at the block houses and the Chapel. There's much activity among the Castilians, re-energised after being freed from the slavery of mining. They are still well equipped, thanks to the large quantity of lead bullet and cannon balls Cardinal Beaton had stored in the months before his death when, as Leslie says, he was any day expecting an attack from his arch enemy, Henry of England.

They set up in the towers and position themselves by the windows for firing down on anything and anyone that's moving below them. It's almost too easy. They pick them off like waddling geese, and a great cheer goes up whenever they hit one of Arran's artillerymen. Soon Arran's troops withdraw.

Another lull ensues. November is the month dedicated to the Souls in Purgatory and, now the excitement has passed, Will feels as though he may well be one of them. Although he hated the mining, at least it was exciting; boredom sets in once more. He wonders what manoeuvre Arran's going to execute next, for surely he cannot allow the siege to continue unchallenged. It's not long before he finds out.

Chapter Thirty-Two

The Great Cursing

On 23rd November 1546, Will is sent up to the top of the block house to oversee guard duty. It's a grey day; grey sky merges with grey sea. They haven't seen the sun for a week; even the constant wind has failed to blow the clouds away enough to uncover it. Water droplets rest on walls, doors and floors, drifting in through unglazed windows and apertures, leaving everything damp and slimy to the touch. What little light there is soon begins to fail as the short day tips into the long Scottish winter night. He strides back and forth across the battlement, swinging his arms, but he cannot remember the last time he was warm.

He's not alone in his vigil, but feels disinclined to speak to his fellows. What can he say to them anyway; that he hates this castle as much as they do? Better to stay silent. That is until Morrison hails him to come see, and they all hang over the parapet puzzling, through the dimness, about what is going on in the streets below.

Arran's guard is lining up in front of the castle, within firing distance but on horseback. Will shouts to his fellows to get the brazier going so they're ready to fire at need, although the horses will likely give the troops the necessary speed to escape any cannon fire, and he judges they are out of range of musket shot. It would be difficult to fire in any case, for darkness is near upon them.

They fuss around the brazier nevertheless, and Will sends a man running down the spiral stairs all the way to the kitchen, as he was once sent, to get a tray of burning embers to light the damp faggots of wood. The wood is supposed to have been kept covered, but someone has neglected their duty. And it'll be his head that will roll if cannon fire is needed and they cannot deliver it.

A trumpet blasts out and he sprints back to the parapet. All the church bells of St Andrews peal at once then fade away. A procession of priests come in pairs down the Swallowgait from the cathedral, carrying torches which they wave back and forth like firebrands. They're singing but the singing is not as in the kirk, solemn yet uplifting; it is a chanting which hurts the ears and sets the body trembling.

The soldiers beneath clash their arms, the noise reverberating off the castle walls, and lower their flags to the ground. By the light of the torches he sees a cleric in full regalia being carried high on a chair. The priests part and he passes through them, then he too is lowered to the ground. He stands in front of the soldiers on horseback, with the priests fanning out behind.

The Castilians have poured from every nook and crevice in the castle and are leaning out of windows and hanging over parapets. They're strangely silent, but it would be difficult to be heard above the cacophony rising from the choir below. Will's whole body vibrates to the sound, his heart beating as though it will burst from his chest and the blood roaring in his ears. He looks to his right and sees Norman Leslie himself standing next to him.

Once more St Salvators leads the way, its church bell tolling; the other church bells follow. Will covers his ears as the satanic crescendo from the choir peaks, then fades. The cleric raises his arms to heaven and slowly lowers them making the sign of the cross. Then he begins to speak.

'The Bishop of Rome, servant of all the servants of God, according to the duty of the Apostolic charge and to maintain the purity of the Christian faith, doth send you his word.'

He again makes the sign of a cross, his arms sweeping wide.

'You are guilty of the crime of high treason, and worse, in following the path of heretical teaching. We *curse* all heretics.'

There is an intake of collective breath from the men surrounding Will. He, himself, can barely breathe at all.

'To preserve the holy communion of the faithful, we follow the ancient rule and accordingly do excommunicate the killers of Cardinal Beaton together with all those persons, whoever they may be, who aid and abet them, in the name of God Almighty, the Father.'

Will is an aider and abetter; this Great Cursing from the Holy Father in Rome includes him.

'Wherefore in the name of God the All-powerful, Father, Son, and Holy Ghost; of the Blessed Peter, Prince of the Apostles, and of all the Saints; in virtue of the power which has been given us of binding and loosening in Heaven and on earth, we deprive Norman Leslie and all his accomplices of the Communion of the Body and Blood of Our Lord, we separate him from the society of all Christians, we exclude him from the bosom of our Holy Mother the Church, in Heaven and on earth, we declare him excommunicated and anathematised. We judge him condemned to eternal fire with Satan and his demons, and we deliver him unto Satan to mortify his body, that his soul may be in torment until the Day of Judgement.'

In the ghostly light cast from the torches Will can see Norman Leslie. Whatever bravado he may show later, Will knows Leslie is tight with fear. He's leaning into the parapet as though he cannot stand upright without its support. No man can be brought up in the bosom of

173

Mother Church and not know terror when they are cast out. The agony of George Wishart as he burned is as nothing to what Leslie, Will and their fellows are condemned to suffer – for they will burn in the fire pits of hell, for all eternity.

The trumpet blasts out once more. The cleric sits back down upon his chair and is raised aloft by his bearers, the priests resume their dirge as they turn away, torches held high, and the soldiers on horseback follow. Soon the space in front of the castle is still; it is over and their eternal souls are damned.

Leslie pushes himself off the rampart.

'May God roast them and guide *their* steps to hell,' he says loudly.

There's a muttering amongst the men but no cheers of support; Leslie's words ring hollow.

Chapter Thirty-Three

Will's Demons

The Great Cursing has left Will bereft. He's always believed that he would pass through the gates of Heaven with ease, and if he helped reform to happen then surely his place would be assured. He tells himself it is of no matter to be excluded, thrown out, cursed – but it does matter. He watches Norman Leslie bluster about how the Pope is the Antichrist, and knows that Leslie too is shaken.

Sitting on a stool in the great hall in the dark of night with the wind howling outside and in, his aching head in his hands, he tries to untangle the politics in his head; even though it was never supposed to be about politics but about faith and salvation. Meanwhile men snore all around.

There's a loud bang and he jumps, overturning his stool and looking fearfully behind him. The glass is rattling loosely in the long window, as though someone is trying to get in. A man by his feet, gives a guttural snort and rolls over, but otherwise the sleepers seem undisturbed. Will chides himself for his feebleness, wraps his jerkin tight around and settles back to his thoughts. It's the same thought sifting through his head; they should not have murdered Beaton, he should have been tried and then justly executed. He sees the

Cardinal's slumped body, the blood spurting, his pleading face as he died. Round and around it goes, until he's ready to thump his own head off the wall.

He decides to fetch his bedding and lie in the great hall. He'll be amongst servants and foot soldiers, but at least he won't be alone, for Nydie has been bid to stay with Young Arran. He bends to light a stub of candle in the fire and places it in a lantern. The flame isn't strong, but if he holds the lantern high it'll light his way enough to keep evil spirits at bay while he walks the dark passages.

The wind shrieks up the turnpike as he descends, and his candle flickers wildly like demons are dancing in its flame. He must walk down the outside stairs, cross the courtyard and climb the stairs above the dungeon to fetch his bedding; the dungeon where the Cardinal's body lies yet, despite the many pleas made by his concubine to release it.

He huddles in the doorway looking out on the wind-blasted yard, and his heart fails him. The midden heap is being blown into all four corners. He'll have to walk through a swirl of shite, and his lantern will surely get blown out. He'd rather the discomfort of sitting on a stool all night than crossing this space.

A figure looms out of the darkness. He bangs his head off the wall and drops the lantern. The man bends to pick it up, miraculously still alight.

'It's you, Morrison,' Will says, trying to still his shaking, as young Morrison's features are revealed.

'Aye, I lost out tonight.'

'Well your watch should be uneventful, we're unlikely to be attacked in this weather.'

'All attention is on what the wind throws at us,' says Morrison, ducking as a long splinter of wood whirls passed his head. 'Although we are here as much to keep our fellows in, as Arran's troops out.'

'What do you mean?'

'We're leaching men; two went last night and one the night before. We know not how they escape the castle, for the posterns are all closed and Carmichael holds the keys. He thinks they may be climbing out the sea tower windows and down the cliff, but it's a risky route for the waves reach high to catch the unwary.'

Will is silent, pondering. Many came to join them last summer, when food was plentiful and they were strutting around the countryside like kings. Then more joined when Henry sent money and supplies, but that is all gone. Now is the time of the true believers, those who have faith in the teachings of Luther and George Wishart.

'Let them go. It is better we have only those who follow Christ's true path among us.'

'I fear we may need the numbers if we're to continue to repel our besiegers,' says Morrison. 'But you, who could be sitting warm by the great fire, where are you going?'

'To collect blankets from my cell above the dungeon.'

Morrison laughs, although Will did not intend humour. Then he grows sombre. "Tis curious that the Cardinal is still in the dungeon below, tucked up tight in his coffin.'

Will doesn't think it curious at all. The Cardinal will haunt them for all time for what's been done to him, both in life and death.

They leave the sheltering doorway and set out down the wooden stairs and across the courtyard together. The lantern is blown out immediately but the moon peeps through, briefly lighting the fast moving clouds above, and the dark shapes of debris dancing around like fiends at play, below. He can hear the waves crashing onto the rocks; the spray leaps high enough to clear the castle walls as they both lean into the wind, pushing their way through to the doorway opposite.

'I will leave you here and continue my rounds,' says Morrison.

He feels bereft when Morrison, with his cool

steadiness, trudges away. He runs up the outside stairs and into the dark doorway. He climbs, feeling his way, for it is black as a ghost's lair. Half way up he freezes. Demons are close, he can feel their touch. They're stroking him, calling him to them and he cannot resist, for he is cursed. The wind howls louder. He's sure it carries the cries of Beaton as he pleads for his life, and he stood by and did nothing. The noise rises to a crescendo of shrieks. There is a loud bang as something heavy thuds against the doorway below. His legs give way; sinking to his knees, he crawls up feeling the unquiet spirit of Beaton following close behind, its stinking breath blowing upon his neck.

He blinks. Around him he sees a fluttering; they're small and white and dance over his head. There's another loud crash, this time from above. The noise frees him from the grip of unquiet spirits. He turns and stumbles down the stairs, falls into the courtyard, the dried shit coating his body with a layer of dust, and flees to the doorway opposite, back up the stairs to the great hall, where he huddles by the dim light of the dying fire. He wonders if he'll ever have a quiet heart again. The Cardinal's soul has invaded his and the Pope has cursed him. He is damned.

When he awakes it is broad daylight; the storm has dropped to a steady blast of wind and his co-conspirators are complaining about how much he stinks.

Chapter Thirty-Four

Truce

Leslie and several others, including Richard Lee who considers his work at the castle done, leave for the court of King Henry early in December. Will watches as they are rowed around the coast to a waiting ship – Arran's fleet have disappeared, they know not where. He feels Leslie is deserting them to seek spiritual, as well as physical, protection from King Henry, who styles himself Defender of the Faith.

'By God's good blood, may they be kept safe on these wintry seas,' says Morrison, as the boat disappears from sight.

Will hawks and spits. 'Aye, and by God's good grace they'll be better fed, warmer and more comfortable than will be our lot over this winter.

Yet, before Yule, Regent Arran sends a deputation to stand in front of the castle with a proposal which lifts their spirits. The Castilians watch the group of three from the castle windows until eventually Melville determines to go out and speak with them. Nydie and Will are ordered to accompany him, but Will clutches at his belly pleading the thraw, for the one thing he's promised himself he must do for his family is to continue to stay out of sight. Morrison goes instead.

Will positions himself, half-hid at a window above, as

the three stroll out to stand before Arran's deputation. They bow to one another, and he sees Nydie nod to his opposite number. The man looks familiar – it's Logie of Clatto from the lands above Garrbridge. Will sniffs; Gilbert Logie is loyal to Arran!

He sees Logie nod back, holding onto his cap which the blustery wind is tugging; his lips move but Will cannot hear the words. It's not long before Melville shakes his head, and the two groups part, Nydie chasing his cap back to the gate while the others hold tight onto theirs.

Will leaps down the stairs to speak to Nydie. 'What happened?'

'They are proposing a truce, but Melville is affecting little interest.'

'Why?' Will covers his mouth, he didn't mean to hit such a high note.

'I think he's reluctant to agree terms with our leaders absent.'

The discussions go back and forth over the next few days.

'Now Regent Arran proposes to seek absolution from the Pope on our behalf,' Nydie tells Will.

He straightens up, his body feels lighter – as though the gloom which has sat heavy upon him since the Great Cursing is lifting.

'While we await the absolution, should the Holy Father be willing to grant it, we have agreed to negotiate the terms of a surrender, which will be favourable to both sides.'

'What does that mean?'

Nydie shrugs, 'I think they do not know – it is what the negotiation will determine, once Leslie, Kirkcaldy and Balnaves return from England. We do have to keep within the castle; they don't want us roaming at will.'

Will is relieved to hear it. He would not wish for a repeat of last summer's behaviour when the garrison plucked what they could from his town.

'In the meantime we are to send hostages as a pledge of good faith.'

'Ah, I thought it all sounded too easy.'

'That is what has taken so long to agree, for they have insisted that Kirkcaldy's sons are among the hostages.'

Three boys, younger than Will, two of them indeed Kirkcaldy's sons, leave the castle later that day. Will thinks, as he watches them go, that yet again he's glad to be the son of a merchant and not worthy of anyone's attention.

Soon there is a strange rumour running around the castle that Henry of England is seeking absolution from the Pope on the Castilians behalf.

'How can that be?' he asks Nydie. 'Henry has denied the Pope and seized all his lands and wealth in England.'

Nydie shakes his head in shared disbelief, but then the tale changes.

''Tis now being said that Balnaves, far from asking King Henry to seek absolution, is requesting him to use his influence to block the absolution that Arran has sought,' says Will.

They roll their eyes.

'Here's the latest on the absolution story,' says Nydie leaping out in front of Will some days later.

Will shoves him on the shoulder and Nydie wrestles back.

'What now?' asks Will when they pause for breath.

'Leslie has heard that the Dowager Queen asked the King of France to seek absolution but the Pope, in return, wants all the ecclesiastical dues unpaid since the Cardinal's death to be given up.'

Will gives a snort of laughter but is relieved to know that the absolution may still be granted. 'Do you think it's true, will they give the funds up?'

Nydie grows serious, 'Who knows if any or all of these tales of absolution are true.' He shuffles his feet

181

considering, and then looks up. 'Regent Arran will not easily hand over funds to the Pope – for his family now control what was once Beaton's rich livings. And why would he to save our souls, when we are his enemies?'

Will considers what Nydie has said. It all sounds worthy of that fellow Machiavelli advising his prince; a ruse, and excuse, for a truce and delay. On their side to give England more time to effect a rescue and on Arran's side, simply to delay – for that is what it is said whiffle-whaffle Arran does best.

Chapter Thirty-Five

The Fight

Shortly after Yule, the Leslies and Kirkcaldy of Grange return from London and are able to re-enter the castle under the flag of truce. They have each been granted a hundred merks and much reassurance about how Henry Tudor is their supporter. Balnaves has stayed at Henry's court, and continues to press for military aid to break the siege once and for all. The English king has also written to Arran, insisting the Castilians must be given safe passage and freed, as his friends and well-wishers to the marriage of the infant Mary to his son Prince Edward. The Castilians are jubilant and dance an impromptu reel in the courtyard, kicking up the muck – which has grown worse again since Balnaves left – with their flying feet.

Will stands on the sidelines watching the celebrations. If Henry is our great friend, he thinks, why has he not broken the siege, and where is the promised relief force? If they had not killed the Cardinal, but held him prisoner, he still swears the English king would have sent an army for the joy of getting his hands on Beaton. He can feel the weight of despair heavy upon him once more, as though he's trapped under a rockfall in the siege tunnel. He reminds himself that their work is God's work, and the good Lord must be supporting them else they would not still be holding the castle. He rubs his forehead but it does not help; the sense of impending doom will not leave him.

'What's the matter with our pigeon-hearted bairn now? Little misery face, does nothing ever make you happy?' says Peter Carmichael, jostling him.

He turns his head and looks down at Carmichael. He feels too weary to rise to the accusation that he's a coward.

'What did I ever do to you that you should so revile me?'

Carmichael sneers, 'I have no time to bandy words with a scunnersome donkey penis.'

'Then why speak?'

In response Carmichael shoves him, and he staggers into the revellers, who push him out of their way. Stumbling into the portico, he's determined to hit Carmichael back and have this out once and for all – but Carmichael has disappeared. He heads up the stairs looking for him but, instead, finds Norman Leslie sitting by the fire, stroking his freshly trimmed beard . He goes to leave but Leslie lifts his head, turns his piercing eyes upon Will, and beckons him to come sit on a nearby stool.

'Ach Seton, you're a lad who doesn't care for merriment, more of the taciturn nature.'

Will shrugs, embarrassed by the description, which he knows to be true.

'Well, you're no so daft. We may be jolly for now but who knows how it will end, and somehow I fear they'll get us out, unless we get the town and surrounding country on side.'

'Surely King Henry will eventually send troops?'

'There are many obstacles to Henry Tudor taking direct action.'

Will shuffles on the low stool, stretching his legs out. 'I would be most grateful if you could explain, for I am confused. When we were planning the attack on the castle, all were agreed that England *would* come to our aid.' He hesitates, uncertain if he should share what he's thinking. Leslie reminds him of a horse Father once owned, which seemed friendly, but, without warning, would turn and bite its rider.

'Spit it out, young Seton, for I'm fairly certain I know what's coming.'

'I did wonder... if we'd kept the Cardinal alive, would that have spurred Henry into action?'

'Perhaps, but on balance I think not, and I'm not saying this only because my Uncle John was instrumental in Beaton's death. Perhaps a wee lesson in Anglo Scots, Anglo French and Franco Scots politics might be helpful to you. I shall make it brief, for no doubt someone will soon come seeking me.'

Will waits expectantly while Leslie leans back and scratches his head.

'King Henry, throughout his reign, has pursued a most ruinous conflict with France, most recently over both the taking and holding of Boulogne.'

He nods. Leslie isn't telling him anything he doesn't already know, for the French siege of English-held Boulogne affected Father's trade.

Leslie holds up his hand. 'Patience Seton, let me tell it in my own way.'

The fire has burnt low and he feeds it with the last of the Cardinal's books, thinking how unhappy Bethia would be if she saw them consigned to the flames. He, himself, would prefer not to burn books but most of the furniture has already gone; they even chopped up Beaton's great bed the other day.

Leslie continues. 'Henry's subjects, taxed beyond measure to fund his wars, are now in desperate straits with no siller and the price of all goods constantly rising. Not that the King of England cares overmuch about the state of his people, it's more that they cannot sustain the high taxes for him to continue fighting, and there's inevitably discontent – that always makes a king nervous. France equally desires an end to constant conflict, whilst still insisting Boulogne is returned, and indeed there was always a possibility that France would sell Scotland out for Boulogne. You're with me so far?'

Will nods.

'It is our misfortune that we took this castle in May, and in June a treaty was brokered between England, France, and others, signalling an end to their current wars. The treaty would've affected us little had it not included a clause saying, *"the serene King of England shall not move any war, without new occasion, against the Scots"*, which I am supposing was the French king's nod to France's ancient alliance with Scotland. And we are not without our uses to him; there's no war so cheap for France as when their Scots allies are involved.'

Will sits up; this treaty is new information.

'Unfortunately, our taking of the castle is not considered new occasion enough; if he wants the treaty to hold, Henry cannot act directly to relieve us. He has created a diversion by drawing Arran's attention away, to the Borders, with the siege at Langholm. Nevertheless, having feted the French in London last August, when the treaty was signed, he's now reluctant to stir things up, especially with our Dowager Queen looking for any excuse to get aid from her French relations to end the siege. So you can see our chances of rescue were never great, although we did not know it. Perhaps, if we had known, we wouldn't have taken the castle.'

Leslie stands up. 'I must go down, but one final thought, young Seton. It would be treason for me to say it, were I in England, but Henry Tudor is dying, Indeed, when I was briefly in his presence, the stench of rotting flesh was,' he swallows, 'unavoidable. As the inevitable draws closer the king is much preoccupied with the next world and matters of the faith, and, no doubt, anxious to be secure that he may easily enter the gates of heaven. There are some fundamental differences in belief between England and us, and it is my opinion that these differences

186

have also held his hand where relieving us is concerned.'

Will purses his lips and nods. 'Transubstantiation: we, unlike England, rightly do *not* believe that the substance of the bread and wine blessed during the Eucharist become the blood and body of Christ's real presence, for it is all a Popish invention.'

'Aye, I see you are well versed in the doctrine. You are a bright lad and I thank you for your loyal support.'

Will blushes and shifts on his stool. It is the first kind words anyone has said to him in a long time, and, in this moment, he understands why men follow Leslie.

'I hope this gives sufficient explanation. And I most fervently hope that we may negotiate our departure with honour from here, I do very much hope.'

He sits pondering as Leslie leaves. He's never heard Leslie so considered, usually it is Kirkcaldy, and even Melville, who provide the calm and rational. He rubs his face and rises. He may as well go and join the celebrations, while they last, but he stands taller, holding Leslie's few words of praise close, like a warm blanket.

It is February now and yet the darkness barely seems to lift, and then hard frosts begin, which at least give bright days and a fresh vigour in spite of the biting chill. One morning Will watches from his post on the battlements as a ship appears, in an unusually calm sea, sailing wide of the peninsula at the Boar Hills. It seems to be aiming for the castle, not the nearby harbour. He calls down to the courtyard and others come running to look.

'Provisions from Henry,' says Morrison, and soon it is being passed from man to man that there are fresh supplies.

'And look how low it sits in the water,' says Nydie.

'Perhaps they bring us ammunition,' says Morrison. 'Or maybe men – a relief force finally come.'

They watch, all eagerness, as the ship tacks in the

light winds. It is headed for the castle, they are certain. It tacks again, the turn taking many minutes. Surely the helmsman is adjusting course to come to them…, but he is not. There is a collective sigh of disappointment as the sails are lowered and the ship is guided into harbour.

They watch it unloading, and Will puzzles as to what the cargo is. They were right, it is indeed something heavy, with men bent double under the weight. Norman Leslie, come to see, is standing companionably beside Will. Peter Carmichael appears on his other side and Will has to force himself to hold steady.

"Tis lead, to make cannon balls,' Norman says. 'They must be desperate for there is a tale in St Andrews that the Queen's men stripped it from the roof of the Great Hall at Holyrood, or so my informant tells me.' He grins at Will as he speaks, inviting him to join in his pleasure at the Great Hall with its rafters and battens exposed to the sky.

Will manages only a grimace in return, for he's thinking about how many cannon balls all this lead can be turned into. Leslie pushes himself up and departs, leaving Will wondering who the informant is.

'Your pretty sister has been helpful,' smirks Carmichael. 'Very helpful indeed…'

Will doesn't know he's going to do it until it happens – he swings his arm and hits Carmichael. Taken by surprise, Carmichael neither takes evasive action nor defends himself. Will is able to land the punch full on his face, feeling cheek bone crunch beneath his fist.

Carmichael staggers, shaking his head.

Will stands fists clenched, transferring his weight from one foot to the other, as he waits. His knuckles are stinging and he clenches his fists more tightly. Carmichael, face flushed, charges at him like an angry goat. Will steps to one side, sticking his foot out as Carmichael passes. Carmichael trips, and, arms flailing, runs into the parapet.

Will sees, from the corner of his eye, the circle of faces watching, men nudging one another and grinning. He blocks them out and concentrates. Carmichael has his fists up as he moves closer. Will holds his ground. He sees Carmichael swing for his belly and, at the last moment, steps back. The punch lands but not as forcefully as it might, and Carmichael is stumbling, off balance again.

Christ's blood it hurts, but Will shuts out the pain. Carmichael turns to come at him but before he can land a punch, Will hits him again in the face. Carmichael's head snaps and bangs off the wall to his right. Later Will's half sorry that he didn't angle the punch to knock Carmichael over the parapet and down to the sea below. Although a mortal sin, it would probably have been worth it to rid himself of that sneering face forever.

Carmichael staggers away from the wall, eyes unfocused, the blood pouring from his nose spattering his clothes, and the stones, a bright crimson. Morrison catches Carmichael, pressing his head back to stem the bleeding. Will stands watching until Morrison gestures him away.

He leaves the roof top, rubbing his knuckles, conscious of sore ribs – he'll no doubt be all bruises around his belly tomorrow. He doesn't believe Bethia is their spy. He knows she gave Richard Lee information about the position of the siege tunnel, but that was only the once, and Leslie will have plenty of sources of information. He's sure Carmichael was only saying it to rile him, as usual.

As he descends he can hear Carmichael shouting after him. 'I'll make you sorry you were ever born, you lickspittle, you, you…fopdoodle!'

Will sniffs and then smiles, stroking his bruised knuckles. He's not a fool, knows if he hadn't caught Carmichael off-guard things may have gone differently. Carmichael will no doubt exact his revenge later. And yet it cannot take away from the most satisfying moment of Will's life so far – the sight of Carmichael, head hanging and blood dripping, like a stuck pig.

Chapter Thirty-Six

Absolution

It is more than a year since George Wishart met his cruel end, and now another end has come. Henry Tudor is dead, although the news wasn't unexpected. Word is that he's been dead since the end of January and they crowned the young King Edward quick, and now Edward's Uncle Seymour is Regent. Leslie says it makes little difference, for England supports them still, and will continue to render assistance. Indeed they have recently borne witness to a pledge of loyalty to King Edward made by Lord Gray, Sherriff of Angus, a doughty reformer who's visited while the truce holds. Will, although he's always hoped for rescue by England, is uncomfortable at the prospect of ever declaring allegiance to that country, even for a generous pension, – he is a Scotsman, after all – and he left the great hall before the Sherriff had finished speaking his oath.

March blows itself out and tips into April. Henry Balnaves returns, much to Will's surprise, for he expected him to stay safe in England while he could, but at least the bailey is clean once more. Will grows more gaunt and miserable as day follows day. And now the Scottish fleet are back in the bay, blockading the castle so they can neither be easily rescued, nor supplies easily brought from south of the border. The last victualling ships

England sent were captured, so all depends on what they can take from the depleted town and countryside. What is more, there's word that the French King Francis has now died, and his son Henri is already speaking to the Scots ambassador about how they may help to expel the Castilians.

'You were aye a dour bugger,' Nydie says, as Will slouches in his corner.

He stares up at James standing in front of him, legs wide apart, as though he is some great lord instead of the son of a local laird who happens to be knighted; as though he is somehow much older, better, stronger than Will. He jumps to his feet and shoves Nydie, hard. How dare he speak thus, as though Will hadn't seen him puking after Beaton's murder, as though Will hadn't wiped his arse when he was too sick to move.

'That's better,' says Nydie regaining his balance. 'Come.' He slings his arm around Will's shoulder and leans into him.

He nudges Nydie away, but James doesn't seem to notice, and after a moment he relaxes into James's easy comfort.

'John Knox is here.'

'Here? They've allowed him entry?'

'While the truce still holds, and he claims to be our confessor, he's permitted to come and go. He's brought three young pupils with him, saying he's safer inside St Andrews Castle than on the outside.'

Will's face lights up. Knox is a great orator and a sound defender of both Luther and Wishart, as well as being a much better preacher than John Rough. He walks eagerly along the portico and up to the great hall.

Knox discourses and Will listens.

'Resistance to tyranny is obedience to God,' he begins.

He can feel the spectre of the Cardinal retreating and the rightness of their actions advancing. It is Arran and all his men who are damned, not the Castilians.

'We are the sword bearers in this violent struggle against good and evil as the apocalypse draws near. Where there is sin we must root it out, for to see sin and do nothing is the worst sin of all. It is our task, set by God, to convince men of the error of their ways.'

But before he can get fully fired up, Morrison comes seeking Norman Leslie, Kirkcaldy or Balnaves, and Knox is interrupted. 'There is a procession come to the gate,' Morrison calls several times, voice growing louder to be heard over Knox's oratory.

What now, thinks Will, slumping against the wall.

They hurry down to the courtyard to hear the news. A document has been handed over and Kirkcaldy of Grange unrolls and studies it.

The Pope has granted the Castilians absolution. Will's heart sings. All will be well.

Kirkcaldy reads aloud the absolution. The pardon contains the phrase, *remittimus crimen irremissible*. Will scrabbles around inside his woolly head for the translation but there's no need, it's already being muttered among them. The Pope has said he "pardons that which is unpardonable". How can that be? Nevertheless it is still a pardon – the Great Curse has been lifted. He feels a smile spread over his face; it is wiped away as quick as it came.

Knox is roaring in outrage. 'To avenge the death of the martyr George Wishart was no sin, and to say our righteous actions are unpardonable is of itself unpardonable. We will *not* accept an absolution such as this.'

Will looks around, some of the garrison are nodding agreement, others are looking to one another.

'The Pope is the whore of Babylon and his church the synagogue of Satan,' bellows Knox. 'We want no absolution from the Antichrist.'

Kirkcaldy and Norman Leslie are conferring. Will watches them, holding his breath. They nod in agreement and Will staggers, losing all strength – as if the marrow is being sucked from his bones.

Knox demands a torch lit and, taking the pardon from Kirkcaldy's hand, holds it to the flame. Will watches the parchment flare, curl and burn. The charred remains flutter across the courtyard, while the Castilians howl their derision. The siege will continue.

Part Four

Bethia

March 1546 to July 1547

Chapter Thirty-Seven

The Roarin' Game

It is bitter cold, the streets rough with rutted mud and icy puddles. The few soldiers which were left in St Andrews have withdrawn, Bethia knows not where, probably to find warmth if they can – and escape the pestilence which has run rife among them since December.

Now there is the truce, and Arran's soldiers are mostly gone, the Castilians have again been wandering freely to steal, destroy and ravage. The townsfolk and those in the wider countryside are angry that they've been left with little protection. Even the Provost, Sir James Learmonth, ever the Castilians' champion, albeit on the sly, said it is enough after he came under attack on his way home to his castle at Osnaburgh.

When Father meets Walter Wardlaw in the street, they, for once, are united in their frustration. Father splutters out his anger. 'Their arrogance knows no bounds, and where is Arran? He took Dumbarton Castle quickly enough and 'tis said it has stronger fortifications than St Andrews?

'This is all very true. It seems that the siege will be allowed to run until the garrison have emptied the town of food and animals, and ravished all our womenfolk.' Wardlaw's eyes slide towards Bethia as he speaks and she shuffles her feet, staring at the ground. 'Can your new friend not give any intelligence?'

'What new friend?'

'Arran's aide,' Wardlaw inclines his head towards Bethia. 'You know who I mean, the younger son from Clatto.'

'Clearly, as Arran's aide, Gilbert Logie is with Arran at Linlithgow,' says Father.

Bethia thinks of Gilbert. She misses his calm counsel, as she suspects Father does too. The last time they saw him he said Arran hoped to get the Castilians out by negotiation, after this truce was brokered – although Gilbert also admitted the truce was influenced by Henry of England, before his death, even showing them a copy of the letter King Henry had sent to Arran and his Council:

If you can be content to withdraw the siege which you have laid at the castle of St Andrews, for our sake and until the matter of displeasure against them were further debated, we would take it for a token of love and kindness towards us and think you esteemed our friendship...otherwise we shall be forced to relieve them.

'The Tudor King hid his threats under honeyed words,' Father had said, and Gilbert nodded in agreement.

She shifts from foot to foot, wishing the conversation over and Father picks up on it. 'We must away home, Wardlaw. It is too cold to stand and blether.'

'Aye, it is bitter, even for March. I will visit soon, with my brother.' He nods towards Bethia. 'For it is high time we got this marriage agreed and hand-fasted.'

Father stares at Wardlaw, who licks his lips.

'There will be more than a hand-fasting – I would not leave my daughter so unprotected. It will be a properly notarised marriage settlement, and a blessing by a priest, or nothing.'

Wardlaw hesitates, staring at Father from under lowered brows. 'Aye well, she'd better do her duty and deliver sons.'

Father takes Bethia's arm. She's shivering as they

walk home, and it's not only with cold. While the truce holds, Father agreed to a delay and Norman was sympathetic, saying that she should not be rushed and promising that he would take good care of her – but the marriage has not gone away.

She feels weary to her bones. There's still no word from Mainard, although at this time of year none would be expected with most ships staying safe in harbour. She should have long given up on him, as it's clear he's done with her. She sighs and decides to block it all from her mind. Who knows what may come to pass in the next month or two; surely she can hold Norman off for that long.

Later she's bent over her sewing, conscious of Mother nodding her approval, when Father comes in. 'The water at the mill lade is frozen and the ice thick enough for the curling.'

Mother draws her shawl tight and leans closer to the fire. 'It is fine for the Dutchiemen to be roaring upon their canals, but surely the men of Scotland have more sense than to be sliding stones around, especially with the town in such turmoil.'

'I'm in need of some relief from turmoil. And likely no one, not even the barbarous beasts of the castle, will be wandering the streets on such a day. Bethia, you will come with me, and you too, John.'

Bethia shakes her head and even John's freckled nose is wrinkling at the prospect, but Father insists.

Once by the pond she expects to be dull as well as frozen. The players take up their positions, faces tense with concentration. The game progresses quickly as there's an icy mist rising, a forewarning of colder weather still. She stands beneath the trees, which give an illusion of shelter, listening to the soothing sound of stone sliding across ice. She wonders why it's called a roarin' game when it's more like a whooshin' one.

She stamps her feet, grateful that she has thick leather

boots, unlike the poor weans they passed on the way here with their bare feet and legs mottled purple, and then catches sight of a figure wandering amongst the trees to her right. Elspeth! May the Holy Mother watch over her. What is she doing here?

Elspeth has spotted her and signals urgently. She looks to Father, but he's crouched on the ice absorbed in studying his next move. She hastens over and gives her a hug but Elspeth flinches at the touch.

'You were beaten?'

She nods.

'Your father?'

She shrugs. 'He thought it was his duty, although he did it most unwillingly.'

'But your face …'

'That was my fault. I moved when I should have remained still.'

Bethia strokes Elspeth's arm. 'When did you return? Did your father find you – he came to our house so angry he was fit to burst.'

The tears leak from Elspeth's eyes but she doesn't brush them away.

'I only wanted to paint… and to be with Antonio.'

'Where is he now?'

'I left him,' says Elspeth, and the desolation in her voice makes Bethia's heart ache.

'Why? Would he not marry you?'

'He already has a wife.'

Bethia wishes Antonio was before her so she might take her staff and beat his face to a bloody pulp – and at least save some other innocent lass from his pretty ways. 'Did you know?'

Elspeth stiffens. 'No, of course not. I would never have gone with him if I had known; I am not a harlot.'

'He should never have presumed upon you.'

Elspeth's eyes are brimming like an overfull glass.

Over her shoulder, Bethia sees Father is watching

them. He tips his head to her, and bends once more to slide his curling stone. She sees Elspeth's father is here too, standing to the right of Father and so well wrapped up she hadn't recognised him.

Elspeth brushes the tears away. 'The wife came seeking him. I did not know who she was… at first. I saw them meeting, from my window. She was pleading with Antonio, a child holding onto her skirts. He passed her some coins and returned to our room: to me.' She gulps and a sob escapes her. 'Antonio claimed she was his sister. I wanted to believe him, but the doubts gnawed at me like a flesh-eating sore.' She spreads her ungloved hands wide, fingers stiff and white with cold. 'If she was his sister why would he send her and the child away when they were in need? Why would he not bring them to us?'

Bethia nods.

'He said it was because we were not married; he could not expose the child to a state of sin. I wanted to believe him, I so wanted to believe him.'

'But you could not, because he had told you there was no impediment to the marriage – and yet he had not wed you.'

It is Elspeth's turn to nod. 'The next day I followed him, although the streets of Antwerp are so overfull of people it was not easy. She was waiting for him by a hostelry near the docks. I saw him pick up the child and toss her in the air, and she called him Papa.' Elspeth hangs her head. 'I am ashamed to tell you that, if it had not been for the child, I may have stayed with him, wife or no.'

Bethia lays her fingertips on Elspeth's. 'It is as well you did not, for if he could leave one wife and child, he would as easily leave another.'

Elspeth picks at her shawl then looks Bethia full in the face. 'I think he truly loved me. He begged me to stay; would not let me from his sight.'

Bethia wants to shake her – but what would be the use. 'How did you escape him?'

'Everyone has to sleep, and I stole the key and crept out then. I went to the docks and Mainard's father was there and he helped me, once I explained who I was.'

Bethia jerks as though a cart wheel has run over her. 'Did you see…'

Elspeth shakes her head. 'Antwerp is a place of such size you cannot imagine. It was only by chance I saw Master de Lange, and I left the next day. The crossing was very bad, indeed I thought, and hoped, it would be my end.'

Bethia bites at her lip. 'What will happen to you now?'

'My parents say I am for a nunnery,' Elspeth says through chattering teeth. 'There are worse things, I suppose. I would still rather the nunnery than marriage to Fat Norman, although,' she nudges Bethia, 'I hear he has found himself a new bride.'

'Do not speak of it.' She grinds her teeth; there was perhaps another chance here when Mainard might have contacted her – and again he did not. She is as weak as Elspeth with her false hopes. She vows from this moment she will give him up.

'I am sorry, my friend. Neither of us have the future we hoped for, although,' Elspeth smiles for the first time, 'they may let me paint and perhaps make designs for altar clothes in the convent, for my style is much improved under Antonio's tutelage.'

'How can you bear to speak his name after what he's done?'

'I would rather have had a few months of happiness with Antonio than years of misery with Norman Wardlaw. You too must make your choice, Bethia.'

'There is no choice; I have no man to run away with – and it is not a wise path, as you have shown. I must do as my father bids, for the sake of our family.'

Elspeth grips her arm in sympathy.

The game is finishing and John returns blue-tinged and chittering from where he's been smashing ice by the burn, and sets off at a run for home.

'You will come and see me, Bethia, before I go? You will not desert me?'

Father is walking towards them, with Master Niven following behind.

'Of course I'll come and see you,' she says, although she doubts it'll be easy, for Elspeth is tainted goods now.

Father nods to Elspeth and holds out his arm for Bethia to take.

'You knew Elspeth would be here,' she says as they walk, the frozen grass crackling beneath their feet.

'Aye, I agreed with Niven you might meet one last time.' He stops walking and turns to face her. 'Elspeth was allowed too much liberty and lost her way. Think on her fate and obey me, my lass, for I know what is best for you.'

Bethia looks down.

'Are you listening?'

She nods slowly.

'Come it is too cold to stand.' He tucks her arm in his once more and they walk in silence. As they draw close to home he says, 'You will not meet with Elspeth Niven again.' He squeezes her upper arm, pinching the soft flesh. 'Give me your word.'

'But Father...'

'Your word.'

'I promise,' she says, tucking her other hand behind her back, crossing her fingers and sending up a prayer to the blessed Virgin.

But some weeks later, when she finally escapes Father's watchful eye, and creeps out to Elspeth's home, Elspeth is already gone.

Chapter Thirty-Eight

John Knox

Bethia and her family are at Holy Trinity to hear the preacher, John Knox. Father says he doesn't know what the guilds were thinking to invite this reformer to speak in their kirk, but she's curious to see this man of whom she's heard more and more talk, especially of how like he is to George Wishart. She hopes he's more inspiring than their usual priest, also come from the castle, John Rough. She studies Knox, head tilted, as she sits in their pew. He may be like Wishart in faith but he's not a bonny man to look upon with stocky build, long nose and protruding lower lip.

Knox says he's been prevailed upon to preach and, although 'tis said he cried noisily and then spent several days in the sanctuary of his room to consider his calling, he clearly embraces his role as a religious leader. He lacks Wishart's humility, and the dull Rough's honesty, and she doubts him.

He stands in the pulpit raised above the crowd so all can see, and talks and talks and talks. She has never known a man who has so much to say and with such belief in the rightness of his words. He lifts his arms often, waving them expansively, the dark patches of sweat beneath his oxters spreading across his voluminous robes, his long beard waggling when he turns his head. The occasional shafts of sunlight piercing the windows, illuminate the spray of spittle flying from his mouth as his voice thunders, ever louder, reaching to the rafters above. She can see this priest truly believes he is a channel through which the voice of God may be heard on Earth. And yet he claims again and again that no mortal man can be head of the Church.

'The Pope,' he shouts, leaning over the pulpit, 'is an Antichrist, hear me all, an Antichrist and can never be a member of Christ's mythical body.'

She's not sure what he means; what she does know is that she's listening to heresy. She wonders that the Lord does not strike Knox down, but if he keeps preaching sedition the Queen's troops most certainly will – and it won't be a quick strike, it'll be another slow burning.

She herself doesn't know what to think. This exhortation is not what's supposed to happen in her church. True, on feast days, she has heard a sermon, but it's usually a story from the bible to illuminate her life and not such unforgiving doctrine. Where is the Mass, the slow meditative rhythm of the Latin, the comfort of a familiar, and much shorter, service? She jumps; it's as though Knox has seen inside her head. He begins to instruct on a new order in which Mass no longer has a place.

'Mass is an abominable idolatry, blasphemous to the death of Christ and a profanation of the Lord's supper.' Knox hammers a beat with his fist upon the pulpit as he declaims his next lines. 'The sacraments of the New Testament must be ministered as they were instituted by Christ Jesus and practised by the apostles; nothing ought to be added unto them and nothing ought to be diminished from them.'

A shudder of shock runs through the congregation. People shift and look to one another. Some push forward so they can see and hear more clearly, others ease their way to the back, ready to escape if need be. But no one leaves. There is something about the power of Knox's belief which holds them all here, whether they agree or not.

'Stand ye still and listen to the word that comes from the mouth of God, lest ye submit to Satan in error. It is not enough that man invents a ceremony and then gives it significance according to his pleasure, as the Papists do. We must follow the scripture and keep the religion that is received from God without alteration. Romans 10 verse 7, "faith comes by hearing, and hearing by the word of God," and lest we forget, "whatsoever is not of faith is of sin," Romans 14, verse 23.'

She looks to Mother sitting next to her, Father beyond Mother and John tucked between them: John is asleep head rolled back and mouth open; Mother is holding a pomander to her nose, and she does not blame her, for the smell arising from the crush of the standing mass pressed close is suffocating. Father however is looking quietly thoughtful. She has seen that look often, it usually means he's considering an opportunity but she cannot imagine how he plans to turn the preachings of Knox to his advantage.

She is also puzzled as to why Knox is permitted to speak. Since the truce it's as though Arran has washed his hands of the siege and allows the protestors their place: perhaps he's not unsympathetic to the cause; or perhaps he's rewarding them for ridding him of his rival the Cardinal; or perhaps he simply does not want to do anything more to antagonise the men who hold his son hostage. And Gilbert Logie is faraway, with Arran, so can provide no insight.

Knox is leaning over the pulpit now, his spittle raining freely down upon the faithful. 'The great Martin Luther, who was so recently gathered unto the bosom of Christ, taught that there is no Purgatory in which the souls of men can be purged after death. Ye either live a life of true faith and enter the Kingdom of Heaven, as

Luther did, or ye suffer damnation, burning in the fires of hell for all eternity. To pray for the dead, and especially to pay indulgences for prayers to be said in their memory, is a vain abomination. Heaven opens only for the faithful.'

She is stunned by his passion. His voice never drops below a shout and he speaks for over four hours, even calling into question the right of the Queen to rule. 'Where a woman reigns and papists bear authority we have a council headed by Satan,' he bellows. The longer he speaks, the hoarser his voice becomes and now there's a plug of mucus, stretching between his lips. She waits for it to break, but it never does. On and on he goes until she leans forward, resting her face in her hands, made dizzy to the point of collapse by his vehemence.

When the congregation finally emerges, blinking in the sunlight, they are unwilling to disperse but stand talking to their neighbours, quietly in the beginning, then louder and louder as people argue the points Knox has made. He follows them out, looking pleased that his discourse has resulted in such debate.

Hugh of Nydie is there with his wife Lady Merione. 'These are solemn and true words spoken by John Knox,' he says, his voice booming out over the crowd.

She can see Father is surprised by the passion in Nydie's voice, indeed does not know how to respond. No wonder young Nydie stormed the castle with Norman Leslie, if his father holds such views. Bethia only wants a quiet life, and wonders why men must make such a to-do about doctrine. She thinks of how careful they all need be to not offend some person of power, or break any laws, spiritual or temporal, without the increased danger to their lives that this new thinking brings.

'Knox is permitted free access. He comes and goes between town and castle as he pleases, and takes our sons the true word,' Nydie says.

'*My* son is in Edinburgh, with his aunt,' says Father.

'Aye, may be wise to stick to that story.'

Bethia feels sick, wishes Hugh of Nydie at the bottom of the mill lade, or anywhere other than here. Now Father will be insisting that her marriage go quickly ahead.

'It was so hot, and so pungent in there, I thought I would faint,' says Mother loudly to Lady Merione. 'Come, you will break fast with us, if you may.'

Father glares at Mother, clearly not wanting his meal disturbed by Nydie's dissecting of Knox's words. Lady Merione, however, takes little persuading to eat before starting the ride back to Nydie lands. Soon they are gathered at the board with Agnes huffing and puffing at having to stretch the meal to feed more people, and the quality forby, Grissel getting into a guddle offering water and towels to the guests to wash their hands, and Mother determined neither Agnes nor Grissel will sit down with them to share the meal.

Bethia sits quietly while those around her chew, poking her knife at the stringy old goat meat Agnes has acquired, despite the shortage of food at this time of year, made worse by the depredations of the Castilians. She wonders if she could flee to Antwerp as Elspeth did. Now summer will soon be upon them there are more ships in the harbour – perhaps she can find one that will take her. She knows it's nonsense to even consider such an escape. She cannot travel unattended and without funds, and her duty is to help her family in whatever way Father commands. Anyway, she is certain now that Mainard is not interested. The hurt is still there, but not so sharp. She sighs again and then realises everyone at the board is staring at her.

'Well, my child, what say you?' says Lady Merione.

'I do not know,' she says, bowing her head and mumbling, for indeed she does not know, either what she can do to save herself, or of what Lady Merione has been speaking.

There's a crash as John upsets his trencher spilling the watered-down ale he drinks. The beaker rolls across the uneven floorboards and comes to rest against the door. He winks at her as Father's hand reaches over to cuff him.

'Leave us,' Father says. Normally he would roar, but he's mindful of Hugh of Nydie's eyes upon him.

John needs no further invitation and goes, and Bethia, after a nod from Father, follows. As she closes the door she hears the Earl of Nydie inquire if she's to be wed soon. She lingers to hear Father's answer. It had been agreed with the Wardlaws that all will be done quietly, but, no doubt, Mother has shared the information with Lady Merione.

Before Father can speak, Nydie does.

'She may do for my son.'

Her heart lifts. Is he suggesting what she hopes?

There's a pause.

'Young James?' Father sounds surprised but there's a trill of delight from Mother.

The door latch lifts and she scurries away. She has met James of Nydie a few times, most recently in the castle. He seems courteous and is certainly better to look upon than Fat Norman – and yet, there's something missing. There is no tug to her heart, not in the way she had with Mainard and sometimes recently with Gilbert Logie, when she's near him. Nevertheless she would far rather marry James than Norman, and surely he is the better match. Mother will certainly agree, but she's less certain of Father. He'll suspect Hugh of Nydie's motives, for she is a step down for his family. She will have a generous dowry though, Mother will make sure of it.

She sighs, all she can do is wait while others decide her fate.

Chapter Thirty-Nine

Nydie

Bethia stands by the West Port watching Father. He's riding towards the ridge above the Kinness Burn, which is the road to Cupar, where he often has trade. But it is also the road to Hugh of Nydie's lands, where she suspects, and hopes, he is going. There has been much discussion between her parents about whether she should marry Norman Wardlaw or James of Nydie.

'James is by far the better match,' says Mother, 'and one day will be an earl too, as was my father. It is most suitable.'

Father sighs long and loud. 'And being the wife of an earl is of small account if he has no Earldom.'

Mother tosses her head, 'Hugh of Nydie is too well connected to suffer because of his support for the siege.'

'God's blood woman, his connections will not save him from punishment. Most of his closest allies are among the garrison, and will likely forfeit their lands themselves. Anywise he has not yet formally offered his son for Bethia, whereas Norman Wardlaw has offered – and, more to the point, been accepted. We should not even be discussing James, for I have shaken Norman's hand and given my word.'

Mother grows pale. 'At least speak to Nydie so we may know his intentions.'

Bethia clasps her hands together and mutters a prayer. A tear runs down her cheek. It is June, and the fierce weather long past, yet there has still been no word from Mainard. He could at least have sent her one message, even if it was to tell her he would not be returning, but then few ships have come this year, and even fewer pilgrims. The tale of the holy city of St Andrews at war with itself will no doubt have been carried over the sea, spread through France and across the Holy Roman Empire.

She stands at the gate watching Father's retreating back. She watches for a long time as he grows smaller and smaller. She becomes aware that the workers on the nearby rigg are lifting their heads to stare at her, and she's being buzzed by flies from the dung they're spreading.

Retreating back through the port, the acrid smell of burning catches in the back of her throat, as she walks up Southgait. The Dominican Friary still has wisps of smoke drifting skywards from the fire which partially destroyed it a few days ago. The talk in the streets is that Norman Leslie and his Castilians torched it. She stands gazing at it; half the roof and one wall has collapsed, leaving the solid stone arches exposed.

A soft hand touches her arm. 'You s-s-should not be w-w-wandering the s-s-streets alone.'

She turns to look up into Norman's puffy face, the spider web of red lines across his nose and cheeks vivid in the daylight.

'The destruction is sad to see.' She waves her hand at the ruin of Blackfriars.

'And in our ane street,' he says, devoid of stutter, his voice harsh in a way she has never heard before. 'We are nowhere near the Bishop's Palace and yet they're arrogant enough to attack here.'

She looks at him with respect, can almost see the man that Father has described as a fierce trader. He takes her hand, tucking it under his arm, and she allows it as they

211

stroll towards her home. It's easier, she thinks, to be with Norman when she is by his side and doesn't have to look at him, although the wheezing each time he takes a step is hard to ignore.

She hears the drone of bagpipes and looks for its source. A piper is leading a wedding procession: the bride head bent, the groom red-faced, the parents smiling, the priest carrying the vial of holy water to bless the bed, the watching crowd shouting out, smirking, nudging one another.

Bethia tugs her hand out, mumbling, 'I will go home now, you need not escort me further.' She doesn't look at Norman. She scurries away, pushing through the watching crowd, past Agnes and Grissel who are calling out as loud as anyone, and into her home. She slams the door shut behind her and leans against it, praying to the Virgin that Father and Hugh of Nydie have come to an agreement.

Father soon returns, saying he hasn't got time to discuss where he's been when she asks. He sends her into the strong-room, which adjoins his workroom, to fetch some papers, while he reads a letter just come. She turns as she opens the strong-room door, and sees him crumple a paper and toss it into the fire burning in the grate.

She is kneeling in front of the iron bound kist when she hears Mother.

'When did you return, Thomas?' There's a crash, as the door Mother must have flung wide, bangs off the wall. 'Why did you not seek me out? I have been most anxious.'

'Whoah, whoah. Hud your horses. Sit down and I will tell you all.'

Father knows she's in here and she waits for him to call her out, to send her from the room – but he does not.

'Nydie and I had a full and frank discussion. He does not think the siege will continue much longer.'

Mother huffs. 'They've been saying that from the beginning and now we're more than twelve months in.'

212

Bethia hears a chair creak. 'Nevertheless the new King of France takes a different view from his father, and is close to our Queen Mother and her family. Both Nydie and I think King Henri will honour the auld alliance between our two countries, which his father all but broke, and send help soon.'

'And surely England might equally send help.'

'They might, but they have had ample occasion to relieve the garrison and have so far failed. In any case, although it matters to those *Castilians* by which means they are got out, it matters little to us – provided the town is left unharmed.'

'Apart from that our son is among them.'

The chair creaks again, as though it is about to split. 'As he's made his bed, so let him lay on it.'

'He is our son,' wails Mother.

'Aye, and because of his rash actions we are likely to find ourselves homeless beggars.'

Mother huffs. 'But what of Nydie?'

'Hugh of Nydie is a man, I have learned, who is impetuous in speech yet slow to act. The suggestion that his son and our daughter might wed was spoken aloud the moment it occurred to him. He barely remembers saying it, and was most surprised to be forced into a discussion of its merits.'

Bethia slumps against the chest and bites on her hand.

'But why were you so long, what were you discussing if not this marriage?'

'Take care how you speak to me, Mary. I am your husband and need not account to you for my actions or time. I have explained, but still you do not seem to grasp the gravity of our situation. Remember when your family was expelled from England, how King Henry took all your land and possessions?'

'I am hardly likely to forget.'

'This is what may well happen when it is discovered that our son is among the renegades in the castle.'

Mother gasps.

'And the same is true for Hugh of Nydie. It would be of no help to our family for Bethia to marry into theirs. Norman Wardlaw is a far better option, and he is aware of our precarious situation; we are already discussing how we may together lessen the severity of any retribution.'

'You have told the Wardlaws where Will is!'

'Only Norman, Walter is a different matter.'

'Well, I hope Norman's discretion can be relied upon, for his brother has a most sinister demeanour. Have you agreed a date?'

'I will speak with Norman.'

'And I will look to her wedding clothes.' Mother sighs. 'We must have a wedding breakfast, I assume?'

'Of course.'

'And with *such* a family.'

Bethia covers her head with her apron and rocks back and forward. There is to be no escape.

Chapter Forty

Bethia's New Home

Fat Norman has bought a new home for them, not any house but a tower house resting on the hills outside St Andrews. Bethia feels strange at the prospect of living away from the hustle and bustle of the streets. It is too quiet up here, although the air smells sweet and there is a view of the bay, and her town.

She stands at an upstairs window gazing at a rare clump of tall old trees nearby swaying in the wind, which must somehow have escaped the depredations of building the Great Michael. She can see a group of saplings have been planted close by, probably by the burgh council. Perhaps they are the new siccamour Father had brought from France, saying if he supplied the trees rather than paying the tax then he knew his bawbees would go where they were supposed to, and not end up swelling Provost Learmonth's pocket. She becomes aware someone is shuffling behind her – Norman is waiting, and sighing, she turns to join him.

He waddles breathlessly following her around as she examines her soon-to-be-home. 'You must order all as you p-p-please,' he says. He's still stuttering when he speaks to her, but much less than before. 'We will have this room re-panelled, I think, for it is broken here.' He tugs on the wainscotting and it comes away in his hand.

'P-p-perhaps you might want a p-painted ceiling, such as your mother had done?'

Mother, following them into the room, humphs.

'Oh, n-n-nooo, I did not mean we might have anything as f-f-fine as your...'

Bethia places her hand on his arm. 'I do not care for painted ceilings.'

Norman flushes with pleasure, and Mother with annoyance. Bethia realises she's enjoying herself. Perhaps she *should* get the painter here and he can charm her with his honeyed, and false, words. She looks at Norman, so anxious to please her – at least he's likely to be a devoted husband.

She stops to run her fingers along the arm of the fine new chair he has bought, presumably for her use since he would not fit in it, and Norman bumps into her.

'Take care,' she snaps.

'S-s-sorry,' he mumbles, stepping back. He still smells of onions but, as his wife, she will insist he washes and changes his raiment regularly. And she'll tell Grissel not to cook onions.

Norman leads her to the kitchens where a grinning Grissel is investigating the chill room and rattling the new milk pans laid out along a cunningly made shelf. Grissel is to join Bethia in her new home and she does not know who is more pleased – Grissel to escape the constant criticisms of Agnes, or Mother to be finally rid of Grissel. The only one, it seems, who is not happy in all of this is her, but perhaps she can find some joy in the house and the freedom that being a wife will give her. She stares at Fat Norman, his belly swelling over the top of his breeches as though he's nine months gone with child, and sighs again. He comes to stand next to her, looking anxiously from under straggly eyebrows, his face as pink as a pig's bottom.

'Are you h-h-happy with the house? Is there aught you would like d-d-different?'

It would be like kicking a child to say an unkind word to him.

'It is a fine house, Norman,' she says, and he smiles wide enough to stretch the skin of his cheeks tight.

'And you think you will b-b-be happy here?'

She looks up into his bloodshot eyes fringed by peculiarly pale lashes. 'I will try.'

She leads the way outside to the kailyard, which is far larger than the yard behind her home in Southgait. Grissel bounces around it, exclaiming with delight at her new domain. Bethia looks at Mother's face, lips puckered as though she's just drunk sour milk, and feels a jab of satisfaction, for it is Mother who has been rushing the marriage, when Father was still taking it slowly.

She wanders out the gate, leaving Norman to show the others the newfangled hand-pump he has had installed for drawing water. As soon as she emerges from behind the garden wall she's blasted by the wind whipping around the corner. It will be cold up here in winter without the shelter to be found in the streets. There are compensations, for the bay is laid out below her, the sea sparkling bright as the jewels Mary of Guise wore on her wedding day. She shields her eyes and gazes out. Then she's running back into the kailyard shouting at them to come.

There are ships rounding the point and sailing into the bay. They count them and when they reach ten they think that is all, but no, after a gap a further six appear, their sails billowing white in the breeze as they follow one another beating across the bay.

'How beautiful they are,' Bethia says.

'Saints preserve us,' says Mother, grabbing her arm. 'England has sent its fleet to attack us.'

Grissel screams and Agnes, unusually, draws her daughter close.

'They have come to relieve the garrison; they will take the Castilians and leave the townsfolk alone surely,' says

Bethia, but she knows that is unlikely even as the words leave her mouth. Indeed the garrison themselves are likely to pillage before departing.

'I think not,' says Norman gazing at the ships. 'Having come this far Henry's soldiers will loot and burn as he did in Haddington and Edinburgh, Dunbar and St Monans these past two years.'

'And I think that is *not* at all helpful,' says Mother glaring at him.

Norman ignores her, eyes on the ships which are lowering their sails as they draw close to the land and the long oars come into use. 'I am by no means certain this is the English fleet,' he says. He squints against the brightness of the day. 'My eyes are not so good, my dear, what colours are they flying?'

She shields her eyes once more, the sun is high and the light dazzling, 'Red I think, with some white.'

'It *is* the English,' says mother, scowling.

'Not necessarily. England would be white with some red.'

'And I think you will find I *am* correct.' Mother turns on her heel and marches towards the house.

Bethia would laugh, if her teeth weren't chattering.

'Let us watch and wait,' Norman says to her. 'We are safer up here anyway.' He looks to Agnes and Grissel, eyes huge and faces white as they cling to one another. 'Fetch us the settle and some food.' He turns to Bethia. 'We may as well be comfortable as we wait; and I had supplies brought up, as I thought we might have need of sustenance.'

'That is thoughtful,' she says. She realises that Norman is no longer stuttering, is quite the man in charge.

Agnes and Grissel appear around the corner of the house, struggling to carry the heavy oak settle.

'Put it down there,' Norman points.

They sit and watch as the galleys slow and the anchors are tossed into the sea. A boat comes out from the harbour, the men being rowed holding onto their bonnets, as Grissel returns balancing a heavy tray in her arms. Bethia stands up to allow her to place it on the settle.

'As I thought, it is the French fleet,' says Norman. He looks up at Grissel. 'Fetch a stool for the tray, girl.'

'I've only got one pair of hands,' says Grissel, quite recovered now she knows they are no longer in imminent danger.

'I think you must teach your servant better manners,' he says to Bethia as Grissel disappears around the corner. She raises her eyebrows at him, and he flushes and gazes at his hands.

'Grissel is a hard worker and most loyal.'

'I u-u-understand, my dear.' He sits up straight as his rolls of flesh will allow. 'But still, she will not s-s-speak to me as s-s-he does to you.'

Bethia feels a weariness. Norman is perhaps not as malleable as she thought, but he is also correct; Grissel must treat him with deference, as befits a servant to her master.

He rocks from side to side to ease himself as he chomps on a slice of hare pie. She realises his size makes it difficult for him to get comfortable. Even the settle is too small to rest his spreading bulk upon and he's probably only at ease when he's lying down. She clutches at her skirt and shakes her head – she doesn't want to picture Norman in bed – she will not think of it, not until the very last minute when it is inescapably before her.

She wonders where Mother is, probably inside looking out from a window. She cannot but smile to herself – Mother must wait until she, Bethia, is ready to leave, and Norman, of course. They watch the activity as small boats go to and fro between the galleys and the harbour.

'They have brought many soldiers with them,' says Norman rubbing his hands. 'Finally we will see some action.'

Bethia points at the castle and the small dots of men

running around the top. Plumes of smoke spiral high, purple against the blue of the sky, no doubt come from braziers lit ready, and more cannons are being turned from the land side to point at the sea.

'I think there's unlikely to be an attack today, when they are but newly arrived,' says Norman; but he's soon proved wrong.

The anchors of half a dozen ships are heaved up and the oars begin to dip in and out of the water. She can see them working in rhythm and hear the occasional shouted command drifting on the wind, although the rowers wielding the oars are hidden from view. The gusting wind makes it hard for them to hold position as they near the castle, and requires much work for the galley slaves. She pities them, for their task is relentless.

There's a boom, the sound reverberating around them. The swallows nesting in the eaves swirl high above, and the gulls take to the skies screaming. Then a burst of smoke is followed by another boom, the French ships are firing on the castle and the Castilians have replied. Their shot lands harmlessly in the sea, but the ships have been more successful and hit land, although they've missed the castle. Dust rises from a house in Swallowgait and, as it clears, they see the roof has collapsed and Norman points to the yellow-red lick of flame.

Bethia covers her mouth with her hand and there's a gasp from Agnes watching behind. Norman pushes himself up off the bench as Mother comes around the corner.

'We must leave immediately and do what we can to protect our properties from damage,' Norman says, hirpling towards the stable yard.

Mother grabs Bethia, pinching the flesh as Bethia tries to tug her arm away.

'You are not your own mistress, not yet, and I will tolerate no more cheek.'

Bethia squirms but Mother leans in, hissing in her ear,

'and we can delay no longer; the siege is about to be broke and you must marry *now*.'

They both stare at Norman's back, the pap, pap, pap of a slow release fart escaping as he lumbers through the archway into the yard.

The church bells are ringing in the town in between the thunder of cannon fire. One of the galleys skews round and they see there's a hole in its side. Another comes to its rescue, although they only take the free men off and the galley slaves are left to row the stricken ship back to harbour, as best they can.

'Come,' shouts Norman from the cart, and the driver assists them up, leaps on himself and spurs the horses down the hill.

Chapter Forty-One

Strozzi

The firing goes back and forward over the next day few days and more houses are hit, but at least the fires are put out before they get a hold and spread through the town. The French fleet takes more hits than the castle does, and they withdraw, out of firing range. One ship has sunk, another run aground and the ones which are damaged come into the harbour for repair. There are French soldiers and sailors in the street, swelling the number of troops already in the town returned from Langholme. The activity to end the siege grows more intense. Rumours abound of the man in charge sent by the new King of France.

Leon Strozzi is said to be a military genius. He is also a Knight of Malta, Prior of Capua, Captain General of the French galleys and cousin to Henri's Queen, Catherine de Medici. It seems Strozzi knows what he is about and will flush the Castilians out with all possible speed. Arran himself is now regularly seen strutting around the streets deep in discussion with Strozzi.

'Whit are they doing?' asks Grissel, when she and Bethia are at the Mercat to purchase what food they can for her wedding feast, before all is gone to feed the soldiers.

There's lots of activity on the tower of St Salvators,

which rises behind the houses in this street. They hurry down the vennel, into Northgait and straight into Gilbert Logie, who is calling up instructions to the men above.

'Ah, my lady Bethia,' he says bowing, 'ever in the midst of danger. And I hear I must congratulate you.' He looks down at his feet, then lifts his head and stares into her eyes. 'When is the happy event to take place?'

She bites hard on her lip. 'It is to be tomorrow.'

'In the midst of chaos?'

She stares at the ground shuffling her feet.

'The groom is eager to claim you…which is as it should be.'

'Have you met him?' The words burst from her.

He jerks his head back. 'Ah, no. I do not think I've had that pleasure.'

She doesn't want to speak of Fat Norman. 'What is happening here?'

'I'm not sure I should tell you anything, for I understand your brother to be amongst the garrison.' He frowns. 'That is something you, and your Father, hid from me.'

She bows her head both to acknowledge that he was ill-used, and in a final acceptance that her marriage must take place. Gilbert is right that he was ill-used by them, but of more import is that it's of common knowledge her brother is within the castle. She wonders how Gilbert knows – and if her whole family are suspect. Her belly constricts at the danger they are in, yet she gives a bold response.

'You need have little fear I can, or ever would, pass information to my brother, for our Father has disowned him. In any case the garrison can see for themselves, they have no need of informants.'

Gilbert is staring as though he cannot drag his eyes from her face. Then there's an almighty crash, as the first planks of the wooden tower fall to the ground. They leap back, narrowly avoiding flying splinters.

'This is not a safe place to be,' he says, taking her arm.

'Why are you pulling the steeple down?'

He drops her arm. 'I see Signor Strozzi. I must go.'

She watches among the crowd as he directs the operation and Strozzi shouts impatiently whenever he's unhappy with progress, which is often. Gilbert does not re-join her, nor does he introduce Strozzi. She studies the Florentine; he looks a little like a much older Mainard with his dark eyes and brown face, and the tight curls of his hair. But he is a man who exudes great authority, and word is that he has successfully broken sieges elsewhere.

The steeple is soon all down, with the fishwives dashing in to grab the wood, which will give them a goodly supply for cooking upon. A group of soldiers strain to turn a windlass and pull a large cannon along the street, then work quickly to disassemble the cannon while ropes are lowered and the cannon sections tied on. They begin to heave from the top of St Salvator's tower, the men below steadying the cannon from swinging widely while those above haul with all their might. She watches hand covering her mouth; if the rope breaks, then the men on the ground will be injured, or killed.

It is as though Satan has listened in to her thoughts. There's a cry from above and suddenly the cannon comes hurtling down, chipping and dislodging the stones of the tower as it falls – but the men are well practised and leap out of the way in time. Strozzi roars at their clumsiness and sends for more men. Grissel nudges her, and she knows they must away, for they have to take some supplies up the hill to her new home, along with the kist full of her clothes and two further kists of bedding, dishes, knives, linen and anything else that Mother doesn't require, ready for tomorrow.

She sits high up on the cart beside the carter, gripping the staff Mainard had made for her. She thought it might comfort her to have something of him in her new home, but she only feels sadness. She will burn it, she thinks, tightening her grasp. Grissel perches on a chest behind, blethering to the stout man clutching a pistol who Walter Wardlaw has sent to guard her. She wonders at this – it is not like Wardlaw to be thoughtful, but then she is soon to be the property of the Wardlaw family.

The men lift the kists off the cart and carry two up the stairs, panting and heaving, sweating and swearing as they go. She shows where she wants them placed but then decides on a more convenient spot.

'Mak up yer mind, woman,' Wardlaw's man mutters.

Grissel comes upstairs carrying a chamber pot. 'Where do you want this?', she smirks.

Bethia laughs, although it sounds false, even to her own ears. 'Out of sight; tuck it under the bed.'

Together they make up the bed, ready for tomorrow. The sheets smell of the lavender which Agnes has laid between them – it is an invigorating scent and yet soothing. Norman will need invigorating, she suspects, and likely by tomorrow night she will need soothing. She shudders.

Grissel ties the bed curtains back neatly. 'My mother says it is no sae bad after the first time, and it is better not to fight it,' she says smoothing the blankets.

'There is still the kist to unpack in the kitchen,' Bethia snaps and Grissel hurries away.

She stands by the window, which looks down on the kailyard, listening to the 'klee, klee, killy,' call of a kestrel circling above. The bird circles grow wider, its cries grow fainter and fade away. It is so very quiet.

Then there are voices below and she sees Walter Wardlaw climbing down off his horse and wonders why he's here.

She is kneeling by her kist shaking out her other dress to hang on the pegs set handily along the wall, when he comes into her chamber. She's surprised she didn't hear him clomping up the stairs, but sees he's in his stocking soles. Why would he take his boots off... she cannot

225

imagine it's out of consideration for her housewifery. He closes the door, leering at her as he draws the bolt.

She stands up, holding her dress to her and backs away. He advances.

'We'll just make it easy for Norman,' he says, 'especially as I'm no sure he's up to the job.'

She's backed up against the bed, sure she's somehow misunderstanding but he's coming towards her, still with that strange look on his face.

She straightens up and speaks loudly, although her voice is shaking. 'Get out of my room.'

He pushes her back on the bed and she screams. It sounds odd in her ears, but she screams again as he clambers on top of her, pressing his hand over her mouth and shouting in her ear. 'Scream all you want; it's my man on guard downstairs.'

She twists under him but his weight is heavy on her, and she can't breathe. Then he kneels to tug up her dress, pushing her legs apart and she can draw in air again. She claws at him leaving long scratch marks down either side of his cheeks. He slaps her, the sound ringing loud in her ears, but she barely feels it.

He's fumbling at his breeches now and she reaches down the side of the bed, searching. Where is it? He's leaning over her and she screams again, her hand frantically searching under the bed; and then she has it. She swings out and hits him as hard as she can, with the chamber pot. He's shaking his head, dazed. She swings again, the crack as the pot hits his head echoing around the room. The pot shatters, showering shards of china over her, its handle still tight in her grip.

Wardlaw's eyes glaze over and, as he collapses, she rolls to one side so his weight only partially falls on her. She pushes and kicks to free herself and scrambles off the bed, unbolting the door and escaping down the stairs. Wardlaw's man is at the bottom barring the way, preventing Grissel from coming up. Over his shoulder

Bethia can see her staff, tucked behind the front door. She charges into him, but cannot reach it.

He staggers but regains his balance and comes at her. Grissel leaps on his back, clawing at his eyes and he grabs her wrists – it's enough time for Bethia to get past and grab the staff, instinctively holding it as Mainard taught her. She pokes Wardlaw's man in the stomach and he doubles over, letting go of Grissel who drops in a heap, then she hits his legs, sweeping the feet out from under him. He topples back as Grissel scrambles out the way and they hear the crack loud in the hallway as his head hits the flagstones. He lies dazed as they both stand, panting and staring down at him. She hits him across the head, and he goes limp. Grissel hauls on his legs, slewing him away from the door, and then they are outside and running down the hill for home.

Chapter Forty-Two

A Prisoner

The marriage is to go ahead tomorrow and Bethia has been locked in her chamber overnight. She opens the shutters and studies the wall beneath her window. If she could climb down the swinging rope ladder from the castle, surely she can climb down the much shorter wall of the house. But she can see no way down; the wall is too smooth and the drop too far. She bangs the window shut and goes to sit on the bed, hands covering her eyes, rocking back and forward. Think, Bethia, think, she mutters over and over.

Uncovering her eyes she sees her wedding dress hanging from its hook on the wall in front of her. It is of finest damask, cut low across the bosom and with a wide skirt and small train. Blue in colour, like that of the Virgin Mary's raiment; blue which means loyalty in love – the rich blue dress she once dreamed of.

She cannot believe her parents are making her do this. Father could have been persuaded but Mother not...

'All women have to put up with men trying to ravish them – stay out of his way in future,' Mother says, when Bethia arrives home, so breathless from running, and fear, she can barely get the words out to tell of Wardlaw's attack.

'What were you doing allowing him into your chamber

anyway; what did you expect? He was inflamed with passion and men cannot control their passions. It is up to women to exert the control: to never lead them astray, or place themselves in a situation where the man may take advantage. What were you thinking, going to the house with Wardlaw, and without Norman to protect you?'

'I didn't know he was coming,' she screams. 'He turned up after we got there. Do you think, for one moment, I would have gone anywhere with that man, especially after the way he stares at me and licks his lips.'

'Now calm down,' says Father. He frowns at Mother. 'I mean both of you. We will all sit down and talk this over – quietly.'

'We cannot delay, you yourself are saying they will break the siege this time, with all these soldiers and ships come from France.' Mother says, holding onto his sleeve tightly, face turned up, imploring.

He removes her hand gently. 'I know, I know Mary but I cannot leave my own child so unprotected.'

'She will not be unprotected – she will have a husband. And it is his job to protect her, not yours.'

Father nods slowly. Bethia knows she's losing him.

'He is not my husband,' she shrieks. 'And you are my protector.'

Father rests his hand on her shoulder. 'Be calm, my lass. I will speak with Norman and make him aware of his brother's transgressions. Much better he deals with it.'

She opens her mouth to object but he holds his hand up. 'I agree Norman's no bonny.' He shakes his head. 'But he *is* a good man, I would not give you to him otherwise.'

'No, no, no,' she screams. 'I won't marry him, I won't. I'll never be safe from Wardlaw.'

'There, there, my child – you must trust me to know what's best for you.' Father looks to Mother. 'Perhaps a purge for the bad humours?'

'I will get Agnes to prepare an emetic, we have some mushrooms dried and ready chopped, which are most efficacious.'

'I won't take them, I won't,' hisses Bethia, through gritted teeth.

'Be calm, my lass,' says Father, patting her again.

Bethia hits his arm away. 'You take it. I was vomiting for days the last time Mother fed me red caps.'

'I think some time for quiet reflection might be best,' Mother says. She places her arm around Bethia's shoulders and leads her out of the room and to her chamber. Then she closes the door behind them and thrusts her face close to Bethia. 'You will wed Norman Wardlaw tomorrow and with no more skittishness. I married the man my father chose for me, as girls the world over must. You will do your duty.'

She whisks out of the room and Bethia hears the key turn in the lock.

'Fatherrrr,' she screams banging on the door. "Fatherrrr….' But he didn't come.

She tries the door, tugging the handle and rattling the latch. It is as firmly locked as the last time she tried it. She looks out the window again, it's very dark out there now and the street below is deserted. She hits the shutters off the wall: bang, bang, bang, bang. If she can't sleep, she doesn't see why anyone else should.

There's a tapping at the door.

'Grissel?'

'Aye, it's me.'

Bethia kneels on the floor and whispers.

'I canna hear ye.'

'Kneel down.' She can see Grissel's eye glittering through the gap. 'Can you get me out?'

'There's no key, it's gone.'

'Mother must have it.'

'What do ye want me to dae?'

'Wait, I'm thinking.' She sits up and rubs her eyes, dare she do this? Then memory of Mother screaming in her face returns. 'You will marry Norman Wardlaw tomorrow, my girl, just see if you won't.'

She lies down, whispering. 'Go to the house by Greyfriars and ask for Gilbert Logie. Tell him I have need of him.'

'What, at this time o'night?'

'Please, Grissel.'

'You want me to tell him you have need of him?' says Grissel loudly, 'and wake his whole house to do it?'

'Shush! No, of course not.'

'Well, how am I to tell him anything at this hour, without banging on the door first?'

Bethia sighs. 'You're right, it is impossible. I must think of another way.'

'I'll go,' says Grissel and the eye withdraws.

'Grissel,' she hisses.

The eye re-appears. 'What now?'

'Take care that the front door doesn't stick and make a noise when you open it.'

'Aye, of course. I'll go out through the back.'

Bethia sits on the bed, hands folded in her lap and one leg twitching. Grissel returns sooner than she expected.

'He's no there.'

'How do you know, did you find out where he is?'

'I got in their back door and a servant, his name is Tam and a good looking one he is too…'

'Grissel! What did he say?'

'I'm getting to it. Tam said they're all meeting – and drinking – with Arran and the Italian lad with the curly hair.'

'You mean Strozzi.'

'Aye, that's the one.'

'So you couldn't pass on the message.'

'No – but ye ken, your father's right. Norman's no sae bad, and it is a bonny house.'

'Go to bed, Grissel.'

She falls back onto the bed herself and gazes up at the curtain looped over the bed frame, all colour seeped out in the grey light. She is trapped, there's to be no escape. She feels as though a weight is pressing down on her chest and her breath seems loud in her ears. She listens to it and her eyes flutter and close, she can't fight anymore. She'll marry Fat Norman tomorrow and pray that he will guard her from Walter Wardlaw.

She opens her eyes and sits up. What's that noise? A rustling at the door, then it slowly opens and her small brother stands in the doorway.

'John, how…'

He waves the key at her, a cheeky grin on his face. 'You need to hide?'

She nods.

'Come on,' he whispers. 'I can show you the best hiding place ever. Even God won't find you there.'

She slides off the bed and follows him, the wedding dress swinging in the draught as she closes the door behind her.

Chapter Forty-Three

The Mine

The streets are silent. They stay close to houses where the darkness is deepest. The cathedral rises before them, blocking out the starry night sky, and John leads Bethia across the broad expanse towards it. They creep along the side of its high wall until he stops, and Bethia trips over him.

'Shush!'

He tugs her in behind one of several towers built into the wall and they crouch low, covering their faces. She can hear them now, voices loud and breathless as they climb the slope from the harbour. One of them starts to sing 'The Frog cam to the myl dur,' and the others join in, roaring out 'Froggie was a courting, a courting.'

John covers his ears. 'They're not Frenchmen,' he whispers.

'Nor choristers!'

The men stagger past, swords clanking against their legs. Bethia and John slowly stand up, and then they are crouching again. There are men moving silently through the cathedral gates; dark shapes – their arms heavily laden.

'It is the French soldiers,' John hisses in her ear. 'They are good thieves.'

'Our town will soon have nothing left,' Bethia hisses back. 'But where are *we* going?', she asks as they stand up.

'You'll see.'

She grabs his arm as he follows the soldiers towards the castle, but he tugs her down into Northgait, and around the back of a house. There is a guard on patrol but they crouch again, hidden by the darkness, until he passes. She stumbles over a bucket and John grabs her arm. They stand still for what seems a long time, but no one comes. John lets go and creeps away. She can't see him.

'John?'

He takes her hand hissing, 'be careful of the rubble.'

She can see the darker outline of a mound piled higher than any midden before them. He leads her around it and into a byre, then points.

'You can stay hid down there, for everyone has forgot about it.'

Her eyes grow large in disbelief. 'The siege tunnel – don't tell me you've been inside it.'

John blows air though his lips. 'Me and the fellows have been down many times. We chase the ghosts away, and you can get into the castle easy. If the soldiers all weren't so stupid, this siege would be over already.'

'Oh, John!'

'Come, it is the best place to hide – ever.'

She shivers as though someone is walking over her grave, and backs away. John takes her hand. 'You will be surprised how big it is. They dug it wide, at least at the beginning. Come see.'

She shakes her head.

'Shall we go home then?'

She shakes her head harder and he tugs on her hand, leading her inside.

The boys are so well prepared they even have a tinderbox and candles stored by the entrance, which is as well, for it's black as Hades inside. She stumbles down the broad uneven steps as John holds the candle aloft, and marvels at how high and wide the tunnel is, especially given it was dug in such haste.

Further inside is damp and smells of mildew, and drips of water land on her head, running down the back of her neck. She shivers as she edges along, tripping over loose stones in the dancing light. The ground levels out and then suddenly there's a wall of rock before them. The tunnel seems at an end.

She looks to John, who holds the candle high and points to a small hole in the rock directly above.

'That's the way in?'

'It leads straight into the castle. Me and the boys have been along it.'

'Oh John, you laddies were fortunate not to be caught, or killed.'

'Hah!' he puffs his chest out. 'We are warriors, and it will take more than a few soldiers to catch us. The Castilians are stupid, they think God's on their side so they don't keep proper watch on their counter-mine; and the soldiers are stupid because they think the Castilians are clever, when actually they're very sick, and those who aren't are very lazy.'

'You've been inside the castle?'

'Only a littleways. They have had the pestilence and we didn't want to catch it.'

'Did you see Will, is he sick?'

'No, we are clever warriors. We see no one and no one sees us. Are you climbing up or not, because the candle will burn out soon?'

She stands debating what she should do, clenching and unclenching her fists. If she goes home she'll be married off and end up the property of the Wardlaws. She won't do it. Not when she knows Father, without Mother's insistence, would have been persuaded to wait. The siege may soon be over, but then again the Castilians have resisted every attempt to expel them – God surely is on their side.

'Hurry up.'

She stares up at the hole in the rock. 'You're certain I

won't get stuck?'

He sighs long and loud, the sound echoing, followed by a silence so complete it is as though the stones have sucked the noise in. She knows he's aware of her fear of confined dark spaces. Will once shut her in a kist and she couldn't breathe.

John echoes her thoughts. 'Remember when Father whipped Will for shutting you in that kist?'

'I'd rather not think about the kist right now.' But she hears the satisfaction in John's voice at the memory of Will being whipped, and somehow it steadies her.

He insists she hold the candle and clambers up the rock face to show how easy it is.

'See, place your foot here and then here,' he says hanging over the edge and pointing. 'It is only a short climb, so stop girning like a bairn.'

She cannot help but smile and sees, in the flickering light, John grin back at her.

'Here, pass up the candle.' He hangs over the edge so his whole upper body is mid-air and grabs it.

'What's that smell?'

'The scunnersome thing is burning my jerkin.' He beats at it with one hand and she hears him sigh, no doubt at the prospect of yet another thrashing for the burn hole.

She tries to climb, holding her skirts.

'Girls and their stupid skirts,' he says.

He drips some wax onto a rock and sticks the candle in it, which makes it difficult to see in the shadows, but frees his hands. Fortunately it's a short climb, barely three times John's height, and he reaches down, finds her hands and hauls her into the counter-mine.

It is so low she must bend double; this section was dug with little care and greater haste. He detaches the candle. They crouch and creep up the narrow trench carved down the middle. The tunnel climbs and curves, and she's eternally grateful for the candle keeping the darkness at bay.

Suddenly there's an opening on the right. She stumbles and nearly falls, but John tugs her into it.

'What is this? Did they dig a second one.'

He shrugs but then she remembers Richard Lee's earlier false starts as he tried to work out where the besiegers were tunnelling in. It must have happened again.

'I can't go any further,' he says. 'They'll see the light if I go around the corner, and I will not douse the candle for then I cannot easily find my way back.'

She draws him to her, and hugs him. 'You have been a loyal and true brother.'

They don't speak of the brother who has been neither, but they're both thinking of him.

'When you get to the end, which is close, there's a mound of rubble you must climb over to get out, but I'll wait here for a wee whilie in case they've filled it in – which would have been wise,' he mutters. 'If you don't soon return I will leave, but Bethia, be brave and climb quickly. I cannot stay long for the candle is near finished.'

She hugs him again and stumbles on like a confused mole. The light fades as the tunnel curves and rises. She bumps into a wall of rubble and realises she's reached the end. She feels with her hands, it's much easier to climb than the clumsy joining of the mine and countermine, for it is a mound rather than a rock face. There's a light above – someone is coming.

Laying against the rocks she hopes it is someone who'll recognises her, best of all Will, otherwise she may have escaped Wardlaw to a worse fate. A face appears holding a torch aloft. There's an exclamation and a voice says, 'Bethia Seton, by God's good heart. What are you doing here?'

A hand reaches down and hauls her out. She staggers as she tries to stand. He places an arm around her for support and she looks up into the sweet-natured face of James of Nydie.

Part Five

Will & Bethia

July 1547

Chapter Forty-Four

The Castle

The besiegers have got their cannons atop St Salvators and more on the abbey tower: fourteen in total, Bethia tells the Castilians. It is as they suspected and, when daylight comes, it is confirmed. The garrison cannot even harry them, for all cannons are set high. Leslie questions her about this Strozzi from Florence, but again, there isn't much she can tell.

'A man who knows what he's about, much like our Richard Lee did,' says Leslie.

'We should never have let him leave,' mutters Carmichael, scowling at Bethia as though she was somehow responsible.

The bombardment begins and Will tells her to move from the Cardinal's apartment. 'There is nowhere safe and you have fled from danger into greater peril,' he says, as they duck their heads at yet another explosion, followed by the rumble of falling masonry. 'But the Sea Tower is, at least, further from their cannons.'

She is shivering but growls back at Will. 'I would still rather be here and risk the cannons than have Walter Wardlaw force himself upon me.'

'I am sure, as Father told you, Norman would protect you.'

'And I am as sure that he would fail.'

She covers her ears with her hands.

Will glances to the ceiling as the room shakes. 'Let's go, quickly.'

She stays in the Sea Tower, cowering as the castle is pulverised. Arran's guns take out the East block house, quickly followed by the Cardinal's private chapel. It's clear the garrison cannot withstand for long, so depleted are they by bad food and sickness; and men escaping.

Will returns and stands before her as she crouches in a corner.

'Norman Leslie is strangely silent,' he says. 'He knows it's he who is seen as the ring-leader. He was called to Edinburgh to answer when we first took the castle and he was named in the Great Cursing; we are only the aiders and abettors.' He rubs his forehead hard. 'I think he is afraid, and I must go and help. We will resist as best we can, but I do not think it will be for long.'

She watches him go, so very tall and now broad-shouldered – and surprisingly calm, resigned even. Her little brother is become a man. He returns soon, bringing her some food.

'What is this?'

'Try it,' he says grinning.

She nibbles a corner. 'It's quite… tender.'

'Aye, rat-meat isn't too bad.'

She goes to spit it out, then thinks better of it and keeps eating, trying not to retch.

Will's smile fades. 'Kirkcaldy of Grange has stepped up and taken charge. He says we are to surrender and we must do it quickly, before the castle is taken. This way we may survive, for the condition with any surrender is that our lives are spared. Kirkcaldy, amidst all his cares, has thought of you – he says you must be hid.'

'Why can I not surrender along with you?'

'Our terms are that we must be transported to France, at Arran's expense, and if it does not suit us there, then we are to be transported to whatever country we desire, but not back to Scotland. Kirkcaldy says you are a gentlewoman and it is safer for you to stay hidden, else who knows what may happen to you. And I agree.'

He turns to leave and she grabs his jerkin. 'We could escape, Will, through the tunnel.'

He shakes his head. 'I'm sorry Bethia, but it is too late – otherwise I would have sent you back already, since I could not leave my fellows now. It's a pity you chose this moment to come through, but Kirkcaldy ordered it blocked when he knew how you entered, and there's been no shortage of rubble to shovel down it. That escape route is now closed and, if I were you, I would heed Kirkcaldy's wise advice and hide.'

She picks at the skin around her thumb nail, already red raw, as she follows Will across the rubble-strewn courtyard. It seems the few other women, servants and whores, are not spared a thought, so she's touched that Kirkcaldy considers her, amidst all his cares. But when they show her, in the flickering torchlight, where she is to be hid, she balks.

'I will be trapped. I will die down there for no one will see me, or hear me.'

'That is what makes a good hiding place, to be neither seen nor heard,' pleads Nydie, and Morrison beside him nods in agreement.

'Come, Bethia, be a good girl and do as you are told. We do not have time for this,' growls Will, shifting from one foot to the other. She doesn't want to embarrass him, can see he's exasperated; but he, of all people, should know her terror of confined spaces. Already she's finding it difficult to breathe and she's still outside the pit.

All is suddenly silent; they've stopped firing. Everything seems to be moving slowly, as though in a dream.

Peter Carmichael struts over. 'Either climb down or we'll throw you in. You should never have come here, you're nought but a nuisance.'

243

She flushes, but it is with fury. They didn't think she was a nuisance when she brought Lee information about the mine.

Nydie steps between Bethia and Carmichael, but Carmichael sneers 'You think you can take me in a fight. Try it, son, just try it.'

'Enough,' shouts Kirkcaldy as he ducks into the room. He wipes his face with the back of his hand, water dripping onto the floor from his cloak.

'Make up your mind, lassie, we cannot wait all day while you dither. The East block house is rubble and we won't hold out much longer. The rain is only a wee delay and as soon as it lets up they'll start firing again. If we don't surrender then they'll take the castle, and it'll be the end of us all. So you have a choice, you can surrender with us, or hide. But if it was my sister,' he nods to Will, 'I would be for hiding her, for who knows what they'll do to a bonny young lass.'

Will nods in agreement. 'Come on Bethia, please.' He grabs her arm and hauls her towards the edge.

'Stop, Will, stop,' she cries. She digs her nails into the back of the hand gripping her.

'Get down that ladder,' he shouts, thrusting his red face into hers.

'But if I go down, how am I ever to get out?'

He drops her arm and rubs his face, spreading the dirt further around it.

'The lass is right,' says Kirkcaldy. 'She'll no be able to climb out without help, and it's better she has someone to aid her escape. You must get in there with her.'

'Yes, Will, stay with me, please.'

Carmichael laughs. 'Aye Seton, in you get, and we'll bring you a gown and a shawl and you can be twa lassies the-gether.'

Will is still. She wonders what he'll do and if she should get between them.

'You sound jealous, Carmichael. Maybe a gown and shawl would suit *you* better.'

She would cheer him for those words, if she were not so afraid.

Carmichael punches Will in the chest, but he barely moves. In the midst of her fears Bethia wants to laugh; what can Carmichael be thinking, Will towers over him. He places his hand on Carmichael's forehead and pushes. Carmichael staggers back and sits down, blinking. Will shoves past James and Morrison, and strides out of the guard-room. She hears the thud as his head cracks on the low archway but he doesn't stop, or even reach up to rub it.

'Enough,' says Kirkcaldy. 'Nydie, you will get in there and, when we have surrendered, you will wait for dark and you will climb out, taking the lassie with you. That is an order.'

James nods.

Morrison takes the torch out of its sconce and peers over the edge of the pit. 'It's difficult to make out, but it should be possible for you to climb out. Fortunately our miners did not make the sides ower smooth.'

Nydie grasps the ladder and climbs down. She can see the white of his face in the gloom shining up at her as he searches for hand-holds checking they can climb out. He calls up. 'There's the start of a passageway here which we can tuck ourselves in. We will manage, Bethia is a stout lass.'

'Fine,' says Kirkcaldy. 'I wish you well.'

She doesn't feel much like a stout lass as she crawls backwards to the edge of the hole, and searches with a flailing foot for the first rung of the ladder, but then she's got both feet on and is descending. She shrieks as the ladder slides sideways, but James steadies it, guiding her down one foot at a time – just as Geordie once did. It seems so long ago. Thankfully, she reaches the bottom and they stand unsteadily, looking up at Morrison's face backlit by flickering torch light.

She cannot stop shivering and James strokes her arm. 'Never fear, the Lord looks after his own true and faithful subjects,' he whispers.

Her shivering slows.

They crouch amongst the rubble as another cannon ball crashes into the castle walls. Morrison tosses a blanket down and Bethia calls up a thank you. As they crawl into the culvert, she sees the bottom of the ladder disappearing. Now they are trapped. Perhaps it would've been better to surrender with the rest of the garrison rather than be stuck like a rat in a half-excavated mine – not like a rat, for a rat would find a way out.

They hear Morrison smashing the ladder to pieces, then all is quiet, apart from the vibration of cannon ball hitting castle. The sound is muffled from so far beneath the ground and soon it stops. It must be raining again, or perhaps the surrender has begun. She shifts trying to find the least uncomfortable position and rolls off a particularly jagged stone. They wait.

Then there is movement above them; someone running across the rubble. They huddle down together, but a voice is shouting for James…

Chapter Forty-Five

The Cardinal's Remains

Norman Leslie is running around the courtyard like a lost dog when Will charges out of the guardroom, blinking in the light and pushing away the thought of his sister's distraught face.

Leslie wants the Cardinal's body brought out of the dungeon and laid to rest somewhere more fitting. Will thinks it's a little late for such concern, but submits anyway. He, and a dozen others, are herded through the narrow entrance below Will's sleeping quarters. It is a place he has avoided since he first discovered it the day they stormed the castle, when he was sent running for embers to smoke the Cardinal out. He shakes his head, remembering how scared he was – even the laddie cowering last winter, convinced he was being haunted by the Cardinal's ghost, seems long gone now.

Ropes are flung down and three men slide into the dungeon. They stand back as a lit torch is tossed in after them. Will, leaning over the rim, sees the deep hollow of carved-out rock worn smooth by its many occupants, and thinks that it is accurately named "the bottle dungeon" with its wide bowl and long narrow opening – from which escape is impossible.

He hauls his head out of the bottle neck; the smell is bad: dank, airless and putrid. Surely the Cardinal can't still be rotting after more than a year pickled in salt. The men below shout up; they need help. Will sighs, grasps a rope and slides down to join them. No doubt they will soon be imprisoned here themselves, and he would prefer it if the Cardinal was first removed.

He's surprised to find Melville standing opposite ready to lift the coffin; does he feel any remorse? Three men each side and still they struggle to raise it – it must be lead lined. Others come to assist, and they balance awkwardly on the curve of the hollowed-out floor. The coffin slips and crashes to the ground. The ill-fitting lid slides open.

He looks down upon the tightly packed body and the Cardinal's face stares up at him. He steps back with a sharp intake of breath, and he's not the only one. He rubs his eyes hard, God's blood, he would swear on his life he saw Beaton's unquiet spirit escape.

The Cardinal's body is lying half on its side crushed into the too-small coffin with the knees bent and head twisted, so his face looks out at the world. The naked corpse is stained and unwashed and Will feels shame that any person, however reviled, should have their remains so ill-treated. Then he remembers George Wishart's body, half roasted and blown asunder so that the crowd were collecting what pieces they could find. He, himself, had carried a mangled finger to place in Wishart's coffin.

They ram the lid back on and get the coffin tied up, and hauled to the surface without any further mishap. He climbs back up the rope and the group, staggering under the weight as they slip and slither in the muck, take it in turns to carry it across the rain-soaked, cannon-blasted courtyard and up the stairs. Will notices that Norman Leslie takes no further part in proceedings; he has vanished, just as he did on the day Beaton was killed.

The coffin is placed in the Cardinal's old chambers, which are undamaged, so far. There's some mumbling about washing the body although Will doubts it would hold together if moved for cleaning. Anyway, Kirkcaldy and Balnaves have returned and the negotiations are finished. The terms they sought are agreed; they are indeed to be transported to France. The planks are already laid across the fosse – he can see them through the archway of what is left of the main gate. Will looks around. He and his fellows are a sorry looking group: scrawny, sick and filthy. He thinks of his sister left inside the castle; James will look after her, she'll be fine.

John Knox comes to stand before them, his rain-sodden robes clinging to his legs as tightly as an importuning miscreant. At least he has stayed, unlike his fellow preacher John Rough, who found reason to leave for England some time ago.

'The Word is the beginning of the life spiritual without which all flesh is dead in God's presence,' says Knox, and the Castilians stand and listen. Knox's voice grows loud as he continues. 'In this time of our great need, we will converse with our Lord and say a prayer together.'

Will realises Knox wants the soldiers waiting outside to hear the prayer and know it is being spoken in English; the words of the Bible available to all.

'Our Father which art in heaven, hallowed be thy name,' Knox begins.

Will bows his head and the text of Matthew rolls over him as Knox calls it out in sonorous tones.

'Thy kingdom come, Thy will be done on earth, as it is in heaven.'

In that moment he knows he is among right-thinking people. It was right to protest, even to kill the Cardinal was right – in the eyes of the Lord. He feels the power of God like a jolt through his body; they are not finished here, this is not their end.

'Forgive us our trespasses,' Knox intones, his voice echoing around the silent courtyard.

Everyone must stand before God, and be answerable for their own failings. There should be no priests paid an indulgence to intercede on a transgressor's behalf. And what of his own failings. He is to be safely transported to France and he has left his sister here, in danger – made her his friend's responsibility. He flushes with the shame of it. Then he's running across the courtyard; he is not too late to correct this transgression.

'And lead us not into temptation...' he hears as he ducks into the guard-room, shouting at James to climb up.

James is quickly out and standing next to Will.

'Hurry, Knox is near finished his prayer and then the gate will be opened.'

'You are not coming?'

'You know I cannot leave my sister. Do not tarry, James, go. They have agreed to the terms.'

Still James lingers until Will squeezes his shoulder and gives a gentle push.

He grasps Will's hand. 'I will miss you, my friend.'

'And I you.' Will releases his hand. 'But now I am for the pit, and you are for France – and the bonny French lassies.'

He scrambles over the edge and drops down beside his sister as James stumbles away.

Bethia's soft hand strokes his cheek. 'Thank you, brother.'

He knows it should be him apologising, not her thanking him for making right what he did wrong. Instead he says, 'We should lie down and be hid. Arran's troops will likely search the castle once it is theirs.' He thinks of the Cardinal's remains. 'Although they may be distracted.'

Nevertheless they tuck themselves beneath the overhang. There is silence and his mind drifts, then he's shaking.

Bethia strokes his back. 'I'm sorry you're trapped in here with me.'

'It's not that,' chokes Will.

'What?'

He shakes some more.

'You're laughing! What is there to laugh about?'

'Can you even begin to think what Father would say, if he could see us now?'

And then she is laughing too and it's a comfort to him that, after a long period of strife, they are united.

She grows still. 'Yet I would not be in this predicament were it not for Father – and especially Mother.'

'I am sorry,' says Will. 'I never thought for a moment that they would create an alliance with the Wardlaws. I truly believed it was all a ruse to get me out of the castle.'

'I wish it had been.'

He squeezes her arm.

'Norman Wardlaw is not a bad man; indeed he is kind. If I have to be married to someone not of my choosing, there are many worse; his brother for a start.'

'And was there someone of your choosing?'

She sighs. 'I cannot speak of him, it is too painful. Let's say that he may have been of my choosing, but it seems I was not of his.'

He squeezes her arm again and shifts to tug a rock from under him.

'Anywise I will deal with Walter Wardlaw as soon as we are out of here. I can assure you he will never trouble you again.'

She sighs, 'thank you, Will. But I would not have you in danger, he is very powerful.'

'As am I, in my own way.'

She thinks of him towering over Carmichael and smiles. 'That is very true.'

They lie still. The rain no longer drips on them and all is quiet.

'Would Elspeth have been of your choosing?'

Will squirms next to her. 'Perhaps, I do not know. We didn't have the chance to discover it.' He laughs. 'Although, since you told me she ran off with the painter,

251

I think I was not her choice.' He grows sombre. 'I think my calling is to live a life where I follow Christ's true path, and anything else is secondary.'

She finds his hand in the dark and pats it. 'You are a good man.'

'I am trying to be.'

'I know.'

They sit up and lean against the damp rocks and sharp stones. It must surely soon be dark enough outside for them to risk escape into the short summer night. Bethia falls asleep, head resting against Will's shoulder. She doesn't know how long she has slept when he awakens her, fingers pressed to her lips.

Chapter Forty-Six

Escape

There are men moving around the guard-room. They tuck themselves as tightly under the overhang as they can and tug the blanket over them.

'There is no one in here,' a voice says.

'Search each place with care, we were told,' a gruff voice orders. 'For who knows what trickery these Castilians may pull.'

'They looked barely able to walk never mind capable of any trickery: flea-bitten, worm-ridden and poxed. Even the great Norman Leslie was like to a starving beggar.'

'No mind, we must still search.'

They can hear the men crunching over the rubble, then a flare of light above as the torch is swung over their hiding place.

'Jesu protect me, what's that?' a voice cries. 'I nearly fell in.'

Her heart is hammering in her chest; Will squeezes her hand and her breathing slows.

The men draw close around the edge, she can feel them. From the voices she guesses there's at least three, standing high above looking down into their hiding place.

'God's bones, were they Protestants in search of Hell? They had no need to dig, it will find them soon enough.'

There's a snort of laughter.

'No,' says one slowly. 'It's the beginnings of a mine. They started in the wrong place and abandoned it.'

'Och well, good to know they had as much wasted effort as we.'

She hears the man hawk and spit above them and mentally thanks Morrison for the thought of the blanket. Unfortunately their captors then decide it'll be a fine idea to test if the pit is truly empty. Stones are tossed and Will jerks as they hit his back and the top of his head, but no sound escapes him. Only one hits her, for Will's body is protecting her. She bites her lip and holds her arm – it feels wet, they must've drawn blood. A torch is swung above them, back and forth.

'Throw it in.'

She grips Will's hand even tighter, she can feel his heart thumping. It is only a moment before the gruff voice speaks, but it feels like a lifetime.

'And leave us stumbling around here in the dark? Don't be a fool, Tantallon. Watch out! I think there's another pit behind you, might be any number we could fall in. Come, we have plenty more places to search but they would be fools to have stayed; to surrender means a life spared, to hide is death.'

'Only if you're caught,' says Tantallon.

She wants to be sick; had not fully understood what a risk they were taking.

The light moves away and the men with it. There is silence in the guard-room once more. Will again presses his fingers to her lips. They hear the quiet shift of a foot on stone. They wait. She's sure whoever is watching must sense their presence, feel the fear seeping from her.

He sniffs and they hear him stumble away. They lie still beneath the damp blanket against the cold stone for a long time. They can hear the occasional call from outside, then it too goes quiet.

'We must get out while it is still dark,' whispers Will. Slowly he pushes the blanket off and rises. Bethia rolls onto her hands and knees and stays there. She's so stiff she doesn't think she can stand. She can feel the air shifting above her as Will swings his arms wide and rocks on his feet to get his blood moving. Placing one foot on the ground, she tugs her dress from under it and pushes off with the other, hands crawling up the side of the pit.

Will presses his lips to her ear. 'I'll give you a lift to climb.'

'I must get these skirts out of the way first.'

She wears only a shift beneath, but she fumbles at her waist to loosen the string and the skirt drops to her feet.

'Wait,' whispers Will as she feels above her for the first protruding rock to grip. 'Let me go first.'

'Don't leave me down here!' She holds tightly onto his arm.

'I stayed to protect you, I'm hardly likely to leave you now.'

She lets go and he starts to climb, but his flailing leg kicks her in the face and he drops back and holds her. She rests her aching cheek on his shoulder briefly, then lifts her head. 'Go,' she whispers.

'If you tie the blanket and your skirt together, they can be a rope to help pull you out. You need only climb the first few feet unaided.'

It's difficult to see anything in the gloom, but she runs the skirt through her hands and ties it to the blanket. Will ties it around his waist and starts to climb. She can hear his breath grow loud with effort and hopes no one is nearby. Then she can see the white of his face as he kneels on the lip of the pit, peering down. She climbs quickly; unhampered by her skirt it's easy. She feels shame at the fuss she made about being hid down there. She can get out by herself, if she'd only remembered what an impediment long skirts are. She's already forgotten her terror at being alone in a confined space, for now the pit seems a safe haven in comparison to escaping the castle unseen. She takes one last look down into the black dark and steps away from the edge.

Will is fiddling with the knot tying her skirt to the blanket and she reaches out to take the bundle from him, barely able to see in the murky gloom. Her deft fingers quickly loosen it. They are both concentrating, neither attending to their surroundings, when he topples sideways, taking her down with him.

'Got you, you protesting bastard,' a voice hisses.

She gets onto her hands and knees, crawling away to avoid kicking feet and flailing arms. They roll in a fighting frenzy while she fumbles for a rock, the largest she can find. But she cannot tell which is Will and which is his assailant in this tangle of limbs. She's afraid they will fall into the pit, but they roll closer to the doorway, where the dawn light is beginning to seep in. She crawls after them; she hesitates, crouching with the stone raised high, ready to smash it down on the back of the assailant's head. But is it Will's or his attacker? Then she sees Will's face looking up at her, eyes bulging, the attacker's hands around his throat. She steadies herself, indeed has begun the downward motion when Will kicks hard and rolls again, so the attacker is under him. She crawls forward and grabs the attacker's hair, banging his head off the stone floor. Will is astride him, punching his face. The body goes limp. They scramble to their feet, breathing heavily.

'Did we kill him?' she whispers.

'I don't know.'

They stare down at the inert body.

She grabs Will's hand, 'we have to go.'

'Wait, we must hide him.'

They haul the man by the legs, deep into the guard-room and roll him, as gently as they can, into the pit.

As they leave she treads on something soft; her skirt, thanks be to Mary. She snatches it up, bundling it under her arm. They creep to the doorway and peer out. It's later than they expect – the dimness caused by a mist creeping in from the sea and smothering the castle. She gives thanks again to the blessed Virgin for her care in summoning a haar which is so dense in the early morning light that they can only see a few steps in front of them. Then she realises they may be hid from their potential captors but any soldiers are equally well hidden from them, and all sound is muffled.

They had talked of the best way to escape while they were in the pit, but now they're not so sure the plan is a good one. They cannot go out by the main gateway; it will surely be well guarded. They can try to escape by sea through the sea gate, but they'll have to cross the courtyard. Their plan is to slip out by the closest postern which leads into the castle gardens. Will fumbles in the gun emplacement, where the key is normally tucked under a stone, as Bethia slips on her skirt.

'It's not here,' he hisses.

She pushes him out of the way. 'My hands are smaller, let me.'

'Quickly!'

'No, it is gone.'

'They must've handed it over when they surrendered.'

They stand staring at one another. Will shrugs and turns leading the way, his hand touching the courtyard wall; she follows closely. She can hear voices from above, someone is coming down the wooden staircase from what is left of the private apartments. She tugs on Will's clothing, jerking him into the cellar beneath it.

'All gates must be locked and if no key found then closely guarded. I am by no means certain all have given themselves up. The merchant Seton claims his daughter was abducted and is somewhere within the castle. We have yet to find her.'

Her heart bumps and thumps like dough being kneaded and stretched. Father must be desperate – and she need not have hidden; she feels utterly weary.

'Father tried to save you by claiming an abduction,'

whispers Will, and then says what she has just thought. 'We need not have hidden.' His tone sounds accusatory.

'It's too late now, I will not reveal myself.' She shivers. 'There is no surety they'll release me undamaged, and who knows what they might do to you.'

Will is silent for a moment. 'I agree.'

'And this way you too can escape; you will not be held prisoner and can come home.'

He stiffens. 'I would never willingly leave my fellows.'

She strokes his arm, 'I know, you are loyal.'

'If we don't get under cover now we shall be found anyway. Let's go.'

She grabs him as he turns to the North. 'Not that way. Did you not hear, they will have the postern well guarded.'

'Where else can we escape, beyond walking out through the main gate and bidding them good morn as we leave?' hisses Will.

'Let's try this way.' She tugs on his arm.

There are more soldiers coming, they can hear them talking and laughing. They flee along the portico towards the great hall, tripping over stones until suddenly they can go no further.

The voices follow them along the walkway and now their path is blocked by a huge mound of rubble where the east block house once stood. They turn to head across the bailey towards the kitchens and the sea gate, but there are voices coming from that direction too. They look to one another, knowing they have no choice. She tucks her skirts up once more, and they scramble over the rubble, climbing as fast as they can, into the sheltering haar, while the two groups of men meet below.

Chapter Forty-Seven

A Loyal Fellow

They are trapped. The mist is beginning to lift and Will can see to where ducks and seagulls bob on a restful sea; it is a long way down. The tide, as far in as it gets, is lapping against the base of the cliff. He looks up to what remains of the ramparts to their left. The top is still obscured, but, as soon as the haar clears, anyone looking out will be able to see them if they attempt to climb down the cliff.

'We must hide until dark – and until the tide is out.'

'Where?' Bethia asks.

'We'll make a burrow in amongst the rubble.'

And they pass the daylight hours, dug in, with stones piercing them on all sides, hungry and thirsty, yet distracted by the fear of discovery. As the sun reaches the zenith of its high summer arc he falls asleep. It is a hot, uncomfortable doze but at least it's a temporary oblivion. He awakes puzzled; he's wet. Opening his mouth he lets the rain drip down his parched throat. The relief is indescribable.

The sky grows dark. There is a crash so loud it sounds as though the cannons have started up again, and then an eerie flash of light illuminates the clouds. The thunder growls and is answered again by a dazzle of light. The world is washed in a sinister grey; all sound is muffled, apart from the storm, and it is all around them: God's wrath. In this moment Will does not care if the Lord is angry; he knows he did right to stay by his sister. Bethia is shivering next to him, and he holds her hand as the thunder rumbles out to sea.

The rain settles in, relentlessly, and soon they're soaked. It rinses the worst of the dirt off their faces and stinking clothes, but the pleasure of that soon passes, and the rain becomes an additional misery.

There is activity below. He wipes his eyes with wet hands, trying to work out what's happening. The view into the courtyard is obscured by the mound of rubble, but they can see the forecourt from here; there are people gathering outside the castle. The rain slows to a drizzle and then stops, as a group of men on horseback ride up, bright in their plumed hats and cloaks.

'That's Gilbert Logie, next to Arran in the centre,' she whispers. 'Sometimes he comes to visit Father.'

'Oh aye.' He nudges her. 'I've seen him before. And I take it that's the great Earl of Arran himself beside Logie. First time I've seen him.'

'If you'd come out of the castle you'd have seen him often enough, but only recently.'

He snorts. 'The boy next to Arran is his son, you remember meeting him – a good-natured lad.' He tugs on Bethia's arm for her head is sticking up swivelling like a little bird's. 'Take care they don't see us.'

She ducks down as he lies low, studying Arran; curious about this Regent of Scotland who took his time breaking the siege. Arran's eyebrows sit unnaturally high, giving him a perpetual look of surprise; the lips protrude fleshy pink from his thick beard, which already shows streaks of white through the sandy red – much like Father's. Arran purses those pink lips as he stares at the gate, which is being opened wide as a troop of soldiers march out. He spits then hauls on the reins, forcing his horse to step back and turn, leaving his son glancing between his father's retreating back and Gilbert Logie.

Will is glad to see Logie reach over and pat the boy's shoulder, smiling down on him.

Behind the soldiers come a ragged group of beggars. Will's mouth falls open. Led by Kirkcaldy of Grange and Norman Leslie, they straighten up as they cross the fosse, heads held high. He can see John Knox, his beard sweeping over his chest, James of Nydie next to him and there's Carmichael swaggering as ever; he cannot but feel admiration at Carmichael's refusal to be bowed.

His heart thumps hard in his chest. They must be taking the Castilians away – to France, as agreed.

He touches Bethia on the shoulder. 'Stay hidden until dark and the tide is out,' he hisses. 'Then climb down to the rocks. You can do it.'

Before she can reply, or stop him, he arises from their hiding place, leaping and sliding down the face of the rubble. They grab him as soon as he reaches the bottom, but he gesticulates towards his friends, his fellows. 'I am one of them, I am a Castilian too – I must go with them.'

The soldiers look to Logie, watching from horseback. He nods his assent and the they let Will step into line.

James pats him on the shoulder and John Knox nods to him. They are marched down the hill to the harbour, the path lined by the citizens of St Andrews, come out to watch the prisoners leave. Will sees little sympathy on their faces, and they chant a Popish rhyme.

Ye priests, content ye
Ye priests, content ye
For Norman and his company
Hae fill'd the galleys full!

He supposes he can hardly blame them. The Castilians did little to endear themselves to the town, which he knows from Bethia, was much put upon during the siege.

'Where is Bethia?' whispers James.

'She is still hid.'

261

'You left her in the pit?'

'Of course not. She was by me, in the rubble.'

'Ahh.' James nods.

'She will easily escape once it is dark,' he asserts, hoping saying it will make it so.

'I am glad you are by my side,' says James. 'It shows great loyalty to our group, especially when you might have escaped.'

'Aye, either that or great foolishness,' says Will. He's glad James can explain it, because already he cannot understand what strange impulse had him leap down the rock face – and yet it felt a betrayal not to join his fellows.

It is only when they reach the quayside, and the hammersmith comes to fit their fetters, that he understands they are to be galley slaves. Carmichael is shouting; they're being cheated, the terms of the agreement have been broke. He thinks, no they haven't. We were promised transportation to France, but no one thought to agree what form the transportation would take. He feels a great weariness. What a fool he has been; he's made all the wrong choices from start to finish.

He notices Gilbert Logie standing to one side, watching. The man has an angry scar pulling down one side of his face, lucky the sword missed the eye. He stares at him and Logie stares back, no doubt also wondering what idiocy made Will re-join the group. Logie straightens his shoulders and comes towards Will. The tone in Bethia's voice when she spoke of him was warm, and his sister, unlike him, is no fool. Will makes up his mind, he must trust to Logie's honour.

'I am Will Seton, brother to Bethia,' he says in a low voice, before Logie can speak.

Logie leans forward to whisper in his ear. 'I know who you are. I am sorry, but I can do nothing to help you.'

'No, no, 'tis not help for me I seek.'

'Where *is* your sister?'

'She's hiding, and I fear for her safety.'

Logie's eyes widen. 'You left her!'

Will leans in to explain, conscious that Logie is shaking his head as he listens.

'I will do my best,' Logie promises.

'You won't imprison her, she was never one of us – did not support us, ever.' Will hopes the Lord will excuse a small falsehood, surely telling the location of the mine barely counted as support.

'Have no fear, *I* will protect her,' says Logie.

Will stares at the ground as Logie walks away. Then he lets out a sigh of relief, by God's good heart Bethia should soon be safe.

Chapter Forty-Eight

Rescue

Bethia lies hid in the rubble, caught between the soldiers patrolling on one side, and on the other, the long drop to the rocks below. Soon it's so dark she can only see the soldiers by flickering torchlight. There is a breeze now; she's shaking with cold and her instinct is to burrow deeper into the rubble for shelter. She shifts to escape a sharp edge pressing painfully into her cheek and sets small stones rattling down the slope. There are calls from below and torches waved. Someone starts to climb; her breath is so loud in her own ears she's sure he must hear it. Then she can hear him breathing heavily as he comes closer, and closer. Another few steps and he'll be upon her. There is a rumble, and he grunts as an avalanche of stones underfoot carries him away from her.

'There's nothing there,' he calls to his fellows, but she lies rigid, for a long time.

The moon rises, a fingernail moon, giving a little light in a black sky, That's good, Bethia, she tells herself, they won't be able to see you. She doesn't tell herself that she won't be able to see her way. But although it is dark now, she knows the sun will soon return. She tucks her knees under her, resting on her forearms. It's agony to move, and when she does fresh stones find new places to dig in. Slowly, stiffly, she crawls to the top and looks over. She can see the water, black and glistening below; is the tide on its way in or out? She can't stay to find out; she must move or she'll be here for another day: that or discovered.

She sits, whispering to herself, 'the Virgin is with you, Our Mary loves and keeps you. Be brave Bethia, be strong.' She says the last, and moves. She moves too vigorously and she's sliding down the back of the rubble mound unable to find purchase. She's at the edge of the cliff and about to go over. Somehow she digs in her heels, bracing to halt the slide before she tumbles onto the shoals way below. She lies on her back, clutching at the stones by her side, waves of fear pulsing through her, biting on her lower lip to stop herself from screaming, and then she can taste blood. She doesn't think she can move.

'Come on,' Bethia, she whispers, over and over. She sits up slowly and tucks her skirt into her waistband as best she can. Turning, she grips with her fingers and searches with a flailing foot for the ledge she spied just below her. Finding it she edges along, it's wider the further she goes. She kneels and drops down to the next long ledge and crawls along it; the sandstone is still warm from the heat of the sun earlier. In this way she descends until it's not far to go. But now she's stuck, where the cliff juts out over the sea, its base worn away by the waves. She lies along the ledge and peers over it. She can't see any hand-holds, nothing to climb down with. She must lower herself, let go and trust that the water is not too deep. She crosses herself, sends a plea to the Virgin Mary and scrambles over the edge. She hangs until her fingers slip, nails tearing over stone, and then she is falling. She hits the water and sinks but there's rocks below her; pushing up with her feet she gets her head out of the water, coughing and spluttering. The water is chest high, and, once she gets her breath, she moves forward, one step at a time over slippery stones. The sea-bed slopes upwards, and soon she is able to clamber onto another shoal of rock. She can hear the sound of water, trickling over the cliff behind her, above the susurration of the waves. She wants to stop and rest, but she knows she must keep moving. She slides into the next gulley but the water is deep here and she cannot feel the bottom. She's shivering, and has lost all feeling in her clawed fingers – she tries but hasn't the strength to pull herself up onto the rocks again.

Fighting to keep her head above water, coughing and choking, she's sinking under when a rowing boat, following the narrow sliver of moonlight, appears. Perhaps it is Saint Andrew himself come to save her – but he's too late; she slips under once more and does not come back up. A hand grasps her hair, then the back of her dress. She can hear his laboured breath as he tries to pull her into the boat. Do saints breathe, she wonders.

'Kick, Bethia, kick hard or you'll have us both in.'

Perhaps Saint Andrew is there, pushing from below, for somehow she finds the strength to give an almighty kick and suddenly she's half in the boat, the man tumbling her legs in after. She rolls onto her back, coughing between taking in great gulps of air. When she finally stops choking and gets her breath she stares up at the scarred, red-bearded face staring down at her.

'Gilbert Logie,' she murmurs.

He leans on the oars, shaking his head slowly. 'You are some lass.'

'How did you know where I was?'

'I didn't know for certain, but guessed you were likely to climb down when it got dark.'

'You saw me hiding?' She is confused. Surely if Gilbert saw her, then others will have too. She hauls herself upright and onto the plank seat. He takes off his jerkin and passes it to her and she wraps herself in it, the scent of male sweat comforting.

'I'm sorry I was so late, nearly too late. I was unavoidably delayed by Arran.'

She can't breathe again at the mention of the Regent.

'Where are you taking me?'

'To the harbour, unless you want me to tip you out here and you can try your luck in the sea once more.'

She shakes her head emphatically. She'd rather go to prison than get back into the cold, briny water.

'What happens when we get to the harbour, what will you do with me?'

Gilbert doesn't answer. He's concentrating on manoeuvring around rocks.

She's shivering violently still and slides off the seat and back onto the foot of the boat, finding herself sitting in a puddle of water; it's preferable to being exposed to the breeze off the sea.

They reach the harbour entrance in silence. The French fleet is moored out in the bay some distance away, but there are a few ships at the quayside. He hesitates, unsure where to tie up. She is more and more baffled. She's expecting to be handed over to a guard, and yet he seems to be trying to land unseen.

The quayside is quiet, although there's activity at one ship where men move back and forth unloading barrels, and reloading others from one of the warehouses, torches lighting their way. They will be hurrying to sail as soon as the sun rises and catch the tide.

He rows gently, barely causing a ripple in the still water and they creep along the back of the ship. He's taking her deep into the far corner of the harbour, away from torch-light and moonlight. They draw close to the quayside, he ships the oars and they glide alongside, where he catches the bottom of a ladder.

'Stand up slowly,' he says but she doesn't move.

'How did you know where I was? I am sure I was well hid.'

'You were, I looked and could not see you.'

'Will told you.'

'Aye, your brother begged me rescue you.'

She nods, grateful to know that Will didn't leave her entirely without help. She's still baffled as to why he so impetuously joined his fellows, but she's never understood his passion for Church reform, and why he would risk his own life to achieve it, however much it might be needed.

Gilbert holds the rowing boat tight against the metal ladder, while she rises unsteadily; but her hands are so cold she cannot grip the rungs. He is unable to help, all his energy on keeping the boat steady. Finally she gets a hold on the ladder, but with knees stiffly resistant to bending, she's struggling to climb. Suddenly a face appears above and Gilbert is fumbling for the pistol tucked into his waistband.

'Bethia…,' the voice whispers, 'is it you?'

'Mainard?' She collapses onto the seat and Gilbert lowers his pistol. 'By God's good grace, where have you come from?'

'What do you do here, Bethia? Why the hiding?'

'I will tell you all later, just please get me out of here – quickly and quietly.'

'Wait,' Mainard says, and disappears.

'Who is he?'

'He was a pilgrim from Antwerp, who once helped me.'

'I don't know what help he's planning on giving now, but we must get out of this boat before we're discovered, and by someone more dangerous.'

She's positioning herself for the climb once more, when a rope comes uncoiling down. Gilbert grabs the end, ties it around her waist and then she's climbing, with Mainard supporting her from above, her soaking skirts clinging tight making it even harder to lift each leg and wet hair plastered across her face making it difficult to see .

Gilbert quickly follows. Mainard has already removed his cloak, wrapping it tight around her, and hands Gilbert back his soaking jerkin. The two men jostle over who will see her safely home. She wants to tell Mainard he's too late, she's promised and about to be wed, but her teeth are chattering so much she can't form the words.

In the end it is Gilbert who takes her through the postern, striding past the guards, to her home. Light is creeping over the roof tops as he knocks softly on the door. It opens and she's handed over to Agnes, who exclaims loudly then as quickly covers her mouth. He nods and departs. Father's head appears around the workroom door. He looks tired, as though he hasn't slept all night. For a moment he cannot speak. He pulls Bethia into his arms and hugs her, even though she's sodden.

'Oh lass, my lass,' he whispers. Then he holds her at arm's length and a more familiar expression of annoyed weariness replaces the tenderness. 'But what were you thinking, to go into the castle, of all places, and at such a time?'

She stares at the ground. She cannot speak for shivering.

'Wheesht,' says Agnes, 'can ye no see the lassie's dead on her feet?' She guides her into the kitchen where Grissel is sat upon a stool topping and tailing blackcurrants. Grissel pauses hands raised above the bowl and shrieks in delight as she leaps to her feet, sending the bowl crashing and blackcurrants rolling across the floor. 'Thank our blessed Virgin you are safe – but how did ye escape, how did ye get out?'

'Leave the lassie be,' says Agnes.

She shakes as Agnes strips her clothes off and orders Grissel to fetch warm water from the pot bubbling over the fire, and then to get the berries picked up before she tramples them all into the floor.

Agnes washes her tenderly, exclaiming over the bruises and ripped flesh. 'Such a state, such a state,' she mutters over and over.

Bethia cannot get her mouth to form any words. She tries to speak: to tell of being hidden in the pit; of climbing out; of the fight with the soldier who they may have killed. None of that was so bad, for she had her brother by her side. What was terrifying was to be left alone, half buried in rubble watching the soldiers coming and going for the rest of the long day and evening.

She shivers and shivers as Agnes sends Grissel for clean raiment, then gets impatient waiting, and wrapping her in a blanket, leads her up the stairs to bed.

Mother, just arising for the day, gasps at the sight of her. 'You foolish girl, now look what you've done to us.'

Bethia is too tired to respond and slides gratefully into the still-warm bed. Agnes holds the door wide and Mother passes through, shaking her head.

She thankfully closes her eyes. She does not expect to sleep but she does, a deep sleep but unfortunately of short duration. She's awoken by doors banging and Father shouting. She doesn't know who he's shouting at, for only his voice is audible. It can't be Will and she hopes it's not John. If it's Mother, Agnes, or Grissel then they are all robust enough to survive his ill-temper, and he won't whip them.

The house falls quiet again and she drifts back to sleep. This time her slumber is stabbed by painful dreams. The body of the soldier comes to life and attacks, she twists away and then she's falling towards jagged black rocks, their sharp points reaching to impale her. She awakens, her mind still thick with dreams. Her hands are throbbing and she pulls them out from under the covers; the skin is scraped red raw, nails torn. She wonders where Norman is. She will tell him why she fled into the castle as soon as she sees him. No doubt Father will want them married, if not today, then by tomorrow. She buries her head back under the covers.

Chapter Forty-Nine

Home

It is afternoon when Agnes enters her room carrying freshened clothes. Grissel follows behind carefully balancing a basin of water and staring at Bethia, as though she's a creature from the land of the faeries.

'Come lassie, your Father bids you rise and get ready. There's a man here to speak with you. I do not know who, I didna see him,' Agnes adds when Bethia looks fearful.

She rises from her bed, submits to Agnes's care and ignores Grissel's questioning looks. Grissel slops the water and it soaks the front of Bethia's shift.

'Pay attention you scunnersome wench,' Agnes growls and gives her a slap on the arm, which spills most of what's left of the water.

Agnes sends Grissel away and fusses around Bethia, brushing the mud out of her hair, fastening her stays tightly and producing a pair of lace cuffs. Bethia looks at them puzzled, she's sure they belong to Mother, and Mother is not usually so generous. She wonders what's going on to warrant such attention to her raiment. She's being dressed like for a holy day and she doesn't understand why; Lammas is still some weeks away. Perhaps it is the feast day of Mary Magdalene. She smiles quietly to herself, knowing that John Knox would not approve of celebrating the saints; especially a female saint;

especially a female saint who was once a whore. She's heard Knox even derides the veneration of the Virgin.

Mother comes to complain of the time she is taking and to say the young man is with Father. They're both waiting to speak to her. Mother smirks as she speaks and Agnes nods knowingly. Bethia feels a rising irritation. What is going on? She is hustled out of the chamber before she can ask.

Down she goes, head bent, the habit of obeying her parents too strong to resist. She enters the room behind Mother and goes to sit upon the settle without lifting her eyes. When she does finally look up she finds not Mainard, whom she secretly hoped for, but Gilbert smiling down at her from his position before the fireplace. Father standing next to him is also smiling. She wonders what she's done to merit such a wide smile from Father.

'This young man…,' says Father waving his hand at Gilbert. There's a knocking on the front door before he can speak further.

Everyone starts, and she looks to hide, fearful that Arran's soldiers have come for her, forgetting Gilbert is one of them. For once Grissel is quick, and the door is opened before Bethia has a chance to flee. Up comes Mainard with a great swirl of cloak bringing fresh air and good health. He's smiling and asking to speak with Father privately. Father does not look pleased to see him, which she wonders at. His family have been useful connections for Father's business since he brought Bethia and Elspeth safely home a year ago.

Father's eyes shift from Gilbert to Mainard to Bethia. 'Mainard de Lange, you are welcome, however perhaps you might return later. We have some pressing family business to attend to. Grissel will show you out.'

Gilbert nods agreement as Mainard hesitates – but he's no longer the shy youth. In the afternoon sunshine spearing through the open windows Bethia notices how confidently he holds himself.

'I think I may guess your family business, Master Seton' he says.' I wish to present my suit… before you take the decision.' He nods to Gilbert and smiles sympathetically.

Gilbert puts his hand on the pommel of his sword. The room feels crowded with both men taking up as much space as they can, like cocks thrusting ready for a fight. If it has anything to do with her, Father had best remind them she's already promised.

She is tired, tired in the very depth of her bones. Perhaps she can slip from the room, return to her old chamber and sleep the sleep of oblivion. Mainard does owe her an explanation, but what does it matter now? Then she starts, she has forgot about Will.

'Where is Will?' she asks loudly, cutting across Father who has opened his mouth to speak. She looks up at Gilbert; if anyone knows he will.

Father glares at them all: Mother sitting calmly on her chair; John's face peeping over the back; Agnes in the doorway carrying a tray of refreshments for their guests; Grissel holding the door wide for her mother; and finally at Bethia perched upon the settle – and answers before Gilbert can speak. 'Will is gone, lost to us. I do not want to hear his name spoke in my house again.'

Bethia looks to Gilbert, but he is gazing at the floor.

'Gilbert?' she asks softly.

'He is safe enough,' Gilbert responds.

Father ushers Mainard out of the room, and the family, and Gilbert, sit in silence. Mainard returns quickly, and alone, saying she is to go to her father. She rises and walks through the door which he holds open. He bows as she passes, and then smiles at her. She doesn't smile back.

Father is pacing up and down. He stops and looks intently at her.

'That is a most insistent young man.'

She waits.

'You have not one but two suitors. If I'd kent what a popular lassie you are I'd be taking bids. Shame about

273

Walter Wardlaw, mind, he's a bad enemy, especially as he'll get the Provost on side.'

He moves towards her and she flinches, wondering what's coming now. He reaches out and strokes her hair.

'You're a guid daughter and I know ye did your best to persuade that fool of a brother home.'

Her eyes fill with tears, as much at the unaccustomed gentle touch as at the thought of Will.

'Father, what is going on? How can I have suitors when I'm already promised, or are you now planning a bigamous marriage for me?'

'Do ye no ken what's happened?'

She shakes her head.

'I thought your mother, or Agnes, would've told you. Norman Wardlaw dropped dead,' he pauses, 'or so his brother claims. I heard tell there was a violent altercation between them and Norman came off worst. Nevertheless that's the story Walter Wardlaw is telling, and we have no way of disproving it.'

Her eyes fill with tears. 'Norman was a good man.'

Father lays his hand on her shoulder. 'It's right and proper you should mourn him lass, but we must get you to safety. I am by no means certain that Wardlaw will not send soldiers here.'

She looks up; it is all so strange.

'It is best you marry, and quickly.'

She can hardly believe it: she was nearly a wife, and widow, and now she's back to being Father's chattel to do with as he wishes.

'I never thought to have a daughter that would be so sought after, and by two men of wealth and standing. Mebbe 'tis better if you leave Scotland for a whilie, lass, until all these protestors settle down to become guid Catholics again, and your role in the siege is forgotten. Although, there is the issue of Mainard's father's crime; it made me much disinclined before, I must say.'

She rubs her face. Father knew the reason for Master de

Lange's pilgrimage all this time, and he never mentioned it to her.

He's still ruminating. 'And yet Logie is of a good family: the Logies of Clatto. He is the younger son and a soldier, mind. Perhaps he can protect us from any retribution for my traitorous son's activities...' He tugs on his beard. '... yet Mainard, I've done business there, only a small amount, but if we're all family then we'll be favoured, protected even.'

She waits as Father ponders aloud. She notices Mainard's father's transgressions are becoming of less consequence.

Father rubs his hands. She does not venture an opinion, but then none is asked. She realises she's safe from Walter Wardlaw and, having failed her family there, she should do what's best for them now. Then she feels a surge of rage at being used as Father's pawn, again.

'I will make my own choice this time, Father.'

His face flushes. 'You are *my* daughter and will do as I say.'

She takes a breath and replies calmly. 'But I am of age, and do *not* require your permission to marry.'

Chapter Fifty

The Choice

'I must speak with Mainard,' says Bethia.

Father stands up but replies mildly, as though he's trying to sooth a difficult child. 'Heed my guidance, lass, for I know much of the world, and you little.'

'I've learnt a lot more this past year,' she mutters.

Father rubs his face. 'I am for Logie. Antwerp is a long way away. We would not see you daughter, if you lived across the sea, and we do not know the provenance of the de Lange family. The Logies are well known to us and have strong connections in Fife, a powerful family and a noble one.' He pauses, stroking his beard. 'It would please your mother, and may help in having Will's transgressions overlooked. Aye, I have decided. You will wed Gilbert Logie.'

'I will speak with Mainard first, we have some unfinished business.' She sweeps past him and opens the door.

Father's lips tighten. 'Wait here while I fetch him. I will give you a few minutes, no more. Then you will do as you are bid, lass, I will brook no disobedience.'

He returns with Mainard and sits down. She thinks to insist he leaves the room, but then decides not. She has a growing suspicion, and it will be easier confirmed one way or the other with him here.

'Father says you wish to wed me?'

Mainard looks startled by her directness but answers civilly. 'I do, yes.'

'Why did you not write to me, as promised?'

He blinks. 'I did. Why you did not reply? I write to you every time my father send a letter to yours, and more in between.'

Father stands up. 'I see no purpose in continuing.' He opens the door wide and waves at Mainard to leave. Both Mainard and Bethia stare at him.

'It was you, Father.'

Father tugs his beard. 'It is an irrelevance, the laddie was not suitable. The sins of the father are visited upon the son, even unto the fourth generation.'

'But to leave me in ignorance – and heart-sore. Why, Father?'

'You kept the letters,' says Mainard slowly.

'More like burned them.'

Father's face goes red, the veins standing out on his forehead, but Bethia doesn't care.

'Why did you not ask for my hand before you left last year?'

'I did not think it right that death and marriage be confused. Was important first to go home with my father, and the Certificate of Pilgrimage, and for all to be forgiven, before I propose.' He smiles at her. 'You are most direct.'

She returns the smile. 'And, fortunately, you give good answers. Her face grows solemn again. 'But why did you not return sooner?'

'When you do not reply to the letters, I thought you change your mind.'

'Then why come now?'

Mainard flushes. 'Something my own father say made me suspect that *he* destroy my letters.' He looks at Father from under lowered brows. 'It does not occur that you, sir, will have objection, especially since you now do much trading with us.'

Father raises his hand and steps between them, but Bethia pushes him out of the way. She looks up at Mainard. 'Do you still want me?'

'Yes,'

'As your wife.'

He nods, smiling. 'As my wife.'

'Stop!' roars Father. 'Have you lost your senses? You're my daughter and you will do as I bid you. You will wed Logie.'

'No, she will not,' says Gilbert from the doorway, the rest of the family clustered behind him, agog. 'I withdraw my suit.'

She almost feels sorry for Father, who looks as though he's about to have a seizure.

'You will take good care of her,' Gilbert says, looking over her head at Mainard.

She turns to see Mainard nodding. 'I will take good care.'

She feels like she's losing momentum, doesn't want them talking over the top of her head as though she is a package to be passed around, from Father to suitor to suitor to suitor.

'I will not be marrying anyone,' she says loudly, then realises she sounds like a petulant child. 'I will make my own choice,' she amends.

'You will do your duty,' Mother screeches, face pink as boiling beetroot water.

Father shushes her, and she thumps down on the settle, but all attention is on Bethia.

Gilbert takes Bethia's hand. 'I will always wish you well,' he says looking into her eyes.

She looks down at their hands joined together; she doesn't know what to say to him.

'I think it will be safer for you to leave,' he says releasing her hands.

'Aye, that's true,' says Father. 'Our neighbours ken where you've been, or at least they guess, and Wardlaw is a dangerous enemy. I wasn't able to save Will. Let me at least protect you – from imprisonment, or worse.'

What he says makes sense and she nods slowly.

'I am giving you to the lad, and if we are punished for Will's transgressions then it may be wise for the family to have a base in Antwerp.'

'I must have Grissel with me.'

Father grunts, but says, 'you will take your servant, as any respectable lass would.'

Gilbert is already halfway down the hallway. She looks at Mainard, 'I must speak with him.'

Mainard stands aside and she pushes past Agnes and Grissel, sees a woebegone John tucked in the corner, but her attention is on Gilbert.

Gilbert's at the front door, tugging it open. She catches his sleeve, saying softly, 'please wait.'

He lets go of the door and turns to look down upon her. The light is dim and she cannot see his face properly.

'Will you come into the kitchen?' she asks. He follows her along the passage and stands waiting, head to one side. There's a smell of burning from an unattended pot over the fire, but she ignores it.

'I want to thank you for saving me. I would be dead in the sea now, if it were not for you. You have been a good friend, and especially when I most needed one.'

He bows. 'It has been my pleasure, mistress.'

She twists a strand of hair with her finger, round and around. What can she say? And he is looking so kindly at her.

The silence grows and yet again he rescues her. 'I will always wish you well, Bethia.' He takes her hand, kisses it and leaves.

There is an empty space where he's been. She stands doubting herself. Agnes bustles into the kitchen and shrieks when she sees the burning pot. Bethia goes slowly back along the passageway. John looks out piteously from his corner and she crouches down in front of him.

'Don't go, Bethia. Stay with us.'

'I am sorry, John, I think I must.'

His lip quivers and he knocks her out the way, charging into the kitchen. There's a shriek from Agnes and the crash of breaking crockery.

That evening Agnes and Grissel pack and fuss, fuss and pack while Bethia sits numb. John returns and leans against her legs, asking to go with her. She hugs him and he squirms away, kicking out, his face wet with tears.

When she's finally tucked up in bed, bolster propped under her head and shoulders, Mother snoring softly at her side, she cannot sleep. Is she doing right?

She thinks of Gilbert's scarred face, his soft red beard, his kind eyes and his sturdy body. She thinks of Mainard, young, tall and strong, and gives thanks she's both willing and curious for a marriage bed shared with him.

Finally, she drifts off to a warm sleep.

Chapter Fifty-One

The Galley

Will is taking a look at his home. He can only see it by bending over the oar and laying across his knees to peer through between the oar locks. From this position he also sees red raw flesh spreading around his ankles already, from the chafing of the manacles.

He glimpses his nemesis, the Cardinal's palace, thrusting out from the cliffs. When he thinks of what Beaton did to poor Wishart, the knot of anger still fills tight his empty belly. He knows they were right to kill Beaton, and he knows they were right to occupy the castle and defend the true word of Christ from the corruption of the clergy. He looks to Nydie sitting next to him, the shared oar resting in his lap, next to him John Knox, his long beard flung over his shoulder. Beyond Knox three others work the oar including that horse penis Carmichael. He reflects that being chained to the same oar as Peter Carmichael is the least of his worries.

His bare feet rest in a mix of sea water, piss and shit for they must defecate where they sit. Nydie is so close that neither can bend their arms fully and, as they are chained to the oars, it is impossible to lie down. Nevertheless he derives comfort from Nydie's presence and great friendship.

The captain shouts in French and the captives look to

one another, checking understanding. A sailor gestures. It is clear they are to begin rowing and, as they pick up speed, the waves splash over the sides soaking them – but so hot are they from the exertion, they scarce feel it.

How long is he to be chained here? Is it for months, years or the rest of his life? He does not know, for no sentence was given. Perhaps *he* has lost the Lord's favour. Then Knox speaks and all becomes clear.

'Let us remember we are fulfilling God's great purpose.'

Will straightens up, as much as he is able.

'The Lord punishes to provoke us to repentance. Suffering is an honour, not a trial – being a galley slave is as nothing to what George Wishart endured willingly. Our affliction is a communion with the passion of Christ, and a test of all the Castilians' resolve.'

And I, for one, thinks Will, shall not be found wanting. He bends himself to the task Christ Jesus has set, and soon he can think of nothing else.

Chapter Fifty-Two

Farewell

The sun is rising as Bethia leaves home, accompanied by Father. She has clung to Agnes, and said her farewells to Mother, who, much to Bethia's surprise, congratulated her on making this match. John cannot be found, but Grissel dances behind, her face wreathed in smiles.

The early morning sky is a purest cobalt blue of a hue no dye can perfectly achieve; the rays of sun reach towards her dazzling, and she has to half-close her eyes to pick her way over the cobbles. A halo of light surrounds her, as though the blessed Virgin approves her, and the choice she has made. The cathedral bells ring out, followed by the deeper tones of Holy Trinity and the more distant call from Greyfriars.

Mainard is waiting at St Mary's on the Rock and they stand before the chapel door to make their promises to each other, in front of a priest. Father takes her arm to walk down the hill; reaching the quay, he nods to Mainard, gives her bags to a sailor and stands before her, while Grissel is helped on board.

Much to her surprise, Father presses a fat purse into her hand. 'May God bless you, child.' He rests his hand briefly upon her head, and turns quickly to leave, but not before she can see him blinking furiously.

The ship has already dropped below the quay as the

tide flows out, and they will be grounded if they do not leave immediately. Mainard holds out his hand and they go on board.

The ship is rowed out, skirting the French fleet at anchor in the bay. There is a jolt as the sails are unfurled and they begin to pick up speed. She's never seen her town from so far out to sea before. She feels a lump in her throat as she looks at the tall spires and tower of the cathedral pointing heavenward, the solid tower of St Rules with its wide spire, the stumpy tower of Holy Trinity and, reaching behind them all, the square turret of St Salvators. She can see small figures working atop St Salvators, no doubt removing the cannon which were hauled up there, with such effort, and wonders if the university will replace the spire that was taken down. She will write to Father and ask. She fingers the coin purse from him; curious that he gave the funds to her and not to Mainard.

The French galleys are raising anchor with much shouted instruction. Her brother will be on board and she hopes Arran is honouring his side of the agreement – safe transportation to France, and fair treatment once he's there. No doubt Father, after much grumbling, will pay a ransom for Will's release. If he does not then she will find a way.

There isn't much left standing of this side of the castle, the damage worse than she realised and many of the nearby houses are in ruins. There's the mound of rubble in which she hid for so many hours – it already seems a long time ago. Then, up by St Mary's on the Rock, she spies a figure waving his cap. Quickly she unwraps her shawl and it streams out a farewell to her small brother. May God's good heart watch over him.

A taller figure has come to stand next to him, placing his arm around John's shoulders as they watch the departing ship together. She wishes Gilbert well, for he is a good man, and loyal with it. She looks to Mainard beside her, and hopes she has made the right choice. She knows so little of him and his family, and the life she's going to; cannot even speak their language. What if his family do not like her? Thoughts flutter around her head like trapped butterflies and her heart flutters with them. She might never see her father again, or John, or Agnes – even Mother. Her chest feels tight, like she cannot get enough air. Be calm, Bethia, she mumbles to herself, you must be brave.

The town grows smaller but the tower of St Rule stands strong. She's going to a new country. She feels a thrill of excitement, like the first time she secretly went into the castle seeking Will. Antwerp is where women are allowed learning – even encouraged to learn, like men – if Mainard has spoken the truth.

The ship changes tack and she's thrown against Mainard. He steadies her, smiling down into her face as the wind tugs her hair free. She leans into him, and they head for the open sea.

Find out what happens next for Bethia & Will....

.....as *The Conversos* continues their story,
the second book of the Seton Chronicles series.

Please leave a review

If you enjoyed this book please take a moment to
share your thoughts in a review. Just a rating and/or a
few words are perfect.

Reader reviews help sell more books and keep your
favourite authors in business!

Glossary

The definitions below give the meaning as used in the book

ane	own, as in my own child.
aye	always, yes.
bairn	a baby, a child.
baith	both.
bawbees	coins, money.
besom	a term of contempt for girls and women; often used affectionately.
blethering	gossiping, chattering on and on, talking nonsense.
caitchpule	'real tennis' court; oldest surviving one is at Falkland Palace
cheeky	insolent, naughty.
clout	to hit; also a cloth.
daft	crazy, stupid.
dinna	don't, as in dinna ken – don't know.
dither	to be indecisive.
dour	pessimistic, humourless.
frae	from, as in away from home.
fuffle	a disorder, a fuss.
gawking	staring, sometimes stupidly.
girning	whining.
glaikit	stupid, foolishly vacant.
glowers	glares, scowls.

gowk	a fool, stupid person usually male.
guddle	a muddle, a mess.
haar	a sea mist.
hae	have.
hirpling	limping, hobbling.
ken	know, as in 'you know'.
kent	known.
midden	dung heap, rubbish heap.
ower	too, over; as in over-much.
oxters	armpits.
scunnersome	exasperating, annoying.
skelping	smacking, slapping.
siller	silver coins, money.
smirr	fine rain
the morn's morn	tomorrow morning.
thrashing	a beating, a whipping.
tocher	dowry.
trauchled	downtrodden.
vennel	an alley, a close.
weans	children.
wheen	a lot.
wheesht	be quiet.
yett	a gate, a postern.
yon	that, over there.

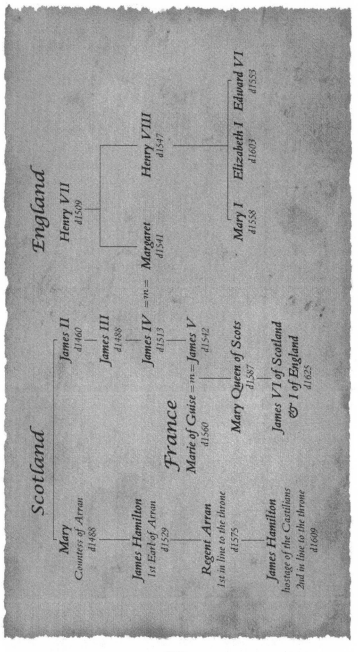

Scotland

England

Mary
Countess of Arran
d1488

James II
d1460

Henry VII
d1509

James Hamilton
1st Earl of Arran
d1529

James III
d1488

Regent Arran
1st in line to the throne
d1575

France

James IV =m= **Margaret**
d1513   *d1541*

Marie of Guise =m= **James V**
d1560   *d1542*

Henry VIII
d1547

James Hamilton
hostage of the Castilians
2nd in line to the throne
d1609

Mary Queen of Scots
d1587

James VI of Scotland
& I of England
d1625

Mary I
d1558

Elizabeth I
d1603

Edward VI
d1553

Acknowledgements

Lots of people have helped me along this journey and I want to thank my family, friends and writers' groups for their ongoing support, even when you were, no doubt, wondering – and sometimes articulating – 'will she ever finish it.'

People have given generously of their time and expertise, and especially Margaret Skea. To my beta readers thanks – my daughter and Keddie Hughes, and my brother – who all made wise suggestions. Maxine Linnell, my editor, thanks too.

Staff at the University of St. Andrews Library and the National Library of Scotland always went the extra mile to find whatever obscure reference I was chasing. Dr Bess Rhodes of St Andrews University was a generous source of information, through her Open Association Course on Reformation St Andrews. And Historical Environment Scotland, what a great organisation: many thanks. If you haven't already visited St Andrews Castle I would urge you to do so. I still get a shiver of excitement going down the mine and counter-mine.

I read widely and amongst the most useful books were those by Margaret H.B. Sanderson, especially Cardinal of Scotland; Jane Dawson's biography of John Knox; articles by Dr Elizabeth Bonner on the Auld Alliance; and Marcus Merriman's The Rough Wooings gives detailed information on the complex politics of the era. I also found the Munro Series by Margaret Skea, and Shirley McKay's Hew Cullen historical detective novels – although both a slightly later period – gave an authentic feel for day-to-day life, as well as being cracking good reads. There's not much historical fiction set in Scotland covering this period, but there's a rich trove set in England, even for the end of Henry VIII's long reign, and especially C.J. Sansom's novels.

Hugest thanks of all go to my long-suffering husband who, as ever, was a tower of strength.

Historical Note

I have tried to follow the historical events of the siege of St Andrews Castle as faithfully as I can. Inevitably some of what happens is down to my own interpretation and, since this is a work of fiction, to the needs of the story. Some events I have altered slightly or condensed, for example the Castilians did not understand they were to become galley slaves until after they were transported to France.

* * *

Let me know if you do spot any glaring inaccuracies, or want to chat about my books. I love a good blether with readers.

You'll also find a couple of stories delving more into the Seton Family, that are free to download from my website.

You'll find me at www.vehmasters.com.

Made in the USA
Columbia, SC
31 August 2023

22330071R00178